Six

A Demon Hunter Romance #1

Carrie Thorne

Published by Thorny Books

Carrie Thorne

https://carriethorne.com/

Also by Carrie Thorne

A Demon Hunter Romance

Six

Wildest

Changed

Echo

Fury (TBD)

Foothills

All the Days After

The Next Day

A Day Late

A New Day

About Yesterday

280 Days (2025)

Day Dreaming (2026)

Again Tomorrow (TBD)

Days of Summer (TBD)

A Beachside Romance Series

Chasing Forever

Running Home

Hiding Away

Standalones

The Christmas Bet: A Double Feature Christmas Standalone.

Enjoy free books, first looks,

review team access,

and occasional hellos from Carrie?

Let's do this: carriethorne.com/newsletter

For my consultant on all things Alaska, from culture to fish to seafaring.
She's also a pretty fantastic twin sister.

1

Coast Guard Vessel Valkyrie, Two Miles Northwest of Wainwright, Alaska. Tonight.

FRIGID WIND WHISTLED THROUGH the open window. Patrolling the eerily calm Arctic waters, Ryan steered the Valkyrie through the Chukchi Sea along the Alaska coastline. He scanned the area for anything that stood out, any sort of unusual activity. Not an ordinary Coast Guard vessel, the Valkyrie crew ran a covert mission to protect humanity from their darkest fears.

Ryan wasn't the captain, nor did he have any intention of becoming so. Just over a year he'd been assigned to the Valkyrie. After making his way up the Coast Guard ranks, he caught wind of trouble off Dutch Harbor... the sort that scared the hide off even the roughest fishermen. Realizing he had the perfect opportunity to use his inherited skills, without committing to a new team, he presented an idea to his captain.

Miraculously, Willa Price hadn't had him laughed when he'd told her about the very real monsters that threatened their world. As the captain of a ship that had sunk for no good reason a few years back, having lost most of her crew to a mysterious tragedy, she was all ears. Nor had the idea of a coastal patrol targeting the paranormal surprised

Admiral Jenks, as he'd been considering something similar for years. Sailors were a suspicious breed, and for good reason. It had taken a lot of time and planning, but about a year ago they had recruited the best of the best, well, the most open-minded anyway, and shipped out on their first deployment.

"How's my favorite demon hunter this evening?" Ryan didn't jump at the sound of Willa's voice, but he was surprised at the interruption from his captain in the middle of the night.

"Keep it down." He mockingly shushed her, scanning the empty bridge, raising his eyebrow in jest.

Despite her rank, she was casual with her XO and the rest of the crew. She had to be on this boat. They saw the weirdest shit in the Coast Guard and were as top secret as they come. Without the tightknit camaraderie, they'd drown fast in their one-hundred percent sink-or-swim expedition.

Willa handed him a hot cup of coffee in his favorite mug, massive and lidless. He braved a testing sip as the steam billowed in turbulent spirals. "Not many awake tonight. Besides, they've already figured out you're different. Ryan, it's time you just told it to them straight. After the Kappa you took out in Bristol Bay last month when it went for Manuel... that was incredible. Remarkably super-powered. I didn't know you could move that fast. Or tear a creature's head off with your bare hands." Amazingly, the pride in her voice outshined any alarm. He'd been so damn lucky to land this position.

Not bothering to hide his scowl, Ryan gratefully savored the bitter heat of the coffee to avoid responding directly, instead muttering, "What are you doing up at this hour?"

"Couldn't sleep. There's something in the air." She tilted her head, gesturing to the still ocean, the calm breeze, the cloudless sky. She looked quite the captain tonight with her dark, salt-and-pepper hair wild from tossing and turning, sleepless in her bunk.

Turning the ship ten degrees south-southwest, Ryan scanned the horizon and nodded. "I feel it, too. You know, for a human, you've got some good instincts."

Scrunching up her nose in delight, she quirked her head to the side in consideration. "Maybe I've got a distant demon hunter in my pedigree."

He gulped too big of a swig of the scorching coffee and cringed as he burned his throat. Distant would be fucking fantastic. His demon blood ran thick as lead through his veins. Briefly running a hand through his military short hair, he set down his drink and scanned the starry sky. Something was up all right.

A minute speck in the distance was rapidly morphing into something threatening. "Shit... do you see that?" he asked, squinting to catch a better glimpse of the bizarre phenomenon.

Moving to the window in a flash, Willa followed his line of sight. "Is that... water?"

Rapidly adjusting course, he tried to turn away from the massive jet of water that was headed straight for them like a ballistic missile. No more than ten yards starboard, the projectile crashed into the ocean and abruptly terminated.

Leaving Willa to take over at the helm, he tore down the ladder and shined a floodlight on the landing site.

Dean ran up beside him to check it out. "Is that...?" The newest member of the crew couldn't even finish the thought. It was too farfetched to consider.

Glowing in the spotlight, Ryan could just make out the figure of a woman. Against protocols, but what the hell, wouldn't hurt him, he dove into the water. A shock of icy razor blades lashed across his skin as he plunged into the Arctic. Within a few quick strokes, he reached the body.

Floating on the surface like an otter taking a peaceful nap, a pale ghost of a woman lay before him. Chest slowly rising and falling, she wasn't dead. Yet.

Ryan's pulse thundered more against the startling realization than the cold. Somehow, before he'd even reached her, he'd known she was alive... despite the frigid temperatures and crazy trip through the air, across what he suspected had been hundreds of miles.

Wrapping his arms around her in a safety hold, he swam them both carefully toward the ship as Dean lowered the hoist. On deck, Dean reached out to take her.

"No, I got her," Ryan abruptly responded. Helpless in his arms, impossibly fragile considering what she'd survived, he couldn't seem to let go.

Any jostling, and her heart might pump faster, the rapid influx of colder blood from her extremities could trigger cardiac arrest. No doubt, she was inhumanly tough, but not immortal. Holding her close against his chest, he pulled them both up the ladder.

Carrying the vulnerable ice cube as steady as he could, he felt the slow movements of her lungs expanding and releasing. He breathed a long sigh of relief, willing her breaths to match his own, her pulse to beat steadily with his.

Harry, the resident medic, came sprinting ahead of them to the infirmary. "How's she doing?" he demanded as he quickly set up for hypothermia protocols.

"I think she's going to be fine once we warm her up. Toss me those scissors." Ryan nodded to Harry, gesturing to the supply cabinet as he set her gently on the bed.

A deep pit formed in his gut. She was dressed in dark cargo pants, a bulletproof vest, and wore holsters for daggers strapped to her legs.

He knew exactly what she was. No other way she could have survived traveling by a massive waterspout, landing in the Arctic. Alive.

Where had that massive jet of water come from? Clearly, she was in the middle of something big. A major op that must have gone terribly wrong. For a moment, as she'd crashed into the sea, he'd thought her a demon. No, he had no doubts now that she was a hunter.

Shaking off the dread that muddled his thoughts, he unstrapped her vest, cut and peeled off her frozen, sopping wet clothes, and shifted her on the heating system that Harry had waiting. The medic had warm IV fluid going before Ryan could even step out of the way. Within minutes of being warmed from the inside and out, color returned to her pale cheeks.

Before she awoke, he needed to ditch her and leave Harry to take over. He wanted nothing to do with a damn demon hunter.

Heading for the exit, he moved to alert Willa of the true nature of their stowaway—if she hadn't figured it out already. They'd stop at the nearest port and drop her before she knew what they were about. If necessary, dump her with the closest vessel. Throat constricting, he fought the impending panic attack.

Nearly at the door, her soft whimper stopped him dead in his tracks.

Turning, he saw her brow scrunched in fear. Fury. In pain or reliving the moments before her arrival here, he couldn't be sure.

In a heartbreaking, gut-wrenching instant, he was back at her side.

Without realizing what he was doing, his hand was gently cradling her cool cheek, whispering that everything was going to be ok. That she was safe and in good hands.

Moron. Like so many foolish men before him, he was suddenly a sucker for a pretty face and a helpless cry. Even though he knew she wasn't vulnerable in the least, he couldn't help but feel protective instincts drenching him like a monsoon.

Berating himself and his initial hatred towards a total stranger, he remembered that Sunshine Hunt hadn't raised him to turn his back on someone in need. No matter his personal feelings against other demon hunters, this woman was barely holding on and needed *his* help.

At least until she was back on her feet. Then she was gone.

Even a demon hunter deserved a fair chance at life.

Maybe.

Fuck. There was something about the woman that haunted him, the idea of leaving her to her fate gutting him to the core.

With worry in his eyes, Dean shifted from left foot to right foot and back again in the medical bay doorway, finally opening his mouth. "You staying with her?"

Another damn sucker.

Puffing his cheeks out as he held his breath, Ryan nodded. "Yep." He exhaled slowly, fighting the dizzying internal battle over whether he should throw the damsel back in the water or hold her hand all night. Torn between the ruthless hunter he was born to be and the peace-loving man he was raised to be.

Voice dry as the damn Mojave in August, he found himself asking, "Mind grabbing me some dry clothes? And maybe some for the stowaway?"

Obediently, Dean disappeared down the hall.

Yawning so wide Ryan could see straight down his throat, Harry rubbed his sleepy eyes now that the urgency was over. A seasoned medic, poor guy had seen way too much death and near death to get worked up over a late-night rescue. "She's stable. If you're parking here for the night, I'll grab some rack time." He smacked his lips with fatigue and scratched his half bald head. "You'll call me when she wakes? I think she's going to be okay..." Harry stared at their patient, his gray unibrow furrowed in deep, stuttering concentration. "Amazingly. She... she's like you, isn't she?"

Yeah, Ryan knew he ought to have spelled it out sooner. Better than the not-so-subtle theories the crew had been whispering. "Yep."

Nodding, Harry backed away and walked slowly out the door. Ryan knew that despite his fatigue, he was bursting with questions, but the medic knew better than to ask now. No way he would have missed Ryan's indecision in how to handle the situation.

Ryan was left alone, dripping and pacing around the infirmary, revisiting his ridiculous internal dispute, even though he knew exactly how this would end.

Efficiently, Dean returned with a pile of clothes and a dry towel. Maybe the kid was worth keeping around. Pulling off his sopping shirt, Ryan dried off.

Dean stepped closer to their patient, sappy eyes admiring the innocent-appearing face. Without looking away, he said to Ryan, "Leah's not your biggest fan anymore. She looked to be about the same size, so I woke her and convinced her to lend some clothes. She was pretty stingy." Dean winced, like he was almost as terrified of Leah as he was of Ryan.

Amused, Ryan nodded. Although hand selected by Willa, Dean had only been on board a few weeks, since they'd left port for their current deployment. He didn't yet realize that Ryan talked tough, but was a total softy. *Thanks for that, Sunshine.*

After changing into dry clothes, Ryan pulled up a chair and parked himself at his patient's side. Plopping his feet up on the side of her bed, he crossed his arms and settled into his chair at her side.

As Dean's footsteps faded in the distance, Ryan quieted the incessant worries that cluttered his mind. Panic continued to bubble under the surface, but as he settled, curiosity and interest stirred. Blinking his eyes slowly, he let his gaze rest on the intruder, hoping he could figure her out before she awoke.

She was ridiculously attractive. For a demon hunter. As her hair dried, he could see the fiery red waves. Not a freckle to be found on that porcelain skin. She'd be stronger than she looked.

Incredible body, too. Not that he'd looked, of course. He'd been delivering emergency medical care. Now that he knew she was ok, he wouldn't be a total cad to remember how spectacularly pert those breasts were, how she had some serious muscle from training, not just genetics.

Not going there, he tried to convince himself. Tried and failed. Miserably.

2

Sitka, Alaska. Six Days Ago.

"Just cut her head off," Quinn offered helpfully to her cousin, each crunching step on the snowy sidewalk bringing a guilty-pleasure smile to her face. Treading synchronously with her cousin, she grinned over their markedly differing styles. They looked like cousins for sure, both shorter than the average demon hunter, with similar features and expressions. But that's where it ended. Quinn had lazily wavy red hair, Lana had wildly dark curls. Quinn's seasoned hiking boots left deep waffle prints behind her, whereas Lana's heeled knee-high boots left delicate imprints.

She shook her head as she imagined anyone believing Lana to be delicate.

Distracted, green eyes aimed straight ahead, Lana flipped her black hair into an elegantly efficient ponytail and gestured with a subtle nod of her head. "Three of them. In Sitka. Are they daft?"

Swaggering across the moonlit, barren street ahead was a tall, dark, and dangerous trio. "And here I thought this would be yet another dull night of research." Quinn sighed in melodramatic woefulness.

Her demon hunting team of five had spent weeks in the damp town for the final stages of one mission. Potentially, their upcoming mission was a critical push against one of the nastiest monsters of them all.

So, yeah, Quinn was glad they'd be as prepared as possible. But this time, she just wasn't feeling it. At least Sitka had been pretty for a few hours, all white and sparkly with the surprising spring snow, but now everything was turning into a nasty, half-melted mush.

Flashing a foolproof—or fool-catching—smile, eyelashes batting over dreamy emerald green eyes, gaze hungry with lust, Lana initiated her favorite ploy. Not so flirty, as she felt downright awkward when she tried, Quinn adapted more of a bored expression, pasting a blasé smirk on her face. Together, they slowed their pace to intersect with their prey as they reached the alley.

The most forward of the trio stepped closer to Lana, with an oh-so-clever come-on of his own. "Good evening ladies." Ridiculously appealing, as vampires tended to be, he pasted on the same fuck-me smile and smoldering look that Lana wore. Quinn tried not to gag. "We're just in town for a few days. Can you recommend a place for drinks this evening? Perhaps join us for a *bite*?"

"What a coincidence. We were just headed to our favorite club. This way." Lana beckoned them to follow her into the dark alley.

Absurdly pleased with their luck, the last of the trio licked his lips, flicking his tongue over his sharp canine in anticipation of a scrumptious dinner. Who fell for this tripe? Quinn rolled her eyes and waved the others ahead, checking the street one last time for any potential witnesses.

Mr. Forward-Blood-Sucker was already making a move on Lana as the trio followed her deep into the alley.

Drawing the Rambo-style bowie knife that had been hidden under her motorcycle jacket, Quinn swiftly reached around the nearest vamp's chin, pulled back sharply, and jabbed the blade into his throat.

He fumbled, struggling to pull her off him.

Anticipating resistance, Quinn sliced. Her stomach roiled at the disgusting crunch through his trachea. After she'd severed most of the major structures, his head hung loosely on his stump of a neck.

Quinn shook the blood off her hand. Why did the whole pointy stick and dusting parts of vampire mythology have to be the made-up part? Humans trying to sleep better at night, no doubt. Nobody wanted to think about the revolting parts of demon hunting. Far less romantic.

The nearly-dead vamp sank to the alley floor at her feet, his bloody puddle creating a red snow cone effect on the slushy pavement. His friend glanced back to check on his progress. Observing the precise opposite of what he was expecting, his toothy mouth gaped open, his pale eyes grew wide as the moon.

Grinning, Quinn beckoned her prey closer.

Nearly to the faded green door at the end of the alley, Lana slammed her head back and clocked her boy-toy in the nose.

Swinging her knife, Quinn used a similar trachea-crunching neck-slice to take out number two, while Lana took out number three with the dagger she pulled from her tall boot.

"Not very tough, were they?" Lana asked as she crouched down to clean her blade on the dead vampire's shirt.

Must have been young. Where were their sires to tell them not to venture down dark alleys with overly eager women? Realizing she'd been splattered in her final strike, Quinn's lower lip pouted out pathetically. "Eww. These were new jeans, too."

Nodding, Lana looked equally grossed out at the mess. "I swear, these nasties were particularly bloody." Her face fell into a heavy frown. "Bet they already had dinner. We were to be a fortuitous dessert."

Born to save humanity from the things that go bump in the night, Quinn took each loss personally. She knew the rest of her team was equally committed to their birthright. Not all demon hunters took their work so seriously, but all were sworn to keep the monsters from flooding the streets.

"I'm going to clean up before dinner. You mind calling the coroner?" Quinn cleaned the mess from her knife, as Lana had done. Dead monster carcasses were becoming increasingly difficult to subtly dispose of. Centuries ago, their demon hunting ancestors had realized they needed help. Already dealing with the dead and undead alike, coroners were their best option for keeping humanity out of the loop, and demon hunter identities secret. Thus, part of routine, and certainly lesser-known, coroner training included recognizing and destroying demon and hybrid carcasses.

"Sure thing. I'll have your beer waiting." Lana was already pulling out her phone. Both eyed the ground and the blood that was turning into a revolting red lake as it melted through the wet snow.

Swinging back to the short-term apartment she shared with Bennett, Quinn freshened up with a hot shower and a change of clothes. Recharged, she ran back through the particularly chill night against the frozen rain that had pelted the soggy ground. Sadly, her motorcycle jacket had been splashed in the mess too, so she had done a brief scrub and gone without. She didn't care for the prickling cold against her skin, but she wouldn't be slowed by it.

Stepping into her favorite place on the planet, aside from her aunt and uncle's house on the hill, and her parent's place outside of San Francisco, or her own shoebox apartment... ok, so she had a lot of favorite places, Quinn took a quick pause in the doorway to inhale the welcoming scents wafting about the ancient wooden structure. The savory grilled yumminess from the kitchen. The rank, yet oddly homey, odor of muddy snow from dozens of sailor's boots. And, her favorite, the indescribable aroma of a massive cedar cabin that had been built by her ancestors, all warmed by the chatter of folks unwinding after a hard day's work.

From behind the bar, her cousin Missy took a quick break from pouring drinks to wave hello. In their family for generations, Missy ran the tavern with Lana and her father. Ignoring the partying fishermen and rowdy Coasties, Quinn pushed through the buzzing crowd to join her team in the secluded nook in the back. In front of a toasty fireplace, cozy leather couches, and plush chairs surrounded a wide coffee table that was stacked with ancient texts.

She sank into the buttery soft leather couch next to Bennett. Her feet landed with a resounding thunk on the dilapidated wooden coffee table as she settled back for another night of lengthy, strategizing debates.

Lana appeared a moment later with her promised beer. Gratefully, Quinn took it and savored the first sip of the smoky porter that warmed her straight down to her toes. Best thing about demon hunting superpowers was her alcohol tolerance. Okay, maybe not *the best*. That sounded terribly asinine. There were many other, far superior perks, little rewards for risking life and limb for the good of humanity. After a long day of hacking and slashing through the creatures of the underworld, a few beers and a double bacon cheeseburger were a well-deserved reward.

And she was a grownup. Even if she had yet to believe it. Although, at thirty-two, she was a wee babe in the lifespan of a demon hunter. Plus, it was still not wise to imbibe to excess, especially when planning an attack on one of the world's most venerable yet mysterious creatures. Staid Bennett would remind her of that little tip, anyway.

They'd been working on this mission for years, yet somehow things weren't coming together. Two years ago, to the day, actually, they'd been hanging out in Quinn's apartment in San Francisco, her windows wide open so she could hear the comings and goings around Alamo Square. On that fateful day, as Bennett referred to it, Astrid, the self-declared bookworm of their ragtag demon hunting team, had nearly dropped her pizza when she stumbled upon the prophecy. Astrid had been perusing one of the older books from Quinn's ceiling-height bookshelf that took up the largest wall of her living room. Who read through prophecies for fun? Well, Astrid did.

She hadn't been looking for trouble, just enjoying an ancient book of prophecies from Quinn's library. For some reason, Astrid had been immediately convinced that it referred to their team. Not any of the other puzzling prophecies she'd read that night. It was just this one that seemed to strike a chord.

Bennett had jumped on board. Headfirst. Why wouldn't he? It was an incredibly romantic tale. Typha, the notorious monster that was said to have taken their demon ancestor prisoner millennia ago, was destined to be slain by a fearsome team, including a star-crossed pair of demon hunter lovers.

Dropping into the deep club chair across the table, Lana's arrival brought Quinn back to the present. "What were you saying about just cutting her head off?"

Quinn took a deep breath and smiled. "Simple plan, but it works on most monsters. Like tonight's vampires."

Sweeping her sleek blond hair over her shoulder, the corner of Astrid's lip lowered in an unhelpful scowl. "Nice try, but that wouldn't even finish the job on the vampires. They won't be truly finished until they're cremated."

"Fair point," she conceded. Raising her glass, Quinn let the ale slosh dramatically, not losing a drop to her smartass theatrics.

"And," Astrid said, clearly prepared for this argument. "As we learned months ago, Typha may have hydra features."

Rolling her eyes, Quinn downed the last of the hefty brew and rested the empty glass at her side. Always a glitch. Never an easy fix. Not that she minded. She actually enjoyed a challenge in her job. Birthright. Whatever. "No one has ever even seen a hydra. Maybe the head regrowth takes a while, like a lizard or starfish. Actually, that makes more sense. Limb replacement rather than heads. Having multiple heads would be awfully confusing. Would it grow extra brains each time? Sounds impractical." The corner of her mouth turned up in an impish smirk.

Astrid attempted to argue, but Quinn shook her head and smiled.

"Sorry, Astrid. I'm cranky and uncertain, and therefore ornery."

At her side, Bennett leaned forward and rested his elbows on his knees. His face serious, he was clearly in full Bennett-broody-mood tonight. "We're ready. I know some of you are uncertain, but we're running out of time. I'm sick of waiting for the final answers to magically appear. We have our route planned, ship stocked, bags packed. Activity in the Bering Sea has been picking up substantially, and I have little doubt it's Typha growing stronger and expanding her sphere. The prophecy is starting to unfold."

Quinn sealed her eyes shut to mask the impending eye roll. Nasty habit. Never complimentary. The trouble with using the gesture so often in jest, was that it came a bit too naturally when the situation absolutely did *not* call for it. "As much as I don't doubt there is something to the prophecy, we don't even know that it is referring to Typha. I mean, yeah, it probably is. But it only refers to a team, two of which are demon hunter soulmates, that will defeat the monster that imprisoned the demon mother and threatens the veil."

Serene in his countenance, as usual, Bennett covered her free hand with his. "Most tales point to Typha as Deandra's captor. Many have tried to defeat her before." His eyes softened as he gazed at his and Quinn's joined hands. "But this, this is what our ancestors lacked."

"I'm not risking all of our lives on a multi-century game of telephone." She freed her hand and tied her shoulder-length red hair into a messy bun. She'd recently gotten carried away and cut some of the layers a bit too short, and a few strands refused to cooperate, falling back into her face. "We are five of the five hundred demon hunters alive today. Even the best of the best, those that studied the prophecy as well as we have, and with more experience, sought her and were never seen or heard from again. Although romantic relationships between demon hunters are rare, we are certainly not the first, nor will we be the last. I'm not sure that we are so special as to have been foretold millennia ago."

Prophecies, legends, rumors... all could be sources of critical information. Quinn had no hesitations about that. The stories came from somewhere. Hell, most of the creatures they faced were well documented in folklore. However, assuming that one coincidence was the embodiment of such an important prophecy, even a rare romantic relationship between demon hunters, was downright dangerous. Flippancy and sarcasm kept her sane, but she was as dead serious as the rest of them when it came to keeping humanity safe.

Lana sat up in her cushy club chair. "Why do you think that is? We're a sexy bunch. I'm not one for eugenics, but the theory could hold true for demon hunters." She grinned, raising a wicked eyebrow and saluting with her double tequila before shooting it in swallowless gulp.

Chuckling in amusement, Quinn rejoined her hand with Bennett's and kissed his knuckles. "Lana, I'm never bored or lacking for strange thoughts when you're around. Maybe it's because most demon hunters are too weirded out by the shared ancestor thing from a few thousand years ago. How many people alive today descend from Genghis Khan that are getting it on with each other? Or even Thomas Jefferson. I hear those guys really got around." She flashed Bennett a whimsical wink.

Bennett pulled her hand back down, linked their fingers together, and rested their joined hands on his lap. "Very funny. Or, it's because demon hunters are more closely related to the mythical world and tend to settle with their soulmates. As we are substantially fewer in number than the general population, it's statistically much less likely that we will find that in another hunter."

Again, Quinn struggled to refrain from rolling her eyes. Yeah, she believed in demons and monsters and everything that went bump in the night. But fated mates, true love, foretold fates... that was more likely to be a story to help lonely people sleep at night. Just because some myths were based in truth, doesn't mean they all were. Even demon hunters could be fantastical in their thinking, maybe more than most full-humans.

Standing and smoothing the wrinkles from her super-slim skinny jeans and lacy top, Lana patted Bennett on the head, messing up his mid-length hair. "You're cute. On that note, I'm going to find a little soulmate sort of action for myself." Swinging her hips, she strode into the thick of the tavern's hullabaloo of happy sailors.

Cousins close in age, Lana and Quinn enjoyed the playful side of life. Lana had more in common with their grandfather, who hadn't married and had children until he was a hundred and twenty, having enjoyed his bachelorhood so thoroughly.

From the darkened corner in their secluded nook, atop his stool, elevated above the rest, Vann kept his arms folded, his lids hooded as he spoke. "Even if you share the love foretold, with the power to defeat Typha, we are still five. A *team of six* is described in the prophecy." The bass of his voice, although barely above a whisper, was penetrating, in stark contrast to the cacophony of the crowded tavern surrounding them.

Laughter reverberated off the walls of the tavern. More so as Lana joined their revelry. Fishing had been unusually favorable in the seas surrounding Alaska for months, maybe even a year now. Experts attributed the good fishing to all kinds of environmental factors, although none had any evidence. Some said it was the declining sea ice coverage, others claimed it was the polar vortex, and more yet said it was another climate regime shift like in the mid-70s.

Quinn and her team knew better. Something was driving the fish, and it wasn't mother nature.

Bennett sat up and took a ruminating pull on his scotch. "Astrid found that number documented once. In one book. We're the closest anyone's been to finding Typha in centuries. With each rising inch of the seas, she grows more powerful. With the timing... Quinn and me coming together, Vann joining us, Astrid finding the prophecy... this isn't a coincidence. We have no choice but to take the risk. I know, with everything I am, that we are the team to defeat her." His chocolate eyes were swirling with gravity, his mouth turned up in a half smile that exuded overconfidence.

From across the room, Lana embraced the handsomest fisherman in the room. Quinn couldn't help but smile. Poor guy didn't have a clue what he was getting into. Out of his league was an understatement.

Astrid shook her head again. Poor thing was going to wrench her neck with all the dissent tonight. "I agree. We are the team described in the prophecy, but we aren't complete. From what I can find, Six cannot be just any old demon hunter. Without Six, defeating her will be impossible. Deandra, our demon mother, is still said to be held in Typha's dungeon. I don't know about you, but I'd rather be disemboweled than end up the captive of such a demon."

Rising from the worn-out sofa, Quinn dropped Bennett's hand. "We've been working on this for two years. But our research has stagnated. No new information in months. Certainly, no sixth hunter looking to join our team. We've read every book, contacted every expert. I agree, things are accelerating, and the time is now, but we're not ready. The boat's ready, our gear is packed, the waters are passable as the sea ice is receding for the year... this feels like it should be the right moment. Let's fly out to Dutch Harbor, as planned, get on the boat, and do a little recon."

Vann nodded, rising from his own chair. Standing nearly a foot taller than the rest, he rested his elbow on Quinn's shoulder. Amused by his teasing antic to exaggerate their height difference, she pinched his ribs. "Agreed. We aren't learning anything more from here. Let's verify her location, check out her lair. See what we're up against. Maybe we'll stumble upon Six along the way."

Quinn nodded in agreement, yet hesitated. "Not sure we're that lucky. We're a strong team, one of the best, but part of what makes us good is caution."

Reaching out her hands, she offered a boost to Bennett. Mouth turned down gravely, he relented and accepted her recon suggestion. On his feet, squeezing her hand in his, Bennett led her outside.

She knew he was disappointed they weren't going all-in against Typha. When Bennett was set on something, there was that little could be done to change his mind. His bravery, his daring, was part of why she'd agreed to move beyond friendship. Going on two years now as a couple, and after a lifetime of friendship, they had a comfortable rhythm.

Outside, the biting wind, unusually cold for the coastal town, sliced across her cheeks and bare arms. Missing her jacket, she shrugged and powered on anyway, ignoring the wintry blast. Among their abilities, demon hunters were extraordinarily resistant to cold. Still, she didn't like it.

Across the street, they politely nodded to the night clerk of their small apartment, and headed up the creaky stairs to their room. In the past, she'd always bunked with Lana and her family, but Bennett had wanted their own space this time, as they were staying so long. While she missed visiting with her aunt and uncle at their grand cabin, she typically saw them often enough at their tavern. Sadly, she was going to miss her uncle on this trip, as he was out on his own demon hunting mission with his team in Australia.

Turning the key in the lock, Bennett pushed open the dense wooden door. Although groaning on its arthritic hinges, the door didn't dare resist the force of his hand. Releasing his other hand, Quinn headed straight across the wide-plank refinished floor to the bathroom.

It took an extra jiggle, but the crystal knob cooperated and granted her entrance. The black and white tile floor was gleaming, almost blindingly shiny. Quinn was grateful for the weekly housekeeping service, and that they had been in today to refresh their towels and soaps. Despite the charming character of the old building, with its plush towels, Egyptian cotton sheets, and massive wood-burning fireplace, she really missed her hole-in-the-wall San Francisco apartment.

Maybe Bennett was right, and there was something about demon hunter relationships that differed from an ordinary pairing. Marriage wasn't an expensive ceremony with tuxedos and a white dress, it was a ritual involving a permanent binding. After the ritual, the hunter's mate would take on some of the demon hunter's abilities to heal and live long lives, in order for the pair to form lifelong partnerships and parent their children together.

It was nearly impossible for demon hunters to have children outside of that binding, when their fertility windows synced with their partner. Being actively fertile only about once a year, at most, demon hunters often took decades to conceive. If on a mission at that time, the window didn't even open that year. Hell, Quinn had only experienced the unusual sensation four or five times in her thirty-two years.

Made sense. Most demons were immortal and would have some serious population problems if they could procreate like rabbits. As human-demon hybrids, like their lifespans, demon hunter fertility was somewhere in between humans and demons. Of course, the occasional nutcase could try to spread their seed far and wide, causing some serious changes in humanity's connection to the paranormal, so limited ability to create offspring made sense for maintaining secrecy. Not likely what Deandra had in mind when she'd created their breed.

Not something Quinn wanted to imagine at this point in her life, anyway. She'd rather follow in her grandfather's footsteps and wait another century. At least another half century would be preferable. Where Bennett may be ready for all that, she was a long way off.

"Quinn, can I come in?" Bennett knocked from outside the bathroom door she'd left ajar.

"Yeah, come on in." She spread her favorite winter-fresh flavored toothpaste over her electric toothbrush. Meticulously, with perfect circles, she scrubbed the pearly whites. Rapid healing, no diseases or infections, physical prowess, three to four times the average human's lifespan... yet Deandra, their powerful demon ancestor that bred with a human and begat the first demon hunter thousands of years ago, hadn't included no-cavities in the special abilities she'd passed to her offspring.

Realizing she was still getting ready for bed, he stepped back and apologized. Poor, squeamish man. At least she wasn't peeing this time. He'd been horrified the first time she hadn't closed the door to use the toilet.

Spitting out the glob of toothpaste from her mouth, Quinn rinsed and dried her minty lips. "What's up?"

"I love you, Quinn," he said, then stopped. He ran a hand over his chiseled jaw, over his perfectly manicured eyebrows—not on purpose, he was born that way—over his patrician nose, down his subtly dimpled chin.

Long pause.

"Love you too..." Pulling out a long strand of floss, she continued her evening routine.

"Have you decided yet?" he asked, his puppy-pitiful chocolate eyes wide with hope. He leaned against the sage-green tile countertop and impatiently awaited her response. Again.

Finishing the back molars, she rinsed her mouth and brushed past him. Moving to sit on the foot of the cushy bed, she pulled her hair out of the messy bun and toyed with the rubber band. "Can we talk about this when we get home?"

Bennett sat next to her. Several inches taller than her slight five-foot-four frame, he was so densely packed with muscle that the bed sank under his weight and threw off her center of gravity. Slipping until she was glued to his side, she sighed through her nostrils.

"I think part of why we aren't ready to face Typha is because we haven't moved forward. When we join, it may set things in motion..." His eyes were dead serious.

Quinn couldn't ignore the sinking feeling in her gut. "The prophecy is very nonspecific. It mentions true love between demon hunters, not marriage."

He continued with yet another reason they should settle down. "My mom decided to settle in at the house in Washington and spend more time back home in England. Dad convinced her to give up the home in British Columbia. It's a great house. As soon as you say yes, I was hoping we could have the ceremony there. Then, maybe move in and start that family we always talked about?"

Quinn was surprised by the uncertainty in his voice. Perhaps all her hedging was taking its toll on his confidence. "This is a really big decision. We're so young—"

"Not that young," he said, shifting to defensive.

"Just... let's talk about it again when we get back. We'll know more about what we're facing then anyway, and maybe I'll be ready then."

He nodded, the corners of his mouth turned down. "Okay. Come on, let's get some sleep."

Rising from the bed, Quinn flicked off the overhead light and shed her jeans and tee before joining him between the sheets. Knowing sleep wasn't going to come easy with the impending mission, she grazed her hand over his chest.

No reaction. Sliding her hand down, she tried to stir a little interest.

"Quinn, stop. We need rest. We have a long journey ahead." His tone was resigned, downright didactic.

With a rapid inhale and release of a useless breath, she pulled her hand away. "Okay," she offered in as bright a tone as possible.

Staring up at the dimly lit ceiling, she tried to calm the adrenaline coursing through her. Something stirred inside her, knowing this recon mission would turn the tides. That things were about to change.

BLARING LIKE AN AIR raid, the incessant beeping of her alarm clock drilled into Quinn's sleepy brain. She could survive with very little sleep, but she really liked a good night's rest. Last night hadn't been as restorative as she'd hoped.

Vivid dreams had inundated her, pulling her into a heavy state of unfamiliar longing. Must have been all that talk of soulmates. Tossing off the blankets, she passed Bennett as he set the coffee pot to brew.

She cranked the shower on hot and let the water cleanse her wandering mind. Something was different. All night, images of heart-wrenching passion, the obsessive need for another, of penetrating emotion, flashed through her mind like memories, but none of it had ever happened.

Her heart thundered wildly in her chest with thrill and desire as he stalked toward her. The corner of his mouth turned up in a flirty smile, silently sharing in a private memory of the night before. Dark eyes met hers. Hands clutched her hips to pull her closer. Soft lips grazed along her collar bone in a blazing trail of need.

Indescribable, gut-wrenching images continued to waft through her mind, bringing an awareness of what love should feel like, the sort the prophecy implied. Whatever happened to her brain during the night, she now knew what was missing.

Drying off, she quickly brushed, flossed, and got dressed. Her knee ticked rapidly as she sat on the foot of the bed, waiting for Bennett to finish getting ready. Like he'd said, but not what he'd meant, deciding would set things in motion.

As he pulled on his boots, Quinn found the courage to speak. "Bennett?" She asked, her voice wavering with a hesitance she wasn't accustomed to, but she was beginning to realize she felt all too often with Bennett.

He grunted, his mind clearly elsewhere. No doubt focused on the plan.

Knowing he was at least half listening, she sighed heavily, then found herself saying, "Now's not the time to shed any doubt. I know that. But something's not right, and it's more than just missing a sixth demon hunter."

"With the increase in demon activity over the past few months, we need to keep moving forward." Again, he wasn't wrong. More fishing vessels going missing. Wildlife slaughtered in unusual ways. The entire coast of Alaska was a hot spot for demon activity the past few months. About a year, really, but things were accelerating.

"I agree, Typha is growing more powerful. We need to intensify our investigation. But... Why you and me? We may both be demon hunters, but we're not anything special." Those dreams, the impending recon mission that felt so much heavier than it should... like a truth serum, she could no longer silence the doubts that had been brewing. *Fated mates*, if that utter bullshit existed, it wasn't the temperate relationship they shared.

He sat stiffly beside her, no longer able to pretend his shoelaces needed such focused attention. Did he doubt as she did? Or did he resent her hesitation? Shaking his head, lips pulled tight, his gaze finally turned towards her, searching for what she knew he wished was there. "Don't say it," he said.

The truth that had been steaming under the surface was boiling over. Filled with restless energy, she rose from the bed and paced the room. Chest aching as she felt the words erupt, she asked, "When has your pulse ever burned when I walked into a room? That you swept me off my feet and needed to make love to me with frenzied urgency? I think…" Her feet froze, and she turned back toward him again. "We're boring." She knew it sounded poetic, but for someone to crush one of the universe's most powerful demon in a love foretold generations ago… a little passion made for a more compelling story.

From childhood friends to lovers. What could be more romantic? They'd be good together the next few centuries. Quinn doubted she would even question their relationship, if the fate of the planet weren't resting on the depths of their love for each other.

"We're not… not *boring*," he said defensively, his spine ramrod straight.

"Yeah, we are." Images of *more* kept pummeling her mind in a blissfully dizzying, heartbreaking awareness. "Have we ever… done it against the door because we were so desperate to have each other?" Her knees suddenly felt weak as she could almost feel the passion stroking across her skin, lips tasting her wet skin, a rumbling voice that soothed every ache and worry. A love she suddenly craved beyond reason.

"Well, no. But, there's always a perfectly comfortable bed around." Ever so practical, he had an answer for everything.

Hot acid formed an obnoxious blurry fluid over her eyes. "Bennett, we're a good team. The best of friends. But, we're not some love that was foretold thousands of years ago. We're just… I think it's time to call it quits." Wiped out, she dropped back onto the bed and sat next to him.

Nodding, his lips drew tight in resigned acknowledgement. "Maybe." Sighing heavily, he rose and moved toward the coffee pot, but hesitated. "Let's... Can I have some time to let it soak in? Keep this between you and me until we get through the recon, so all of our heads are on straight?"

"Sure," she said with a nod. "Sure." Quinn felt the tension easing from her aching limbs. Somehow, despite the awful throbbing in her chest, she felt... relieved. Hope bubbled under the surface. A weight lifted from her shoulders.

She should be weeping, distressed at the loss of a certain future with her childhood friend. Instead, something opened up inside her.

3

Circinus, Zhemchug Canyon, Bering Sea.

"THERE, THAT SHADOW, SEE it?" Lana linked arms with Quinn and pointed to the cloud-darkened patch of ocean in the distance.

The Circinus listed to the side as they neared the obscurity. Gripping the wheel firmly, Quinn kept her feet braced wide and steady. A frigid gust kicked up from the water, frothy caps licked over the approaching waves. Sea air filled her nose, the briny scent familiar and comforting... which was abruptly negated by a whiff of brimstone that burned her nares.

"I'd say that's our target." She rubbed her nose in a futile attempt to drive the noxious odor away. Never easy, not even the approach. A lock of short hair pulled out from her tightly knotted braid as the wind whipped around them in increasingly torrential cyclones.

Dashing up the stairs to the bridge, Bennett settled at her side and put a hand on the wheel to help steady them. "Come in from the southeast. The wind's not as strong that way."

Quinn gently nudged his hand away. She was all for asking for help, but only when she needed it. Which was rarely. At least, not when at the helm of her boat.

Well, her mother's boat. Part of her fleet of charters. It had taken a serious bit of begging to convince her mother to let her take it up to the Bering Sea, to the largest and most mysterious canyon in the world.

"There's a whirlpool to the southeast that I'd rather not get caught in."

"Whirlpool? Fuck. I've never seen one that big." Bennett squinted into the distance.

He wasn't wrong. That was the biggest damn whirlpool she'd ever seen, like a gigantic meteor had just crashed down into the center, but the deep center and ripples just kept going and going. "Does Typha have a friend? A pet?"

"Like a pet kraken?" His voice raised a few pitches.

She really hoped he was joking, but she knew he didn't joke about these things. At least, not in the last few years. He used to be rather fun loving but had grown serious as he reached his late thirties.

When she didn't respond, he nudged her. "You're the one who loves sea monsters, what do you think?"

"Yeah, kraken. Too small for a leviathan, thank goodness. And, judging by the debris we've passed, it's not just storms protecting her domain."

"Then why isn't it coming after us?" His tone was unbearably grave, his skin remarkably pale.

Quinn found her own voice uncharacteristically serious. "Because she wants us to get close. We should have done the fly over that Vann suggested."

Shaking her head, Lana said, "I wish. Not even I'm crazy enough to fly in this weather." Releasing her arm, she left to join the others below.

Bennett stood at her side another minute. "I'm glad we're here. The closer we get, the more I feel we need to be here."

"You're right. We needed to get close to see what we're up against. This close enough for you?"

Gripping the side, he shook his head. "Not quite. We need to find her lair first. See if we can confirm what she is and be sure she's alone. Maybe even get a feel for where Deandra may be so we can figure out how to bust her out of there."

"You raise an excellent point." She smiled, glancing at him briefly. Things had been awkward on the flight over, but as soon as they'd set out on the Circinus, they'd settled. Despite the heartbreak, they were already finding the friendly rhythm they'd always had. She knew she'd made the right decision.

"Thanks," he said, squeezing her shoulder amicably.

"For?" She couldn't help but ask, after dumping someone a few days prior, *thanks* was not something she expected to hear.

"For not saying anything. For letting us just be normal, I guess."

"We've always been good friends. I'm glad we can still be us."

"Me too. We'll tell the team when we get back home."

Smiling softly, Quinn felt almost relaxed. Maybe things would be okay after all.

With his notoriously powerful yet inaudible gait, Vann came to stand behind her. Jumping, she wanted to smack him, but didn't dare release the wheel. "You scared the shit out of me. Stop sneaking up on people like that."

He grinned, clearly enjoying annoying her.

Bennett chuckled, clearly having seen him coming. Backing away, Bennett said, "Gear up. As planned, let's haul ass once we've gotten a feel for the place. But I don't want to be caught unaware."

Nodding, Vann agreed. "Full combat ready, just in case."

Bennett headed below deck.

"All good up here?" Vann scanned the hazy horizon.

"Just peachy." Quinn chuckled, not taking her eyes off the boiling sea in front of them. The increasing brimstone stench etched foulness into her sinuses. "Still thinking full recon inside is a good idea? I smell a trap."

"Walk in the park," he said. Smartass.

She rolled her eyes, finding a smile despite the nagging worry. As neighbors and the only two of their group that lived in San Francisco, Vann and she had gone on dozens of hunts without the others. He probably could have guessed exactly what was going through her mind right now.

"Seriously, I think we're on the right track. Trap or no trap, if we don't make the most of this little recon venture, we'll never be able to stop her. I'll go get your gear out. Double swords today?"

Quinn nodded, hating the buzzing nerves under her skin. Still, she knew they were right.

He flashed her a cheeky wink and headed down to grab her weapons. As always, she was grateful for her team. Demon hunting could be damn stressful. For the sake of other teams, she hoped hers was not unique, that others shared the ability to goof off. Without that lightness, the dark may as well take over.

Each would be prepping with the gear they preferred. Vann would be strapping on the biggest broadsword you'll ever see. His great-great-grandfather's, and he was quite proud of it. It had sliced through a number of monsters over the years. Astrid and her sleek twin swords. Lana favored her battleaxe that was taller than she was. Bennett and his traditional sword and shield like the knights from his noble pedigree.

Quinn tended to choose at the last minute, reading the terrain first. She had taken out more than a few demons with whatever she could find. Baseball bats, wood cutting axes, crowbars... often her own fists. Paid to be flexible.

From deep within the gloomy fog that had encompassed them, rocks arose from the sea, from out of nowhere, morphing into jutting spikes of basalt and wrecked ships. Scattered in the riotous seas, they formed a veritable cemetery, a stark memorial to her ancestors that had failed. Dialing down the speed a bit, she wove between the pointy objects that threatened the boat's hull. Her mother would kill her if she wrecked it.

Well, she'd likely be more upset if anything happened to Quinn, but Fiona was rather protective of her fleet. And, Quinn knew her mother trusted her as much as any of her captains. Maybe more, as she'd taught her to drive ship before she could even see over the wheel.

From behind her, Astrid interrupted her thoughts. "Quit wool-gathering while we're in the middle of a mission," she teased, without the shit-eating grin Vann had offered, but equally light-hearted. In good spirits, as usual, although intense, Astrid took a bit more to laugh than the others on the team.

"No time like the present to ponder one's existence."

Wind whipped across the boat, sending it reeling from side to side. Astrid grabbed her stomach and gripped the handlebar next to Quinn for support. "Why did we have to become so specialized in monsters of the Pacific? I always get seasick, dammit."

"You're a freak of nature. I mean, a freak of demon hunters, being the first I've ever seen to get an upset tummy. Here, you finish docking. It'll help. I'll go get suited up." Quinn stepped aside, and Astrid gratefully took the wheel. There weren't many others she'd trust with the Circinus, but Astrid was more than capable—out of stubborn determination more than anything.

"I don't exactly see a dock ahead." So literal for someone so brilliant.

Quinn pointed at the only access point on the island that was growing ever larger before them. "There's a nice, almost sandy spot ahead. This hull can take about anything, aside from rocky rip-a-hole-in-your-hull traps like these rocks, so just park on the beach."

"Beach it? Isn't the Circinus a little big to park on the beach?" Astrid's eyes grew wide.

"Probably. Not seeing much other choice here. No way we're going to anchor here, and I sure as hell don't want to tie on to one of those unnatural, headstone-like-rocks or wait alone out here while you all go check things out. Demon hunter muscles come in handy for more than just taking out monsters. It won't take more than one or two of us to get off the beach."

"Got it." Astrid nodded with hesitance, her tightly braided hair not daring to come loose. She looked grateful to have a job to do besides risking retching out her lunch.

Sauntering down the steps, swaying with the ship, Quinn found Vann ready with her gear. Enjoying the easy pre-battle banter with Vann and Lana, she pulled on her modified bulletproof vest and strapped a collection of daggers to her legs. She glanced over at Bennett and saw he wasn't wearing the armor she'd made for him.

"Hey. Get your vest on. Vann and I spent weeks on those," she shouted over the screeching gust that nearly pushed them over the side. "I even wrote all of our names in them, so I didn't end up in Vann's extra-large or he in my small one. Clever, huh?"

Vann nodded. "She added a smiley face in mine. Did you get a smiley face?"

She shook her head. "He thought it was a dumb idea, so he didn't get a smiley face."

"I can't move in that thing. It's not like she'll be shooting at us." Bennett adjusted his shield over his arm, tightening the straps. "Besides, I'll be able to block anything she throws at me."

"I didn't enjoy the near impaling when we took out the sphinx-thing last year. This would have stopped it." She admired her clever creation. Way lighter than the old chainmail and plate armor of her ancestors.

"Or, you could have just answered his riddle." Bennett gave her his classic *duh* look.

"As if. I think it was mocking me. When an evil dude asks you a riddle, and the answer is a sharp stick to your chest, he's clearly not looking for an answer."

"Which is why you prefer cutting a creature's head off, before it has a chance to talk?"

"Works on sirens. Give it a try sometime."

With a jarring crash, the boat pulled rapidly onto the narrow strip of sand without slowing, and the Circinus jolted, resting tilted on the beach. Astrid's voice carried light and lilting down from the bridge as she hollered, "Uh, we're here."

Half onshore, the boat should be secure, and only a little challenging to launch when they were done.

Checking each other's gear one final time, the team hopped out of the boat and landed on the sand with five resounding thuds. In a vee formation, weapons sheathed but close at hand, they hiked up the sandy slope that transitioned into pure rock as they neared the sharp incline of the mountain.

Ominous as the thundering clouds above, before them stood a massive basalt peak, dazzlingly shiny from the never-ending rain and frequent lightning strikes. Awfully substantial, considering they hadn't seen it until they were on the shore. Lana cleared her throat. "I think this was a great recon mission. Good job guys."

Voice scratchy with hesitance, Astrid shook her head. "We're here. May as well go a little further, at least until we know what we need, besides a better docking plan." For all their joking, the worry humming over their heads was telling.

A narrow opening a few hundred feet off the ground was clearly the only entrance. As they approached the forbidding structure, a narrow, switchback stairway became evident. No one needed to say anything, they all felt the menace in the air. Banshees, vampires, things that didn't have names at all... no match for Typha's intimidation tactics.

Nearly to the top of the stairs, Lana broke the silence again. "Glad I've been getting on the stair master lately. How many steps do you think we climbed?" Despite her regular exercise and demon hunter stamina, like Quinn, she still inhaled deeply to take in extra oxygen for her burning muscles.

Bennett pulled up his wrist to check his beloved smartwatch. "Eighty-three floors. Good news: I've exceeded my step goal for the day, too."

Quinn laughed from her position in the rear, panting from exertion. "That's it then. We can all go home."

Their amusement faded as they gathered in the narrow entrance. Black as the moonless night, even with her above-average vision, Quinn couldn't see a thing. Leap of fucking faith. Or something. The only sound their breathing and steps on the slick floor, even the rain and thunder quieted as they entered the cave.

"Anyone else think this was way too easy?" Lana whispered, an unmistakable panic in her voice.

"I'm now one hundred percent sure we've walked right into a trap." Quinn said, expecting a *Raiders of the Lost Arc* boulder to come rumbling down the hall and smush them all.

Bennett looked cool as ice. "Probably. But we're here. Let's make the most of it."

A hundred feet in, a glowing blue haze illuminated the path. Above, there were large swiss-cheese holes in the ceiling where the moonlight shined through. Quinn moved up next to Vann and said under her breath, "What do you think made those holes?"

He tilted his head down towards her and spoke as softly. "They look like waterspouts, but we're too far above the ocean for that."

"Huh." Toes curling in and her gag reflex suffocating her, she sure hoped they weren't snake holes or something and Typha was really an echidna and these were travel tunnels. She hated snakes. If she had to see someone with snakes for hair, that image was never leaving, and turning to stone would be a blessing to save her from a lifetime of nightmares.

Half a mile or so of silence, save for the sound of rain dripping all around and the echoes of their own footsteps, a fierce snarl filled the air. The blue glow thickened ahead. In the distance, a large shell dominated the room. Throne. Shell-throne-thing. Classy either way. Luckily, it looked empty. As a unit, they froze in place, staying in the shadow of the hallway.

Ahead, off to the side, there was a large caldron and worktable. Squid tentacles and other sea creature parts floated in large jars on the nearby shelves. At the far end of the room, there was a wavy, blurry sort of glass-like wall, but she couldn't see through it. Finally, off to the right was a staircase.

Bennett gestured it was time to go with a subtle nod of his head. Agreeing without the slightest hesitation, they silently walked back towards the exit.

Thunder rattled the room as boulders crashed at the far end of the hall.

Quinn whipped her head around to see what had caused the sound. Rocks tumbled to the ground in an isolated collapse in the hall.

Sprinting toward the exit, ignoring the remaining loose debris that still fell and littered the ground. Each tossed rocks and boulders out of the way, knowing they needed to get the hell out of there. Fast.

Before they could clear the exit, a piercing voice echoed directly into her brain, somehow psychically or magically bypassing the auditory system. Resisting the urge to cover her ears, as it would be fruitless anyway, Quinn scrunched her face and ducked against the intrusion. The others reacted similarly, and she knew she wasn't alone.

"Don't go so soon. You've made it further than any of your predecessors of the last few centuries. And, you actually have part of what you need to challenge me."

Well that wasn't reassuring. So much for their sneaky peek.

Bennett held his shield protectively in front of the group and spoke for the others. "Great, then why don't we just leave you in peace, and we'll come back at a better time."

Her shrill laughter could have shattered glass, if there were any around. "Let's have a little fun first. It gets so lonely around here."

Lana cocked out her hip, ready to toss out insults. Quinn stilled her and spoke first. "You have been around a lot longer than we have, ruling the Pacific. We want to protect the people and the sea life you threaten. If you cross back over, we'll leave."

"Ah, but there is always a food chain. And, I do get bored now and again. Where would I be without sailors to dine on and whales to drive mad? It's not like humans aren't destroying the oceans all on their own."

From deep in her chest, rattling her ribs, Quinn heard a different voice, pleasantly lyrical. "*Go now, please. You can find him, but not here.*"

Looking to the others, Quinn didn't see them reacting to this new voice. She didn't know how to respond, but suspected the voice was truly trying to help. Likely not wise to trust a second voice to speak directly to your brain, but this one sounded so... maternal. Muttering under her breath, she tried to answer. "The sixth?"

Everyone shot their heads in her direction. Not much of a whisper, she supposed. The soothing voice resonated through her again. "*Yes. Now, go. I can distract her, but you must move quickly.*"

Panic ringing in her ears, thundering in her chest, she knew that the voice was on their side. Deandra. Returning to the pile of boulders, she continued to clear the exit. "Hurry. Let's go."

Typha's sharp laughter echoed off her skull so harshly she could barely hear herself think. Suddenly she stood behind them. Nearly twice their height, almost painfully beautiful as the tales they'd read, with dark eyes and darker hair, nearly blue skin, but with a half dozen tentacle-like arms. Unnatural, her appearance just made little sense, even for a demon.

Lashing out in the blink of an eye, Typha lunged at Lana, gripped her in arms three and four, shook her like a dog with a rabbit in its jaws, and tossed her aside. Crashing into the wall, Lana crumpled to the floor.

"*She's too strong. Fight, and I will find a way.*" Not reassuring when the kind voice in your head sounded like she was brewing a migraine.

Quick exit impossible, they drew their weapons. Slashing and hacking, the team attacked, surrounding Typha from all sides. With a quick slash from a sleek sword, Astrid knocked off one of the creature's arms. Shrieking like a banshee, Typha's stumpy arm gushed out black blood before the early growth of two new limbs grew from the bloody stub.

"Definitely part squiddy-hydra," Quinn hollered in the chaos.

Arms aching, fire burning in her limbs and lungs as her swords grew heavier with each useless hack and slash, her daggers all ricocheted off the creature's side... she knew their escape was impossible. Bruised, concussed, slowing, the team fought desperately.

Turning back to the exit, Quinn shoved more rocks away as the rest of the team, those still standing, gave up on offense and switched to defense.

With another massive blow, Typha tossed Vann against the wall next to Lana with a gleeful laugh.

Slashing out with one of her many arms, unnaturally sharp and serrated, she sliced Bennett's shield off his arm, taking a chunk of skin with it.

As he recoiled, another arm sliced into his abdomen.

Quinn shrieked in terror as she watched blood and entrails protruding from his abdomen. His head lifelessly turned to the side as he slumped to the floor.

"No," Quinn shrieked as she made her way towards Bennett's crumpled form.

The voice sang in her chest again. "*They will be okay.* You *must go now.*"

"I can't leave them," she roared, tears streaming down her face as she stomached the depth of their losses.

Rumbling beneath her like an earthquake, minimum 7 or 8 on the Richter scale, even Typha looked confused as the few still standing searched for the source.

From beneath her feet, the ground opened up. A massive missile of water blasted her out a swiss-cheese skylight.

Flying high above the sea, she rode the water for hours.

Until, like the flick of a switch, the lights shut out around her, and all was dark and silent and cold.

4

Valkyrie. Now.

AT 0634, QUINN'S EYES fluttered open. She read the time from the red numbers on the clock built into the far wall, glowing brightly in the dim, windowless room. She tried to sit up, but her head throbbed, and her body ached all over. A heavy, but very toasty blanket covered her body. Under, she was... naked?

"You're finally awake." The sexiest voice she'd ever heard rumbled through her ears, vibrating through her weary limbs, filling her veins with pure heaven. She almost didn't care that the words were dripping with sarcasm.

Sitting up to her elbows—nearly losing the blanket—she grabbed it in the nick of time before she flashed Mr. Sexy Voice. Hair wild around her face, she pushed her overgrown bangs out of the way to see the source of the deliciously deep timbre.

Damn, he had a nice face, too. Calculating steel-gray eyes... yeah, he was a smart one. Chiseled, masculine features. Military short, deeply brunet hair. Her eyes strayed downward, assessing more than was appropriate, but she had trouble focusing on anything else. Snug t-shirt that hugged some spectacular muscles, with USCG written across the front. Arms folded across his chest impatiently. Leg ticking with quite probable irritation.

Crap, she had crossed a line.

Psychic or something, he answered with a very serious scowl before she even needed to ask. Sexy voice, spectacular body, good face... but a lousy attitude. "You're on board the US Coast Guard Cutter Valkyrie."

"Taking me to Valhalla then?" She was totally joking... or maybe she wasn't?

Something flashed in her brain. Huh. Why would her first thought be that she was on her way to Valhalla, and actually mean it? Although, if she'd died and gone to heaven, the view was certainly better than what she would have imagined.

The corner of his mouth quirked up in humor, then quickly faded. "Not today. We're a few miles off the northern coast of Alaska. Pulled you out of the water last night." His eyes flashed with something dark, more of a gunmetal gray now, and boring right into her.

"Why was I in the Arctic?" She breathed slowly to fight the panic bubbling under the surface. Scanning the unfamiliar room, her brow scrunched in stark confusion. The bleak desert in her brain wasn't giving her a clue. "I guess that would explain the heated blanket." She nodded, accepting at least one facet of her predicament.

"You tell me." He stared into her, unflinching, asking dozens of silent questions that she couldn't answer.

She shrugged, head shaking, brow scrunched and mouth pulled tight, her expression flashing *NO IDEA,* in big, silent letters at him.

"Ok, we can play it that way. Who are you?" He shifted and leaned back in his chair next to her. His feet, with some awfully massive black combat boots, rested on the foot of her bed next to her blanketed feet.

"Really not playing here. I'm..." *Dammit. Double dog dammit.* Didn't know her own name, but she knew what the hell this bullshit was, that was causing the thick cobwebs in her hippocampus.

"Fucking shit, I have amnesia." Struggling to not panic, she focused on his face, the warmth of the blanket covering her, her pulse pounding through her toasty limbs... anything real that she could grasp.

He scowled, but instead of looking as shocked as she felt, he sank deeper into his chair and folded his arms behind his head, leisurely closing his eyes and settling in for a nap. Not very helpful. And she'd had such high hopes, considering he'd been heroic enough to a pull strange a woman out of the ocean in the middle of the night.

"Nice try," he said flatly, his eyes closed in disinterest.

"No, dammit. This is stupid. Just fucking stupid." She cussed and sputtered some more. He raised an eyebrow as he glanced at her, but he still didn't appear concerned. "Fine, I have amnesia and a sailor's mouth, but come on. Throw me a bone here."

Sighing, he reached to grab a pile of wet clothes from a nearby table. Long arms with massive biceps, dang. Nice definition, too.

Okay, whoever she was, she was a desperate horn-dog. This was getting ridiculous.

He sifted through the wet pile, not seeming to care that drips splattered onto his clothes and the floor. "I don't know shit about clothing brands, but these look nice. Oh, and you had a bulletproof vest. Explain that one for me." He rolled his eyes without looking at her, but continued to study her clothes.

"Not helpful," she muttered, sitting up proudly in the bed. She really didn't think she was a cop, but worth considering. The blanket, only covering her front, left her no backside modesty as she leaned forward to see the wet pile of her mysterious belongings. His eyes flashed to her exposed rear, lingering a moment until she adjusted the blanket to cover her back.

Scowling, he looked more irritated with himself than her this time.

Looking back at her clothes, he inspected the vest further. "Ah, cute. You wrote your name in here. Quinn. And a smiley face. No last name. Guess you're Quinn Smiley."

"Hardy har har." She nudged his foot with hers, appreciating that he might actually have a sense of humor. Sadly, the name didn't ring a bell.

Finally, he faced her directly. "Quinn, I'm Ryan." He extended his hand in friendship. Hopefully friendship. It could also be one of those pull-you-in-so-I-can-punch-you-in-the-face handshakes. Not that she'd experienced many of those. Probably. Hopefully.

Taking his hand, she shook it firmly, letting herself enjoy the zing she felt at the connection. He didn't let go. Maybe he felt it too? She had to hold tight onto the blanket with her free hand or she'd flash him with the front half while she was at it. Although, she suspected he'd seen it all last night anyway, as her clothes were cut to bits.

"Nice to meet you, Ryan," she said in her perkiest voice, ensuring he knew this was a friendly handshake.

"Yeah, nice. Anyway, you're on a government vessel. Fuck with anything, and I throw you back in the Arctic." Definitely the teeth-baring gorilla sort of handshake. Oh well, her hand was still securely held in his big, warm hand, and she felt quite at home despite the lack of hospitality.

Stop it, she yelled at herself. A bit pathetic, to be attracted to an overbearing, albeit attractive, jerk. Irritated with herself as much as with the irksome man, she finally pulled her hand away. "Okay, so I don't know much about me, but I'm pretty sure I'm a decent person."

"We'll see."

She scowled at him.

He shrugged, sighing heavily. "Really, you might be. You probably are. But give me a break. Not exactly a trustworthy entrance, splashing down into the arctic wearing a bulletproof vest and combat gear. I'm not putting my crew at risk."

Closing her eyes, she tried to remember something. Anything.

"We are hell and gone from civilization. We're on active deployment, scouting the coast, with a few resupply stops along the way in Dutch Harbor, Kodiak and then Sitka, so we'll probably drop you somewhere along the way. Worst case, you may be stuck with us for a month or two, if you can't figure out who you are."

He returned to his comfy position leaned back in his chair with his feet on her bed and closed his eyes.

"Ryan?"

Brow slightly scrunching, he grunted in response.

"Ryan? I'm hungry. And I'm naked." At least she could take care of the basics and get started on figuring out where she belonged.

His eyes remained tightly closed, but the corner of his mouth quirked up again. "I'm okay with naked. I'll call for food though. Just give me a few minutes to catch up on sleep. Thanks to you, I didn't get much rest last night."

Kicking out her foot, she shoved his feet off her bed. He fell forward at the jarring drop and glared at her. The glare was unconvincing, as his dark eyes twinkled with amusement. "Fine." He moved across the room and grabbed a pile.

Less than cordially, he tossed the small stack of dry clothes onto her lap. *Could have offered sooner, jerkwad.* The bra tried to bail as the pile landed precariously, but she caught it with a quick motion, nearly dropping the blanket.

Staring at him, she waited for him to leave so she could get dressed in peace. "Ahem," she hinted loudly.

He didn't move.

"Ahem." She cleared her throat loudly and meaningfully, directing her eyes towards the door in an obvious request for privacy.

Arms crossed, legs planted firmly in place, he raised an eyebrow at her. Damn he looked good when he made that irritating face. "Nothing I haven't already seen. Who do you think cut those clothes off you last night?"

"I figured. But come on. Now I'm conscious. No longer medical, just creepy."

"So, now I'm creepy?" He smiled with pure attitude, his eyes wide with amusement.

She muttered under her breath, "Defensive ass."

Grinning wickedly in surprised humor, his eyebrow was halfway to his hairline now. "What did you call me?"

"Ryan. Will you ever so kindly turn your back so I can have some privacy?" She smiled as serenely as possible. It was not a familiar expression. Apparently, she wasn't a serene person. Although, smartass seemed to come to her as easily as breathing.

Finally, he turned around, but didn't leave her much space to change. Quickly, not trusting him to stay put, she slipped on the bra—not a bad fit and quite pretty, and the t-shirt—way too big. She scrounged around, knowing there must be more left than just jeans.

"Ryan?" She tried out her sweet voice this time. Didn't seem to suit, but worth a try.

"Yes, Quinn?" He seemed to realize this was not her natural demeanor and chuckled at her, his head turning slightly towards her so she could just see his adorable grin, but he politely kept his eyes averted.

"I hate to be a bother, but did anyone donate any underwear?"

"Nope."

Infuriating man. Nice backside, though. That was the kind of ass they wrote sonnets about. None specifically that she could come up with, but worth considering. If she never found out who she was, perhaps she could make her fortune with nice ass poetry.

"Are you sure?" she pleaded, less sweet and less serene now, but remaining as pleasant as possible, lest she chuck something heavy or sharp at him.

He sighed dramatically. "Really, no underwear. You're lucky anyone was willing to lend you clothes. Leah is letting you borrow the bra and jeans. She's about your same size. However, she wasn't willing to share her underwear with a stranger, so you're going commando."

"Okay. I get it. Weird thing to share, I suppose." She laid back and pulled on the jeans. She hopped up and slid off the bed. Landing on her feet, she started to feel human again. Man, she felt good for someone that was pulled out of the Arctic a few hours ago. And that likely had sustained a serious head injury. Who got amnesia, anyway? Such a cliché.

The shirt was gigantic, and clearly didn't belong to this Leah person. At least Leah wore great jeans, and the bra was delicate and lacy. Way more girly than anything she wore. At least, from what it felt like. She ought to buy more like this. Nice to feel pretty. She tied a quick knot in the side of the shirt so it fit cuter. "Okay, you can turn around."

Ryan turned toward her and hesitated, his mouth briefly gaping open, but he quickly slammed it shut before she could think anything of it. He was back to scowling at her again. "Don't ruin my shirt."

"What?"

"That's my shirt. You're stretching it out with the knot."

That would explain the heavenly smell. All fresh air and nice cologne. "I was swimming in it, so I fixed it. If you didn't want it ruined, you shouldn't have loaned it to me."

"Okay. I'll take it back." He stepped towards her, hands out as if ready to take her shirt right off now.

With a quick squeal, she dodged him. Not that he was actually going to take the shirt off her, right? Damn, she really wanted him to. When was the last time she'd had sex? This was getting downright absurd. "I'll buy you a new one when I find my wallet."

"Deal." He flashed her an adorable wink that made her want to take the shirt off right then and there for him.

THE WOMAN WAS INFURIATING. Adorable, smartass, gorgeous. Fully dry, her hair was brilliantly red now, a playful style, brushing just over the top of her shoulders and so soft he had the strangest urge to run his hands through it. She wasn't like any demon hunter he'd run into.

Still, looks could be deceiving. He'd trusted Greg, his demon hunter mentor, and that was precarious in the end. He wasn't making the same mistakes Greg had. Even for a gorgeous set of midnight-blue eyes that twinkled with pure orneriness.

"Come on, let's get something to eat." He subtly nodded his head towards the door.

She sidled up next to him in her bare feet. "Thanks. I'm so hungry I could eat a horse."

Completely deadpan, he looked down at her and said, "We don't serve horse on the Valkyrie, as a general rule."

"Aren't you Mr. Smartass himself? I'll eat whatever's available, I mean."

Dumb idea giving her his shirt. No idea why he'd done it. Oddly possessive gesture. *Dumbass.*

Stepping out into the fresh air, Quinn didn't jump at the cold metal on her feet or the chill in the air. She followed him down the steel hallway. Well below freezing, but she barely winced. Yep, pure demon hunter. The strange and deadly circumstances of her arrival, her lightning fast reflexes to catch that bra and manage to not drop the blanket, now she wasn't even blinking at the cold.

Too bad she didn't seem to know what she was. If she did, she knew at least to keep it secret. He suspected she didn't have a clue. As long as she didn't figure it out until after she left, or more importantly, she didn't figure out what he was.

"We should get you some shoes," he said. "Yours are still on Willa's boot dryer."

She glanced down at her feet. "Excellent point. I don't need to lose my toes. Although it's not pleasant, the cold doesn't seem to bother me. Well, aside from the hypothermia last night."

Whoever she was, she was incredibly refreshing. He couldn't help but smile with her, at her dry, quirky humor. "Yeah, besides that." Nearly holding his hand out for her, he caught himself in time, before he did anything so obviously foolish.

His quarters were just around the corner, which he preferred to the crowded galley. Sneaking down the path, careful to walk softly on the steel floor with the sprite tiptoeing behind him with her delicate feet, he led them into his room before anyone saw. Most would be eating breakfast about now, anyway. He wasn't ready to bring her around the entire crew just yet.

Harry had quickly discovered that she was different, like Ryan. If Quinn didn't even know what they were, he really didn't want the crew telling her. Not that they knew what a demon hunter was, exactly. Yeah, he really needed to explain himself before the circulating rumors got worse.

Suddenly self-conscious, he picked up the stray clothes and other tidbits from around his room and stuffed them into a drawer. The room was small with minimal standing room and little more than built-in furniture, including a couch, desk, narrow closet-dresser combo, and his bunk. He'd tried to warm up the place with a big-ass poster of the coast where he grew up in California at the foot of his bed. The lack of space should feel suffocating, but he didn't mind.

Until now. Radiant, Quinn's very presence brought the room up a solid ten degrees. No place he could stand without risking touching her. Shoving his hands in his pockets, he did his best to *not* let them bump into each other.

She looked around suspiciously. "So, you cook in here?"

"Nope," he replied simply, letting the answer hang in the air. Man, he really enjoyed messing with her.

Her stomach growled like a grizzly waking from a long winter's hibernation. His wasn't far behind. Finally, he picked up the phone and called Cook. "Send two plates of breakfast to my quarters. Yeah. Long story, but our stowaway is here, too."

"Stowaway," she muttered, blinking profusely in irritation.

"What else am I supposed to call you? You're not part of the crew, nor are you a guest."

"Innocent victim, perhaps?" Hands on her hips, she remained fierce, but her midnight-blue eyes were showing signs of weariness.

"We'll see about that," he mumbled.

She plopped down on the couch and pulled her feet up, hugging her knees. The snarky expression faded to resigned, almost sad. That, then sight of her icicle toes, was too much.

He silently berated himself. He wasn't a complete asshole. Grabbing his coziest socks from his drawer, he sat next to her and pulled her feet onto his lap.

"Sorry." He warmed her toes up between his hands.

Staring at him with midnight-blue eyes, soft and kind, she didn't say anything. Could have, as he'd already found her to be pure smartass. Once he was satisfied her toes weren't going to fall off... not that they would, but he could at least make her comfortable, he pulled the thick socks over her feet and halfway up her calves.

"Thanks," she said, not moving her feet out of his hands.

A knock at the door interrupted them. As if caught red-handed, he slid her feet off his lap and hopped up to get their breakfast.

Willa stood outside, holding a tray of food and coffees. "I've come to meet our guest." She smiled as she entered with the two-person feast.

Ryan quickly pulled out a pint-sized folding table he kept tucked in the closet. Willa set the tray down and sat in his desk chair. The place was cramped with the three of them.

"Welcome aboard the Valkyrie. I'm Captain Price. We're different from the other Coast Guard Vessels, certainly more casual. Please, call me Willa."

"Thanks, Willa. I'm Quinn—" A troubled smile followed the brief introduction. Whether she was truly amnesic or not, she was awfully convincing. Ryan planned to figure out exactly what she remembered and what she didn't before he let her wander the ship.

"She's got amnesia." Really, he tried to be serious, but bit his tongue before he said anything sarcastic. The tone was enough.

Quinn whacked his arm. Ouch. Yeah, stronger than the average human. He may have to say something before she hurt someone. Another reason he didn't want her around the crew just yet.

Pulling the lid off the covered tray, he handed her a cup of coffee and took the other for himself. "Her name was written on her vest, otherwise we don't know a thing about her."

Willa scowled at him in curiosity, watching their interactions with a hawk-like intensity. No wonder she was captain of the most autonomous ship in the fleet. "Quinn, you must be really... tough to have survived such an ordeal."

Ryan watched as Quinn's wheels spun in her brain. Tough was right. She took a slow sip of coffee and finally shrugged. "Apparently."

"What do you remember?"

His sympathy bumped up a notch as she gripped the coffee cup tight in her hands, her eyes a little glassy. "Not much. Nothing. Shit, I don't have a clue. I remember waking up on this boat. Before that... I couldn't tell you much about me at all. I know what amnesia is, and that to forget this much is extraordinarily rare. I feel sad, a sense of hopelessness, even, like something awful brought me here. I couldn't tell you who, but I miss people, mostly loved ones, I assume. I'm pretty sure I have parents and friends and that I like them. I'm pretty comfortable on a boat. Feel like I've spent a lot of time on boats."

Her stomach grumbled again, this time so loudly it echoed from wall to wall of his quarters. Thank goodness he had private quarters. Because of the need for maneuverability, speed, and limited crew, the Valkyrie was one of the smaller cutters. With his rank on the ship and rather unique abilities, it was pretty obvious he wouldn't bunk with the rest of the crew.

Taking pity on Quinn's helplessness, which he suspected was quite uncharacteristic, he traded out her half-consumed coffee to hand her a plate of food. Offering him an appreciative smile that about broke his heart in half, she dug into her breakfast. Suddenly starving himself, he grabbed his plate as well.

With her knowing gaze again, Willa stood and turned to leave. "I'll let you two eat and get some rest. Ryan, I'll be by in an hour or so for a briefing. Quinn, your boots should be dry by then, so I'll bring them by for you. And, I'll round up some more clothes for you. It may be weeks, maybe a month or two, before we can get you home, especially since we don't know where that is."

Quinn nodded politely. "Ryan mentioned it may take time."

They ate their breakfast in silence. As much as he'd doubted the amnesia story to begin with, he was having a hard time convincing himself she was playing him. Clearly a stubborn, opinionated smartass, she'd have no qualms in telling him off... or diving right back in the ocean and swimming back to wherever she came from.

No one said it, but it was more than just getting her home, the delay. Even if they were standing in the middle of a room of family and friends, would she know it? Were she an average human, they could drop her off at a hospital or something. You couldn't just drop a clueless demon hunter with medical professionals.

He'd eventually have to tell Quinn what she was. At least he could answer that one for her. Maybe it would trigger more memories.

Not yet. Not until he knew what sort of demon hunter she was.

5

"So, bathroom?" Quinn smiled up at Ryan. They'd devoured their breakfast, but still had some coffee left in the massive carafe. Ryan had immediately refilled his mug to the brim. He must not have slept at all last night.

"Yep." He didn't bother to hide the shit-eating grin this time. She had already figured out that he enjoyed messing with her, but he was quickly making a sport out of it.

When she started to wiggle from full bladder, he finally hopped up and opened a door next to his desk that she hadn't realized existed. Thank god, his own toilet, sink, and shower. She was afraid she'd have to go down the hall in her bare feet again.

Although, she did enjoy Ryan's hands warming her toes, his unexpected gentle touch, sliding his cozy socks onto her feet. As much as he enjoyed irritating her and didn't seem to trust her as far as he could throw her, his gruff exterior and smartass remarks were an adorable cover to an internal teddy bear. She suspected he wouldn't be too thrilled to hear her assessment of him.

Gratefully, she dashed into the head and emptied her very full bladder. Huh, she had a pretty spectacular bladder capacity.

IV fluids and coffee. She was lucky she didn't overflow the system. After quickly washing up, she popped her head out. "Mind if I get a shower? I smell like I bathed in the ocean. Which, I sort of did. And, do you have a spare toothbrush?"

"You are one demanding stowaway," he muttered with a playful grin. From the cabinet, he grabbed a spare toothbrush and a towel for her.

"Floss?" She grinned with her pleasantest smile, eyes wide in cheery hopefulness.

"Wow, even getting picky," he teased again, his expression morphing to a full smile. "Top drawer."

She pushed him out the narrow doorway. Stripping out of the borrowed clothes, she took a minute to check things out. Female, check. Amnesia didn't exactly make her forget that little tidbit. Huh, not a single scar. She must not be very adventurous, which really didn't sound right.

No stretch marks, perky breasts. Nope no kids. Well, not biological anyway. She cringed to think how awful it would be to forget one had children. No ring on her finger, no tan lines or indents where a ring would have been. Good sign, since she'd been lusting after Ryan since she woke up. She'd hate to be an infidelitous-amnesic-stowaway.

Maybe she was a dentist? She had impeccably maintained teeth and was apparently quite particular about her dental hygiene. Not bad looking. She liked what she saw. Nothing Hollywood or model material, but she was okay with that. Too short anyway.

Turning on the water, she stepped inside the narrow hunk of molded plastic. How did Ryan fit in this tiny shower? Washing quickly, she mentally pondered her circumstances as she cleaned. Must always be efficient in water usage on a boat. Yeah, she must do something with boats, but she really was more convinced it was someone close to her, like a parent, as she felt like she was being instructed in a thoughtful but firm voice while she recited boater safety and efficiency tips.

So, she was the daughter of a sailor and a worked as a dentist. She really didn't feel like a dentist. Ryan had spare toothbrushes and dental floss and impeccable teeth, and he wasn't a dentist.

She must be from Alaska, as she had an impressive tolerance for the cold. Not that she liked it. Certainly pale enough to be from the northern latitudes.

Dammit all, how did she know all the signs to look for, but not the answers?

Tossing the borrowed clothes back on, her scowl rapidly morphed into a grin as she recalled the look on Ryan's face when he saw her in his shirt. So adorable. He was clearly battling the same attraction she was. But he was a gentleman.

Ha, he really wasn't. Might have watched her get dressed if she hadn't insisted he look away. Rather depressingly, there was something he didn't like about her. One moment he was trying to get her to smile, the next he was glowering. She was amiable and polite. A bit sarcastic, but so far, she liked what she knew of herself.

QUINN STEPPED OUT OF the bathroom looking fresh as a spring rain. Her skin was still pinked from the shower, her damp hair so dark and wavy it looked like lava flowing onto the sea floor. Somehow, she looked like she would be intense with the midnight-blue eyes, but there was always amusement behind them.

Shit, who thought that nonsense? Certainly not him.

"Ryan? What is it you don't like about me? I mean, it's not exactly my fault you pulled me out of the ocean. At least, I don't think it is." Hands on her hips, Quinn tapped her foot as she stood in the bathroom doorway. And, her amusement was gone.

No good answer to that one. It wasn't that he didn't like her. "Nothing personal. Splashing down into the frickin' Arctic in the middle of the night... that's not exactly the sort of arrival that brews trust. Whoever you are, lovely as you seem to be, I have my crew to look out for."

Sighing deeply, her head hung low, she brushed past him and dropped to the couch. Resting her hands over her temples, she closed her eyes. "I know. I know. You're not wrong. I'm beginning to suspect that I'm not exactly normal. Who can survive what I did and recover so quickly? Why don't I have a single scar on my body? How did you survive your little swim in the Arctic to come after me? If I could just remember *something* prior to my bizarre arrival on your boat..."

Shit. He wasn't one of those guys that couldn't handle a woman crying. Anyone could cry all they wanted. It was more of the sad-angry-amnesic demon hunter angle that made him a little uncomfortable. "I'm not sure you want to remember. Before you woke up, you looked to be having some epic nightmares." Demon hunter or not, she was hurting. Bad.

"I can't even remember the nightmare. What if I never figure out who I am?" And now the tears started. Well, tear. Just one. Then a fierceness took over. Her body tensed, fists at her sides, and her brow flexed tight as she searched her empty memory for a glimpse of the events that brought her here.

Leaning against the closet, he crossed his arms and feet and sighed deeply. His chest rising and falling under his arms, he nearly choked on the ball of turmoil that was lodged in his throat. "Honestly, I'm not sure. It's only been a few hours. Give it time."

Time? More time meant a longer stay on the Valkyrie. With him. Driving him crazy with a gut-wrenching internal argument, deciding if he wanted to toss her overboard or woo her.

See? Woo? What kind of guy says woo?

"I'm sure you don't have time for babysitting." She looked up and raised her eyebrows at him.

"No, I don't. However, I consider this more guard duty than babysitting. In the old days, we'd lock you in the hold, then drop you at the nearest port. A stowaway that won't even tell us her full name." He raised a single eyebrow at her, hoping she'd smile again. Already, he missed the amusement behind those midnight blues.

She raised the corner of her mouth in an already familiar expression. "Guard duty, huh? I'm a threat?" She paused.

He started to speak, but she stopped him.

"Wait, no, don't answer that. Of course I am. What sort of person wears a bulletproof vest as she blasts through the air on waterspout, apparently, and can survive a little swim in the Arctic circle? I get it. I wouldn't trust me either."

She was right. He couldn't trust her. Especially... especially because the more he got to know her, the more he genuinely liked her. If their roles were reversed, he'd bet his next three paychecks she'd be just as distrustful and he just as frustrated. Well, she probably didn't have as much reason to be wary of another demon hunter, but any fool would be cautious.

Theoretically, any number of demons, vampires, werewolves, most other human-demon hybrids could have similar abilities, but he knew she was a demon hunter. Fate would be cruel enough to dump a ridiculously attractive demon hunter in his lap.

"Ryan?" she asked, looking up and forming a genuinely sweet smile this time.

He realized he'd been staring at his feet for who knows how long. Too long. When he looked up at her, he saw the amusement growing in that dark blue gaze again. "Yes, Quinn?"

"Thanks."

"For?"

"Everything. Pulling me out of the water. Letting me stay. Putting up with my predicament. Just... I trust you, somehow, even if you don't trust me yet. I probably shouldn't, but you've taken good care of me so far. Maybe someday I'll pay you back?"

And this was why he hadn't thrown her overboard. Yet. He wanted to say it was the sweetness of her smile and the wittiness of her personality. Maybe it was that slight attitude in her turned-up nose, lush bow-shaped lips, and... well, shit, those spectacularly pert breasts and... ok, lust was definitely a factor.

He was an idiot. At least he was a self-aware adoring idiot.

"Stay put. I need a shower, too. You weren't the only one in the ocean last night." Glancing around the room, he realized she could easily find his stash of weapons and take over the entire ship in a matter of minutes. "Stay put. Don't snoop."

Mocking him with adorable sarcasm, she saluted. "Aye, aye, Ryan. I promise to not leave this room or do any snooping." She laid back on the couch, stretching out with her head on one arm and crossed feet on the other.

"Okay," he said. Didn't exactly have much choice. He was definitely not bringing her into the closet-sized bathroom with him. Nor was anyone on board strong enough to stop her if he arranged for someone else to keep an eye on her.

Taking the fastest shower possible, just managing to scrub out the dried ocean from his hair and wash away the stiff layer of salt that was caked onto his skin, he quickly wrapped the towel around his waist and swung the door open to check on her.

Safe and sound. She lay curled on the couch, deeply in sleep. Must be exhausted still. Hypothermia, even for a demon hunter, was no joke. Took a hell of a lot longer than the average human for it to hit, but even a demon hunter couldn't stand it forever. Every muscle in her body had been working overtime to keep her blood pumping. Demon hunters may be obscenely hard to kill, but not impossible.

He'd know.

Although she was asleep, he left the bathroom door open a crack so he could keep an eye on her in case she woke while he got dressed. Hanging his towel on the rack, he noticed hers was neatly folded and hung, taking up just under fifty percent of the towel rack. Her toothbrush was in the holder alongside his. The hand towel had been straightened, not a drip of water lingered in the sink. She was either a neat freak or trying to avoid wearing out her welcome.

Moving to the desk chair, he slipped on his socks and boots. Her brow was scrunched together, and those sad whimpers escaped her lips now and again. Every so often, her breathing would accelerate, then calm down again as a tear streamed down her cheek.

Probably a good thing she didn't remember whatever shit was bouncing around that gorgeous head of hers. Whatever had sent her to his doorstep was clearly the stuff of nightmares.

Ryan flicked the lingering drips of water from his hair and stood abruptly. Whoever the hell she was, she couldn't stay here. Those were some nasty memories, and he had an awful hunch it was a big, bad, vicious sort of demon that would be capable of giving a demon hunter nightmares and wiping her memory. Her team would be looking for her. Even if she was trustworthy, chances were, they were exactly the sort he'd been avoiding.

Just as he was about to open the door, a knock sounded from the other side. Glancing to Quinn, he was reassured she hadn't stirred. It took a lot for a demon hunter to sleep that hard. Even though she didn't know what she was, her survival instincts would be deeply ingrained.

He softly opened the door and stepped out. Voices echoed down the path. Willa stood before him, holding Quinn's dried boots out. Snagging the boots from her, he gestured for her to follow, staying in sight of his door.

Checking the area, he ensured they were alone. Clenching and loosening his grip on Quinn's combat boots, he tried to think of what to say. How to inform his captain of the trouble he'd brought on board.

As usual, Willa beat him to the punch. Yeah, she must have something far back in her DNA. She was a little spooky sometimes. Speaking just above a whisper, she stated rather than asking, "She's like you."

In a similar soft voice, he responded, "Mostly. None are exactly like me, thank goodness. She's more of your run-of-the-mill demon hunter. The sooner we get her offloaded, the better."

"Does she know what she is?"

He shook his head and sighed heavily. "She's totally clueless. Smart though, she'll figure it out soon enough."

Willa rolled her eyes. "We can't exactly leave a demon hunter with amnesia to find her way alone. She'd shock the hell out of any medical care we could find for her, or accidentally hurt someone if we just left her on the street."

Nodding, he begrudgingly agreed. "As much as I hate to admit it, waiting until we get to Sitka gives her time to remember, or at least to learn what she is. If nothing else, my mom can take her in if she stays chill. In the meantime, I don't want her out of my sight. She seems harmless, but I want to be sure before we let her roam about."

"I think she's okay, but I agree, it would be foolish to trust any stranger that we fished out of the ocean. But you can't be with her twenty-four-seven. You've got a job to do. And, can you imagine the headlines if anyone found out we held an injured woman hostage... in my XO's private quarters?"

He snorted, "We'd generate a lot more serious of headlines if anyone caught wind of what we do around here. I'll give her privacy, but no one else on board could handle her if she turns out to be up to no good."

"And your job?"

"When she's not with me, she's got to have a guard that can come get me if she tries anything. Agreed?"

"On it. I'll have Kyle stand outside the door for today. You head up to the bridge. We've been tracking what looks to be a whirlpool. If that weren't enough, a distress call is coming from the area."

"Dammit. I should have figured it was something when we changed course so abruptly. How big? Are we talking kraken size or more Charybdis?"

Willa rolled her eyes at him, moving away from the metal pole she'd been leaning against. "Of all those myths, has anything ever quite been what we expected? Of what the stories tell us?"

He gave her a wink and backed up. "It's the best we've got on what we might be headed into. The stories get more and more twisted and unbelievable with time. Case in point: we've been named demon hunters, courtesy of you humans, but have you ever actually seen a demon? A bit more of a biblical term than suits. Monster hunters or paranormal protectors would be more apt, but, thanks to the tales, we're stuck with the misnomer."

She chuckled and strode in the direction of the crew's quarters to find Kyle. "Even you have to admit, demon hunter sounds so much cooler. As do the clever names and stories we attribute to the monsters."

Man, he knew he'd been lucky in this assignment. He'd run away to the Coast Guard to use his abilities in a positive way. Without inheriting a mountain of cash like those that descended from generations of demon hunters, he'd needed to find a real job, anyway. More, without the support of a team, he wouldn't survive on his own. No, he liked his human crew much better. And, cost wasn't an issue, as his ventures were on the US dime.

Up on the bridge, Leah was at the helm. Always cold, she'd shut the windows. That's why he preferred to work at night when everyone else was asleep. He could blast the room with arctic air. Damn stuffy in here with the heat blasting.

"What have you got?" he asked as he moved to her side. Manuel was nearby, studying wave patterns on his computer.

Leah shrugged. "So far, no visual."

Pointing at his screen, Manuel seemed to have more info. "Check this out. Just a few small whirlpools, but could be something. It's not somewhere you'd expect natural whirlpools."

"Small, huh? Maybe nothing major, just some visitors that got lost on the wrong side of the veil." It had only taken a handful of battles to figure out what most demon hunters didn't realize... or didn't care about. Not all the demons they fought were malicious. Many were just lost or didn't realize the risks of crossing to this side. Destructive either way, and his job was to protect humanity. One way or another.

Returning to the bridge, Willa came up the stairs. She spoke softly so only he could hear. "Ryan, it's time."

"Time?" he raised a puzzled eyebrow at her and ran his hand through his short hair.

"It's up to you, what and how much to tell them, but having her on board is risky, the crew needs to know enough to understand she's more dangerous than she seems." Willa was dead serious. She had a point.

He'd been considering saying something since their last deployment but had been putting it off. Those raised by demon hunting parents, that had a team to back them up, they guarded the secret with their life. People feared what was different. Acceptance was tough to earn as it was, but for someone as different as he was...

Half of the crew was already crowded in the bridge. Might as well get started. This crew was as close as he was ever going to get to an honest team. "Uh, guys?"

Wow, real official XO. Half a dozen pair of eyes bored into him, waiting for him to vocalize what they suspected.

"You probably already figured out that I'm not exactly like you."

Manuel jovially chuckled from his post. "No shit."

Leah nudged his side. "Spider bite? Superhero serum? Alien?"

Yep. He should have spoken up sooner. How many theories had they compiled? "Ha. Funny. Now, you know everything we do on this ship is classified. This is more classified. Like, no one outside of this ship can know. Not your mother, not your partner, not your fucking next milkman. Nobody, or you're off the ship, dishonorable discharged."

"Shit, man. You're serious," Leah said, darkly squinting while she braced the wheel.

"Dead serious. But that woman we rescued, she's like me. Demon hunter. Half human, half demon, born to fight monsters. Unfortunately, that demon side comes with some, uh, violent tendencies. You meet anyone else like me, like Quinn, you keep your distance."

Nodding, a few seemed to absorb what he'd said. Again, Manuel wouldn't let him get away with anything. Chuckling, the big guy's cheeks were scrunched in a huge grin. "So you're like Buffy?"

Ryan rubbed a hand awkwardly through his short hair. "Sort of. Descended from a demon ancestor bent on protecting Earth, not a chosen one thing. A few hundred of us in existence." Well, none exactly like him.

Sauntering up the stairs with coffee in hand, Dean rubbed the sleep from his eyes and nodded. Barely nineteen years old, with a patchy stubble growing on his chin, yet he didn't even flinch. "Yeah, figures. No way you could have survived your little swim in the Arctic as an ordinary human."

Laughing, Manuel clapped his hands. "I think I still hold the strongest sailor title around here. Demon blood don't count, but not to worry, Ryan, I'll beat you at arm-wrestling one of these days."

Finally relaxing, realizing they weren't going to toss him overboard for the freak that he was, Ryan joined in the teasing, "Nice try. Keep up that sort of talk and you'll be swabbing the deck every night for the rest of this deployment." He responded to a barrage of questions about demon hunters, their purpose, and their skills, but neatly avoided anything personal. "Okay, everybody back to work. We've got some monsters to track." Dashing downstairs, he went to bring the rest of the crew up to speed while he was still hyped up on the relieving sensation of acceptance.

A few hours passed before they reached the whirlpool. Cluster of whirlpools, as it were, back on the bridge. So far north, the sky glowed an eerie blue. Feet braced wide, he held on tight as the ship crashed through increasingly erratic waves.

Good thing he didn't get seasick, or he'd be working to keep his lunch down.

STRETCHING OUT THE LAST of her nap from her heavy limbs, Quinn wrapped the blanket around her shoulders and looked about the room. She'd almost forgotten where she was. Wouldn't that have been a bitch, to keep forgetting stuff?

Ryan must have laid the blanket over her. And put the pillow under her head. For a distrustful jackass, he certainly was sweet. She didn't blame him for not trusting her. Whatever she was, she was not normal. It didn't take a complete memory to recognize *dangerous*.

The ship rolled with some unusual wave patterns that seemed to come out of nowhere. No porthole in the room, she couldn't tell if it was dark or light, stormy, or just turbulent seas. Looking around, her face fell as she realized her shoes hadn't been delivered. Willa seemed to be a decent human being and had promised to bring them. It was clearly Ryan's fault she had nothing but his oversized, yet very cozy socks on her feet.

Giggling to herself, she considered what they said about the size of a man's socks. Wow, she could remember the stupidest shit, but nothing useful.

Without snooping—it wasn't snooping if you didn't touch any-thing—she explored his room. There was a sweet picture over his desk of him wearing a crisp new Coast Guard uniform with his arm draped over an adorable woman dressed in jeans and a breezy linen blouse, with wildly wavy blond hair. Must be his mother. She leaned into him with such pride. Yeah, he was a good guy, he just didn't want Quinn to know it.

Curious, she creaked open the metal door to scope things out. Not that she was planning to leave or anything, she just wanted to see the sky.

A very handsome, innocent face greeted her. He couldn't be more than twenty-two or twenty-three. "You're to stay put, Captain and the XO's orders," the actually rather stern face said, his arms crossed over his chest and feet planted wide against the rocking of the ship. It was tough to take him seriously, with his hair in a rebellious disarray, thanks to more than his fair share of cowlicks on his scalp.

Smiling her sweetest, most manipulative grin, her eyelashes batting a bit more than necessary, she lied easily. "Ryan had wanted me to come join him as soon as I was awake. And, as you see, I'm awake."

Skeptical baby blue eyes squinted right back at her. "He didn't mention anything like that to me. You're going to have to stay put until he's off duty."

"I'm bored. You could come in and visit." She was beyond bored. When one lacked memories to reflect on to keep the brain busy, life was really dull. She couldn't explore and she couldn't snoop. Twiddling her thumbs was only interesting for so long.

As she only had about eight hours of memory, most of which she'd slept through, she had little more than thoughts of Ryan to fill her brain. And that was a terrible idea. She'd seen enough soap operas, as much as she hated to admit it... actually, how did she know that? Either way, she knew people with amnesia really shouldn't date anyone. Never ended well when they discovered they had been happily married before the accident. Or had been psycho serial killers.

Crashing violently, the boat slammed across waves coming at them from everywhere. She could feel a slight spinning, as the helmsman fought against a circling current. Breath rushing rapidly in and out of her lungs, she said, "Whirlpools. We need to get out of here."

Her guard smiled in smug delight. "Captain knows what she's doing."

A high-pitched shriek reverberated through the gunwales of the ship, piercing into her skull. Her gut roiled as something triggered inside her she couldn't identify. Instinctively, she shoved through the open doorway and ran past her guard to investigate.

Another ship, looked to be a fishing vessel, was a hundred yards off, spinning circles on the top of the ocean. A long line connected it to the Valkyrie. Engines roaring so loud the ground beneath her vibrated, they were pulling the other vessel out of harm's way.

Slowly, they made progress, and the other vessel righted itself and followed in their wake. Surrounding it, mostly in the center of the whirlpools, were... white caps? No, they were moving wrong.

A bizarre looking creature leaped onto the lower deck with an icy splash. Its face, arms, and legs were structured like a human, but white seaweed-like webbing and flaps draped from its appendages. Oddly pretty, in a creepy, it's-trying-to-kill-us sort of way.

The screech echoed again, and from her perch overlooking the scene, Quinn was ready to dive over the rail. Her guard caught up. He grabbed her from behind, locking his hand around her elbow.

As she strained to resist the urge to knock him flat and go after the creature, she heard him yell over the hollering winds, "Stay put, we've got this."

Against every instinct that screamed in her mind to go after it, her muscles tensing, senses focusing, heart pumping as her adrenaline kicked into overdrive, she listened and stayed where she was.

For now, anyway.

A gnawing ache trembled through her limbs. Spikes zapped through her skull as she clenched her fists at her sides. Ignoring the threat became physically painful, a bizarre sort of torture she couldn't explain.

Running out onto the deck like an avenging warrior, Ryan slashed out, slicing into the creature's torso. Fast. Almost gracefully brutal in his attack. He didn't hesitate.

Enraged, the creature's lovely face scrunched in horror and it bared its cow-like teeth, gnashing, ready to crunch him into a pulp. Growling back at it, Ryan punched the monster with his free hand.

Reeling, the creature was knocked backwards, but lashed out at his leg with a tentacle limb that appeared out of nowhere, pulling Ryan to the ground next to it.

Quinn couldn't hear over the gusting wind and rumbling engines, but Ryan was roaring a demand at the monster, as if he wanted to talk rather than fight.

It didn't seem to be listening.

Rolling to the side then pushing off the ground, Ryan kicked its face to free himself from its grip.

Howling, it released him.

Without waiting for it to counter, he flipped to his feet.

The creature struggled back to a standing position and flailed its limbs at him like a windmill.

Furious, Ryan wasn't messing around anymore. With a calculated swing of his sword, he beheaded the creature swiftly and efficiently.

He could have done that right off, but he had given it a chance. Acid churned in her gut, as she realized she wouldn't have hesitated to take it out.

He rolled his shoulders and tossed his sword to the ground, its steel clanging as it hit the wall of the ship. Grabbing the slimy remains, he heaved its massive, limp body back into sea. He flicked a heap of clear goo from his hand, cringing in disgust before plucking up the head and throwing it overboard after the body.

Another head, still attached to its body, poked out from the center of one of the smaller whirlpools in the distance.

"Go. Home." Someone was hollering from above, right before an ear-splitting crack, and a glowing flare landed inches in front of the creature.

Thunderless black lightning flashed all around. Crackles echoed across ocean. The whirlpools slowly calmed, the waves evened out, and the wind quieted.

Shaking off a glob of slime from his arm, Ryan turned and caught sight of her. Scowling, his eyebrows dropped low over his gunmetal gray, nearly black eyes, he bit his cheek and shook his head at her.

Smiling innocently, she shrugged a wave and dashed back to the room.

A few minutes later, the door swung open and Ryan stormed in, slamming the metal door behind him. Before the echo from the crash of the door finished reverberating, he had his shirt peeled off, and he wiped the colorless slime from his face using the inside of the t-shirt. He cussed and growled as he seemed to smear it around more than clean it off.

Pissed at the slime or at her, probably both, his dark scowl landed on her. "What the hell were you doing? I thought I said to stay in here."

Shooting a fiery glare right back at him, she righteously folded her arms across her chest, her foot tapping against the floor. "I'm not going to sit around while you have all the fun."

Fun? She was getting weirder by the minute. Who found beheading gooey sea creatures fun? And why wasn't she more disturbed by what she had seen?

"Just... stay put. I'm going to take another fucking shower." After tossing his shirt onto the bathroom floor in front of him, he was halfway out of his pants before she realized he wasn't closing the door.

Great. Now he was torturing her in a very different way. It was official, he had the best damn ass she'd ever seen.

Probably. So she didn't actually remember ever seeing one, but she really couldn't even imagine a finer one.

Head tilting to the side so she could watch from the couch, she admired the view, and his lack of modesty, as he stepped into the shower. Through the frosty fake glass, she didn't hesitate to watch the impressive silhouette as he soaped off the slime, even giving an extra scrub to the naughty bits.

When one had so few memories, it was worth investing in as many good ones as possible. And, the sight of Ryan fuming and naked was definitely worth building a foundation on.

Despite his mood, she couldn't say she was the least bit afraid of him. He was clearly all bark and no bite... and the bark didn't seem natural for him. The bulk of his anger seemed more self-directed than anything.

Crashing open the shower door, nearly knocking it off its hinges and shattering the faux glass, Ryan ripped his towel off the rack. Peeking out at her, Ryan's lips quirked up in a brief, devious satisfaction before he pushed closed the bathroom door.

Yep, he was totally doing this on purpose. He finally came out with his towel draped loosely around his hips. Damn, not just a nice ass. That man was ridiculously well built. Solid, too. No wiry limbs for Ryan. He did a lot of heavy lifting, that was for sure.

Quinn bit her lips together to silence her whimpering sigh.

From the drawer under his bunk, he fisted a pair of navy-blue cargo pants and a fresh t-shirt. Sadly, he pulled the tee over those gorgeous abs.

The towel clung on for dear life. Why didn't she have telekinetic abilities? One good breeze and her view would improve substantially.

Raising that roguish eyebrow at her, he interrupted her moment. "Mind covering your eyes?"

She snorted indelicately. "Thanks to your little tantrum, I've already seen most of the goods. Come on, I have so little going on in this empty brain."

"Tit for tat," he teased, those dreamy lips forming a wicked grin. Recalling that he'd turned around when she'd insisted that morning, she'd be a good sport. Must be the amnesia, and really only having one person that she'd spent more than two minutes with, but she rather enjoyed their banter.

"Fine." She rolled her eyes and turned her head, but got distracted by the gap that briefly opened in the towel. Not quite the view she'd been hoping for. "Your leg. It got you."

Across his thigh, a puffy red laceration spanned the length of her hand. The blood was nearly gone thanks to the shower, but it still looked painfully inflamed. He shifted the towel and revealed the entire mark. "Hurts like a son-of-a-bitch, but it'll heal. Just a flesh wound."

"No, that looks terrible. Let's get you to the medic." Quinn felt her pulse pounding through her, a waking nightmare boiling under the surface.

Moving closer, she knelt in front of him and inspected the wound. Running her fingers along the edges of the redness, she felt a deep anger rising, reacting more intensely than she should.

Images flashed of a deep laceration into his abdomen instead, and how much worse the injury could have been, of someone crumpled lifelessly on the ground.

As quickly as it had entered her mind, the trace of memory was gone. The tightness in her chest, the tunnel vision lingered, and she struggled to stay conscious.

Ryan adjusted his grip on the towel and knelt down in front of her. Lifting her chin, he looked her in the eye, his expression gentle. "Hey. It's ok. Like I said, just a flesh wound. Trust me, I've had way worse."

Nodding, she gulped down the thick worry, controlling the tremor that vibrated through her body. Holding onto his softened gaze, she soaked up the glow of silver in his eyes.

"Ok." She nodded and rose to stand.

"Quinn?"

"Yes, Ryan?" she asked as she moved back to the couch.

He paused. Rising to his feet, gripping the towel firmly, he shook his head, clearly changing his mind on whatever he was going to say. "Never mind. You've had a hell of a day."

The dizziness began to subside, and she leaned back into the couch, taking a long, heavy inhale. "Getting fished out of the Arctic probably was not the start of it, either."

"Agreed," he whispered. He plucked his cargos off the floor and, with a sweetly wicked smile, he asked, "Mind covering your eyes?"

At his subject change, she pulled herself out from under the suffocating dark cloud and instead covered her face with the pillow. "Are you going to tell me what's going on around here?" she asked, her voice muffled by the pillow that still smelled deliciously of Ryan, fresh and salty and masculine.

"Well, I'm putting pants on, and you're hiding your face to maintain my sense of modesty. Willa wasn't exactly pleased that I'm making you bunk in here. But I can't trust you yet, and I sure as hell don't trust anyone else to keep a close enough eye on you."

"Your guardsman certainly was bossy and insisted that I stay put."

"And, did you?"

"No," she admitted, her voice still muffled.

Without warning, the pillow was yanked out of her hands and he tossed it back on his bed. Static adhered her hair over her face. She brushed it aside and scowled at him.

He dropped to her side on the sofa. His voice softer, serious, he leaned back. "I really need you to stay put until we figure out what to do with you. As you said yourself, I need to know I can trust you before you can wander the ship. What you saw today... we're not your average Coast Guard vessel. We handle the more obscure rescues and threats. For your safety, and my crew, *please* don't leave the room without me. At least until we figure out more about you."

A sigh heavy on her chest, she leaned closer and rested her head against his shoulder.

He stilled at the contact.

"Makes sense," she said. She drew air in slow and even as she collected her thoughts. She really needed a hug after everything she'd been through, but this was as far as she dared push. "I appreciate you pulling me out of the ocean. Whoever I am... I'm not sure either of us wants to find out."

After her urge to go kill the thing that had jumped on board, she was a bit... horrified with herself.

The anger, the guilt that hung heavy over Ryan like a thick blanket after he'd sliced its head off in one easy swing was heartbreaking.

She'd been ready to tear the creatures apart, limb by limb, but he'd been so human about it. Made her worry that he didn't trust her for a good reason. That she was the real monster around here.

Briefly, he rested his cheek against the top of her head before pulling away. "I'll grab us some dinner. Sit tight."

Lana, Sitka.

"SHE'S DEAD," BENNETT SNAPPED. Again and again, since he'd re-gained consciousness in Dutch Harbor, and the few days since they'd arrived back in Sitka, he insisted that they'd all gone completely nuts in this fruitless search for Quinn. Drove Lana nuts, but she understood his heart was shattered, both in regret and in grief.

But everyone grieved in different ways. She resisted the urge to stomp her feet as she paced their isolated corner of the tavern. Her grandparents had built the place from the ground up, initially just for demon hunters, but eventually opened it to the public. Today, it was their Alaska hub. Like Quinn's hole-in-the-wall apartment in California, and Bennett's family home in British Columbia. Astrid was originally from back east and hadn't declared a home base on this side of North America yet. Vann still lived in Quinn's building where they'd met a few years back. He was a bit more private than open-book Quinn and didn't exactly offer for them to hang at his place very often.

"Quinn wouldn't give up on any of us." Vann's voice rumbled, his tone fierce, shaking the walls of the empty tavern. A few hours before lunch, the doors hadn't opened to the public yet, thank goodness.

Spinning around, Lana flipped her dark curls out of her face. "Ex-actly. She *didn't* give up on us. Hell, Bennett, your guts were spilling onto the ground, the rest of us flattened, and she stood up to Typha. Alone. Swords drawn, she was going all-in for guts and glory to avenge the rest of us."

Pensively in the corner, Astrid shook her head. "Someone was talking to her in there. Didn't you hear her? She said something about the sixth."

"Here we go again. Back to that prophecy. Clearly, it's wrong. Quinn's gone. We lost." Bennett gripped the arms of the worn club chair, his knee rattling a mile a minute.

Lana dropped onto the couch, restless and preferring to pace, but she needed Bennett to hear them. He'd been so caught up in his obsession with this prophecy, convinced that he was the chosen one, that his and Quinn's love could end Typha. No offense to Bennett, she was sure they loved each other, but it wasn't exactly the sort anyone wrote books about.

"The prophecy isn't just about the love between two demon hunters. Typha said we had part of what we need, and someone was in Quinn's head talking about the sixth. Without Quinn, we're down to four." Her own knee rattled faster than Bennett's in their shared restless anxiety.

Astrid finally looked up from the ancient text she'd been pouring through since they'd been back. Her finger had turned black from reading with such tenacity, reading every word with an intensity Lana had never seen in her.

Manner calm, despite the clear excitement brewing in that big brain, Astrid spoke softly, silencing them even more than Vann would have with the gravity in her voice. "I don't know why I hadn't found this part of the passage before. I think we weren't meant to. Yes, it says six, as we'd seen before, but there's more. The sixth is different than we are, unique among demon hunters. There's a mention of seven as the key, but, nonspecific, like maybe not even a person. Maybe Deandra is the seventh?"

"It's a *prophecy*. As distorted and inaccurate from the telling and retelling, just like the stories of the creatures we fight." Lana stood and paced again. She quit caring that she was making them all dizzy with her erratic movements.

She flipped on the switch behind Astrid, illuminating the dim tavern. Immediately, she regretted the action. The dark circles under her friends' eyes, the regret in their tightly clenched jaws... felt like a slap in the face. That un-fun sort of wake-up call.

Still as a statue, Vann said, "Bet it was Deandra, the mother of all demon hunters, that sent Quinn from us, distracting Typha long enough for us to get out of there. Typha looked furious when Quinn blasted out of there. I think the *part* she was referring to was Quinn."

Astrid nodded. "Exactly. And, hopefully, Deandra sent her to number six. So, if we find Quinn, we find Six, maybe Seven, although Deandra makes sense as the seventh, then, if this new information is true, we can go for Typha once again."

"How in the hell did we go from Quinn was hearing voices to, Deandra blasted her on a water spout to Six?"

Bennett rubbed his hands over his face, his eyebrows ruffled and expression unsteady as he said, "Because I was right. That recon set things in motion. We searched for two fucking years for Six, and *nothing*."

Lana flipped the irritating dark curl out of her face again. "We've met all the others in existence at some point or another, and I didn't get the right vibe from *any* of them. Certainly, they all have the same powers we do, nothing unique, and I feel like we'd know if they were destined to join us in taking down one of the biggest baddies of them all."

"Actually," Bennett said, not looking at anyone in particular as he calculated. "Makes sense. Quinn's friendlier than the rest of us, convinced most of us to join. If anyone could recruit one or two more demon hunters, it would be Quinn."

Lana snorted, gripping the back of Bennett's chair. "Really, no offense Bennett, but I think we'll still be missing the 'destined soulmate demon hunters' that will be a critical part of taking Typha's power down a few notches." She cringed, hating to say it, but he just wasn't hearing them. Even Quinn had been unconvinced.

Turning slightly in his chair, he looked up at her and shot her a nasty glare. "What's your problem? If Quinn were here, you'd see that we're the real thing."

With a twirl, she parked on the arm of his chair. He pulled his hand away in the nick of time and his brow scrunched as his irritability deepened. Lana set her hand on his shoulder, hating how much he was hurting. "But she's not here. If Vann's right, she's with Six. If we can find Six, we'll find Quinn. Whatever the prophecy, I want my cousin back."

Valkyrie, Norton Sound.

QUINN'S LATEST DULL READ dropped onto her face as she lost her grip on it. Not sleepy, just losing interest. Willa had loaned her some charts and history books to see if she could figure out where she'd come from, but it was incredibly boring. As instructed, she'd attempted to retrieve her memories while they explored the region, inspecting vessels along the way.

A cold blast of air rushed in as Ryan rescued her from her doldrums. He chuckled when he saw her pathetic sprawl on the couch. Piles of charts neatly rolled on the floor below her, one foot on the back of the couch and the other on the floor, her hair in a wild tangle... she looked deranged.

"I can't look at another dang chart. It's all wiggly lines and words. I now have the entire region memorized and don't have a clue where I've been within that map." She added the thicker book of Alaskan history that bruised her throbbing nose to the stack beneath her.

Setting a collection of books on the desk, Ryan pulled one out and handed it to her. "Here, I snagged a few from the library for you. There's more in my top drawer if you're interested. Fiction. Not helpful for your memory, but maybe more entertaining."

"*Moby Dick*? No thanks. I'll stick with the maps." She begrudgingly accepted the book, but added it to the rest.

He flashed her that mischievous smile and grabbed two other books from the stack. "Better?" He tossed her a well-worn *Harry Potter*.

She pulled back her foot and curled up onto her half of the couch to give him more space to sit, out of genuine appreciation. "You're a lifesaver. Thank you."

Quinn watched as Ryan unlatched his desk chair and pulled it closer, dropped onto the couch at her feet, and plopped his feet on the chair. He opened the Ken Follett he'd taken for himself and his eyes started to scan the page. Finally noticing her staring, he glanced sideways at her and asked, "Yes, Quinn?"

Smiling, she bit her lip and slid her feet closer. "I'm bored. My empty brain is as interesting as the middle of the Sahara, but without the dunes. I'm too bored to read."

Marking his page and setting down his book, he rotated toward her. Rather than pushing her feet away, he lifted her legs and draped them over his. "How can you be too bored to read?"

Her mind suddenly became more barren than the Atacama Desert, and not because of the amnesia, but the easy, unplanned affection, and she struggled to think of what to say. "I love to read, but I think I need a bit more sensory input than paper and ink. Tell me some of your memories, as I'm fresh out of my own. Where did you grow up?"

His hand wrapped around her foot, sending electrified shivers straight northward. "Arcata, California. My mom, Sunshine, left a nearby commune when she met my father and agreed to have me. Determined to give me a fairly normal life, she settled us in Arcata."

"What were you like as a kid?" She rested her arms behind her head, propped up on the pillow so she could watch his expressions as he spoke. His face softened when he told her about his mother. She'd seen the photo, clearly a neat lady and proud mama.

Sighing, smiling, he rolled his eyes and mindlessly rubbed her foot. "You're not going to be satisfied until you've listened to me talk until my voice goes hoarse, are you?"

"Nope." She grinned, enjoying the smile that spread to his dark eyes that we framed by those thick lashes. Not to mention, she was luxuriating in the zing from his long fingers tracing the contours of her ankles.

"I was a pretty normal kid. Played outside, on the beach collecting as many treasures as I could put in my pockets. Every so often, I'd try to sneak home a shore crab to keep as a pet, but Mom always caught on and made me put it back, saying the poor thing had a life of its own to live."

"Just you and your mom? What happened to your dad?"

"He couldn't stay. So, it was always me and Mom."

He was pretty matter of fact about his absent father, but she didn't push. Enjoying seeing him so at ease, unhurried and temporarily not acknowledging his distrust in her, she didn't want him to stop. For now, he didn't seem to object, or even notice the soothing, mindless foot massage he was providing. Like a satisfied cat stretched out in a patch of sun, she absorbed the rich timbre of his voice that was newly laced with content. At her urging, he shared story after story from his youth.

Quinn could picture the sweetly impish boy, the awkward teen, all leading to the fearsome, gentle warrior he was today. Not that he'd word it that way. He was adorably modest. She could listen to him all day and all night. Actually, that's about all she *could* do anyway, unofficially imprisoned in his bedroom. Still, it wouldn't be a burden.

Watching his eyes light up as he recalled the clever mischief of his childhood antics, those delicious lips as he smiled when lost in memories, she was a goner. Not that she had anything to compare to, but she couldn't imagine enjoying another face so well. Or another voice.

"Tell me about your first kiss." She raised her eyebrows and grinned playfully.

Shifting her feet off his lap, he started to get up. "And, we're done here."

Wrapping her legs around his waist, she pulled him back down. Somehow, she was successful. Dang, she was strong. Surprise flashed dark in his eyes, before the neutral gray kicked back in and his brow settled. If she wasn't mistaken, there was even a flash of silver in there.

"Please? I don't remember mine." She leaned up and sat criss-cross-applesauce, facing him and watching his eyes crinkle as he considered her question.

With a soft shake of his head, he gave in and leaned back into the couch. Looking off into the distance, he smiled softly. "Stephanie Kane. Homecoming my freshman year of high school. She was two years older. I'd developed ahead of the other guys my age, reached six feet by my fourteenth birthday. Girls had noticed, and I didn't mind. Anyway, while everyone was distracted by the homecoming court arrival, we snuck behind the photographer's curtain."

"How was it?"

His cheeks blushed pink, and he looked up at the ceiling, a self-effacing cringe on his face. "Wet. Messy. Terrible."

Quinn couldn't help it. She fell back on the couch and began laughing hysterically.

"Hey, I'm sure yours wasn't any better." He laughed right alongside her, his humor glowing deeper as her giggling spun toward ridiculous.

Stuck in a delirious giggle fit, she laughed until her abs hurt. Eventually, she caught her breath, wiping the tears of mirth from her cheeks. Looking up at Ryan, she caught him watching her, that corner of his mouth turning up.

His hand slid along her calf and rested behind her knee. Watching, waiting for her to catch her breath, he lightly squeezed.

Her heart skipped a few beats as she thought he was making a move. Until that mischievous grin, the amusement in his eyes, revealed his intentions. "No," she squealed, already giggling again, ineffectively trying to pull her leg from his grip.

Tormenting her, he relentlessly pinched and tickled at the backs of her knees, sliding up to her thighs, her abdomen. The more she tried to wiggle off the couch and out of his reach, the more he pulled her into his grip and the sillier they both became.

As both were laughing so hard anyone passing by his door would think them completely demented, he stilled his hand. Limbs entwined, their breathing slowed, and they carefully untangled.

Ryan leaned against the back of the couch. His smile slowly faded. Hers followed close behind. Catching his breath, he ran his hand through his hair, scowling up at the ceiling.

Goofing off, flirting like a couple of reckless kids was stupid. She didn't have a clue who she was, or what Ryan was. It didn't seem to matter that she was rescued from such an unusual circumstance, that no human could have survived. That she had a taste for violence. That he was clearly no ordinary man.

He was just so damn pleasant to be around. Easygoing but intense. Filled with happy memories, but feared himself as much as he feared her, and she was going nuts wanting to ask why. For now, she accepted their carefree afternoon as a win.

WHAT THE HELL WAS he doing? She was nothing but trouble. Somehow, despite his better judgment, and knowledge that she was a cold-blooded slayer of monsters, he found himself laughing and flirting and behaving like an eager cadet on his first shore leave.

Both formed a silent agreement, returning to their books and absolutely not touching each other. Didn't make a difference, he still wanted to scoop her up and find out if those lush lips were as succulent as they looked. He struggled to focus on the words of his book. He hadn't read this one yet and had been looking forward to losing himself in the story of the World War II spy.

Thanks to Willa, assigning him to figure out more about their stowaway, he now had the occasional day, like today, where his shift was obnoxiously short. He liked to stay busy, but he preferred solitude. Extra time with Quinn was not helping him to stay chill.

While he pretended to be absorbed in his book, he listened to each steady breath she took, let the smell of his soap on her skin tickle his nose, and let himself glance over to see her sweet smile as she enjoyed a humorous passage. An hour or two of satisfying tranquility passed quickly.

A gnawing hunger was growing deep in Ryan's belly. Starving, he realized they hadn't eaten dinner yet.

He glanced over at Quinn. She was engrossed in her book. But, sensing him watching her, she finished her paragraph and looked up from her book.

With no more than an amused twitch of her lips, her midnight-blue eyes rested on his and stayed. Warmth pumped out from under his ribs, filling his veins with a very new, incredibly stirring, and fantastically terrifying sensation.

Neither said a word, but it was painfully obvious this was uncharted territory for both of them. Even though she had no memories, this easy familiarity, the zapping electricity that held them together despite hardly knowing each other, was not something he'd imagined possible. It was the stuff romantics wrote about, and he'd scoffed at.

Stopping that yearning dead in its tracks before his imagination could really take off, Ryan shifted his gaze away.

Her stomach growled nearly as loudly as his.

"I'll scrounge up some dinner," he said as he looked anywhere but at her.

Stalking out of the room, desperate to breathe in some icy northern air, he escaped.

ROLLING OVER IN BED, Ryan let his eyes settle on Quinn as she slept across the room on the sofa, peacefully curled up in one of his t-shirts, wrapped up in his softest blanket. Thankfully, she didn't seem to be entrenched in her normal nightmare. Instead, the corners of her mouth were turned up in a sensual smile.

Shifting restlessly, she rolled away from him and threw her leg out of the blanket. Ryan's breath caught as her shirt pulled up just enough, revealing an inch or so of her spectacular rounded ass. Glued to the tempting view, he mentally pulled that shirt up just another inch. As if on command, as if she were dreaming what he had all night, a sweet moan passed her lips, and she stretched, just enough to give him a brief glimpse of more.

Groaning, Ryan poorly endeavored to avert his eyes. He really, really should. She wouldn't, were their roles reversed. He tried to not imagine her soft moan was her dreaming of exactly what he was imagining... pulling that shirt up a little more, gripping those hips and taking her from behind...

Rolling back over again, Quinn turned toward him. Her eyes fluttered open and immediately locked onto his. Lips slightly parted, she took a corner of her lower lip between her teeth, practically panting with desire. Yeah, she'd been thinking *exactly* what he had just been imagining.

He tried to say something. To pretend nothing had happened. That they hadn't both just spent the last eight hours held prisoner to their dreams, acting out what they couldn't and shouldn't in reality. Finally, insatiable hard-on and all, he rolled out of bed and ambled to the bathroom in nothing but his boxer briefs. No sense hiding it. The ravenous expression on his face when she awoke would have told her everything, anyway.

Quinn had been amazingly patient. The last few days, she'd taunted him enough that he knew she was feeling ok, so he wasn't too worried. Hell, she'd tormented him with a few glorious glimpses at that incredible body as she went to and from the shower each day in nothing but one of his shirts, or stretched out on the sofa as she awoke, as she had that morning.

It was glaringly obvious the chemistry between them was off the charts. He could feel her eyes on him as he moved, her gaze on his mouth as he spoke, watching in secret when he was pretending to be asleep.

And vice versa.

He couldn't seem to keep his eyes off her. He was quickly getting in the habit of peeking at her throughout the night, poorly attempting to convince himself he was just ensuring that she wasn't getting into trouble.

No, she wasn't trouble. Well, yeah, she was, but not the way he'd feared. She was trouble of the sorts that could make him forget who and what he was. But he didn't worry anymore that she would harm the crew or him.

Although she badgered him each night until he shared a few of his own memories, she otherwise spent a lot of time in her head. Either she was freaking out with an identity crisis, or she was suffering from painfully evolving unrequitable desire like he was. Or both. Regardless, she had to be freaked. He was, and he only had the latter to worry about.

Most of the day, he stayed away, finding something that needed his attention around the ship. With difficulty, he dodged Willa's meaningful looks. She had to know he was avoiding Quinn.

Dreading going to bed tonight and dreaming of nothing but her again, he volunteered to take the late shift at the helm tonight. Although he pretended it was just to take his turn to the crew and to Quinn, he didn't try to fool himself. To clear his head, he'd work the next week solid without sleep if he had to.

Peacefully curled up on the corner of the sofa, wearing his t-shirt and one of her two pairs of borrowed jeans, she was engrossed in yet another book when he returned for a forced break that evening. The woman was voracious. She'd already gone through most of his own books, the ones he'd borrowed from the ship's library, and had a stack ready to gobble up that she'd borrowed from Leah and Kyle.

Not being a total ass, he'd let a few select crew members come to visit now and again. They were all swiftly becoming her defenders and were pushing him to let her have a little more freedom. And, he suspected, a few, like Willa, were playing chaperone. He was only a little offended. It's not like he would try to take advantage of a memoryless, lost woman... at least, no more than she would of him.

They sat and read for an hour, ate in silence through dinner. She was particularly quiet tonight, and he ached for her. Despite her isolation, she never complained. Tomorrow, he'd start bringing her out, try to help her find something to do. If he was going stir crazy, she had to be miserable.

"Quinn?" He opened the conversation with her by name, as he'd gotten in the habit of doing. He hoped she might at least come up with a last name, eventually.

As much as he didn't want a fully aware demon hunter on his ship, he knew she played an important role in the protection of humanity and needed to find her way back to her team. If they were still alive. No way she would have been on such a big op without a solid team.

"Yes, Ryan?" She answered him back by name, as usual. Maybe he just liked hearing her voice every time she said his name, the sweet way she drew out the *y* and the *a*.

"I'm going back on. My turn for night shift. You need anything?" He sharply double knotted his boots and rose from the couch.

She smiled and looked at him, her nose crinkling up in amusement. "No thanks. I've got a good book to keep me entertained. For all I know, I've read this book twenty times, but it's fresh and new now. Although, I admit, I am coming down with a raging case of cabin fever. Be careful, it may be catching." Most would be angry or frustrated or in tears over their situation, but she managed to work in a disarming joke whenever she caught him worrying.

Not that he worried about her. "I know. Look, in the morning, I'll bring you out on deck? I can see about finding you a job or something. You must be bored to death."

A bright bouquet in a drab room, her smile blossomed...

Shit, who thought like that? Yeah, he needed to get rid of her. Soon. Before he turned into a goddamn poet.

"It's a date—I mean, I'm looking forward to it." She gave him a wink that said she wasn't embarrassed by her slip.

Was she embarrassed by anything? Certainly not by his immodesty during, as she'd called it, his tantrum when he'd flashed her with most of the goods, just shy of the full monty. Nor when she'd caught him watching her sleep.

"Sleep tight." He winked back as he slipped outside, not letting the corners of his mouth turn up into a cheeky smile until he was out of sight.

Hearing some of the guys hooting and hollering down the hall, he quickly adopted a scowl before he was caught looking enchanted by the resident stowaway that he'd been keeping hidden in his bedroom. Yeah, he really needed to bring her out more, especially now that he was certain she wasn't going to harm anyone.

Two hours later, the moon high in the sky, he sipped his coffee as he looked out at the vast, tranquil sea. As intensely blue as Quinn's midnight eyes, the northern ocean at night was a sight to behold. Shit. Yep, poet.

Riotous laughter bounced through the gunwales of the ship. The crew was apparently having a wild time. He'd heard rumors of a poker game planned for tonight. Bummer. He liked poker night.

But he would have felt guilty leaving Quinn alone while he joined the crew for entertainment. Bringing her out for the first time for poker night wasn't what he had in mind. Something more sedate would be easier.

Kyle strolled up behind him, still an eager newbie, even though he'd been with them nearly six months now and wasn't nearly as green as Dean. Grinning widely with a bit of a blush on his cheeks, the cowlicks in his hair wilder than usual, he gestured for Ryan to step out of the way. "Yo. Get out of here. My turn at the helm tonight."

"What are you so happy about? You must be ready for your precious beauty sleep by now. I got it."

"Normally, yeah, I hate the damn night shift. Tonight, I'm a bit too wired to get any rest, so Willa said I should swap you out. May as well put that energy to good use."

"What's got you so happy?"

"Nothing much. Just a fun time below deck. Go join them. You'll be glad you did."

Brow quirked up in suspicion, Ryan didn't wait around. Moving at a fast clip, he suspected he knew exactly what had Kyle grinning smittenly.

Same reason he'd hardly been able to wipe the smile from his own face lately.

That laughter resonated down the halls again, rushing at him like a flash flood. Rounding the final bend, he abruptly slowed his pace and strolled casually into the rec room.

No poker. No cards at all. *Fast and the Furious* was playing on the TV in the corner, but no one was watching their usual favorite tonight.

Elbows bent, hands linked, Quinn was gritting her teeth in feigned exertion as she lowered Manuel's hand toward the table in an epic arm-wrestling match, hovering at forty-five degrees. Show off.

No dummy, she was trying to make it look like she was having trouble. He knew she wasn't truly breaking a sweat, and the tremor in her arm was completely fake. Her petite frame tiny to Manuel's massive build, his arm wider than her thigh... yeah, full confirmation to the crew that she was like Ryan.

She looked awfully pleased with herself, eyes twinkling in amusement, surrounded by the crew laughing more heartily than he'd seen in weeks. He couldn't find the will to be mad at her for escaping her prison. As much as she hadn't complained and seemed to be enjoying their quiet evenings as much as he did, she had to be beyond restless.

More, he hated that he hadn't given her the benefit of the doubt that he'd wished for so many years ago.

His unconventional captain stood across the room and flashed him a smile. Scrunching up her face, she shrugged and mouthed unapologetically, *Sorry.*

Manuel's arm trembled for real as he pushed the last of his energy into his beefy arm. As his strength gave way, his hand finally hit the table. The crowd went wild, hooting and hollering. Quinn leaned back in her chair and beamed, her cheeks flushed from humor rather than exertion.

Clearing his throat, Ryan interrupted the jovial crowd, silencing the room abruptly. While most merely muffled their laughs as they gave him their attention, Quinn at least had the decency to look guilty. "I've been feeling much better this evening. Willa suggested I come join the crew for poker night."

"I'm so glad to hear that you're finally feeling up to getting out, after your ordeal," he said with empty sympathy, then raised an eyebrow as he scanned the room, noting the lack of cards and chips, but a plethora of guilty, smitten expressions. "No cards tonight?"

If he didn't know better, he'd swear he was surrounded by drunken sailors for their blushing, immature giggling.

Manuel stood from his spot at the table. Smacking Ryan roughly on the shoulder, he gestured to the table. "Your turn. Dean's been pumping iron lately and decided he could take us all. So far, our mystery guest seems to be the champ. I almost had her beat. As reigning champ, you may just be the one to take her."

With a feigned sigh of surrender, Ryan slid into the chair across from Quinn. She scrunched up her nose in giddy challenge, surrounded by adoring fans that were entranced by their new heroine.

Ryan put his arm up in ready-position, body relaxed, unintimidated. Walk in the park. "Don't break the table," he whispered.

Eyes squinting, the corners of her mouth turned up ever so slightly as she silently taunted him. Arms up, they gripped their right hands firmly, palm to palm.

Adrenaline propelled through him at the connection of their tightly joined hands, his heart pumping out molten lava until the room felt about a hundred damn degrees. No doubt about it, Quinn felt it, too. Hell, it was so electric, the whole crew likely felt the kickback from the blast.

Not breaking eye contact, one side of his mouth quirked up in a wicked half-smile, he asked, "Does the winner get a prize?"

Eyes full of mischief, she wiggled her butt in her chair and taunted, "Satisfaction?"

Man, if only she knew what he had in mind when she said that. "Something more tangible."

She shrugged innocently. "I have absolutely nothing to offer. Not even my memories."

"Okay. How about this: I win, I get to pick a reasonable prize, as soon as you have anything to offer, of course? You win, I'll give you a tour of the ship tomorrow."

"Deal."

Before the countdown could even begin, she applied a gentle, testing pressure.

Hand clasped firmly with hers, he was feeling the strain. That was a first.

She gained an inch on him before he pushed back like he meant it. The sweat on her brow genuine from exertion this time, she poured everything into the game. For the first time in history, so did he.

Locked in the middle, both strained and pushed and didn't make a damn bit of progress. She was ridiculously strong, even for a demon hunter, and he was stronger than most he'd met. Her admiring fans cheered her on, chanting her name in rhythmic unison.

Enjoying the challenge, Ryan wasn't fazed. She was quickly charming the hell out of all of them, him included.

Realizing this could last all night, and they'd all need to get some sleep eventually, he needed a solution. And, he really didn't want to lose in front of his crew.

Not that he feared losing their respect. As XO and a decent guy, he could quickly regain their loyalty. But she was smug enough. Adorably so, but still, he really wanted to win.

And, he knew exactly what he wanted for his prize.

Subtly, he moved his left hand under the table. Fingertips grazing along her leg, he found her hand and brushed his thumb across hers. She flinched at the new sensation. Tracing the contours of her hand, gently squeezing her leg, he knew she must be feeling the same trail of fire at the subtle, intimate contact.

He felt her resolve slipping. Hell, he felt his own slipping, too.

Her eyes locked onto his as she caught on to his intentions, her midnight blues sparkling in anticipation. Unable to resist, he flashed her a taunting wink.

Considering, she smiled at him with a mysterious look on her face.

Slackening her arm, she discreetly let her arm lower to the table under his.

Equal sounds of disappointment for their new heroine, contrasted by cheers of support for their XO, the crew hollered until their voices bounced off of the Aleutians on the horizon. Eyes still locked on his, Quinn slowly let go of his hand.

She finally released him from her thrall and stood. After rounds of high fives, Ryan quietly backed out of the room.

Quinn seemed to read his mind. "Thank you all for a wonderful evening. Goodnight," she said with a honeyed smile.

TRAILING BEHIND RYAN, SLIDING her hand back into his, Quinn floated with the gentle rocking of the ship. Neither brought up the fact that she'd completely gone against his orders. Initially, she was afraid he'd be furious that she'd left the room without clearing it with him first. But he wasn't that kind of warden, apparently.

Hands still joined as they entered his quarters, he released her long enough to close the door behind them. Eyes flashing dark as night, before she had a chance to think, he tugged her close.

Brushing a stray lock of red waves out of her eyes, his voice low with a steering ache, he said, "Look, Quinn, I'm really sorry about before."

Puzzled by the words of apology, relishing in the warmth he embodied, her heart pounded in a rhythm as erratic as her emotions. She looked up and squinted in question.

"I know I've been locking you up in here like a damn prisoner." The guilt flowed from his words like nectar, sweet to her ears. She knew he wasn't an asshole, but it was nice to hear it from his lips.

"I'd be furious with you for taking so damn long to realize I'm not out to harm anyone, but I get it. I'm not... I'm not human." She captured his eyes with hers, his deep gray irises swirling with black. "Neither are you."

Sighing heavily, he brought his hands up to cradle her face. "No, we're not. I didn't trust you. I'm sorry for doubting you." His thumb grazed over her lower lip, sending tingling shocks in a heavenly trail.

Lost in his dark eyes, she couldn't feel anything outside of him.

"What changed?" she asked, breathlessly locked in his gaze.

"Couldn't say. I just... you're more than I thought you were. There are some like us, who would risk the safety of the crew for their own needs."

"Thank you for trusting me now. If it helps, I think I needed the downtime. I would have kicked your ass if I felt threatened, or snuck out sooner if I needed to."

"I don't doubt it. Still, I'm sorry it took me this long to realize you deserved the benefit of the doubt."

His eyes rested on her lips, sending that thrill vibrating through her in anticipation. "Damn right I do. What made you so distrustful?"

He bit his cheek and released a heavy sigh. "Long story. Not one I want to think about right now. Ever, really, but I'll tell you someday. Right now, I've got something else I'd rather focus on."

"Yeah? What's that?" She stood on her tiptoes to get closer, hoping he was on her same page.

Leaning in, slightly, his statement a hopeful question, he said, "I know what I want for my prize."

Her lips curved into a wicked grin. "I let you win."

"I still won," he said, baiting her, silver flecks dancing in his eyes.

Anticipation about killed her as he studied her, waiting.

She rose to her toes, tilting, her gaze falling to his mouth. "Not sure you were playing fair."

"Have a problem with that?"

"Hurry up and kiss me and I might agree to a rematch."

Lightly at first, his lips brushed over hers, where his thumb had been only moments before. Stoking the fire that had been brewing since first hearing his voice that morning, knowing she'd found what she was looking for even then, the kiss set something off inside of her. Breath heavy in her chest, light as she floated on air, she clutched her hands in his short hair.

As the balance between them flowed steady and intense at the light connection, he lowered his hands to her waist and pulled her tighter against him. Insistent, becoming demanding, he kissed her more deeply, sweeter than she had anticipated. Than she'd thought herself capable of. More than lust. More intense, intimate, turbulent.

As the kiss deepened, his tongue caressing hers, the moment evolved into something that struck a chord deep inside her, a yearning that began before she found herself on his ship.

Tongues parried wildly, inseparable, hands searched for skin. Neither was in control. Before she knew it, she was climbing him like a tree, desperate to get closer.

Lifting her, fluid and grasping tight, he clutched her hips and held her. Her legs wrapped around his waist. He slid one had under her top and splayed his hand over her low back, each point of contact anchoring her to him as they devoured each other. Pouring herself into him, taking him in return, she felt herself growing stronger, more assured, more *everything*, as he gave her all of him.

Slowly pulling away, savoring the taste of each other before acknowledging the moment needed to end before either fell in any deeper, she melted as he indulged in one last kiss, and then another, and then finally lowered her tenderly until she stood on solid ground. Still entwined, they held on to each other until the world stopped spinning quite so fast.

"Quinn?" he asked as she nuzzled into him.

"Yes, Ryan?"

"I can't... we can't..." he said breathlessly, his voice trembling with an ache that mirrored her own.

"I know. For all we know I'm a psycho murderous bitch who's married with five children."

His deliciously deep laugh warmed her to the bone. "I doubt the first part. The second, yeah, that's a big part of the reason we shouldn't."

Still locked tightly in his arms, neither ready to separate, she could at least solve part of that. "Well, a woman's body isn't so much of a mystery that I can't answer the last of it. I guarantee this body hasn't grown or fed any babies. Yes, I checked. And, I don't think I'm married, as I don't even have evidence that I've ever worn a wedding band or even an engagement ring."

"I'm pleasantly reassured." He chuckled, then said with a hungry grin, "If we don't figure out who you are in the next few weeks, I say fuck it, and you just might have to let me do a little examination of my own."

"You know, I'm not sure if I'm disturbed by that statement or a little aroused." She chuckled against him.

"I meant it seductively, but it came out more than a little weird." The humor in his voice, the light chuckle that vibrated across his chest, was exactly what she needed. "Let's get some sleep."

Too tired to bother with formalities, they stood side by side in the cramped bathroom and brushed and flossed together with sleepy eyes and exhausted brains. This amnesia shit was a real bitch.

For the first time, she took a long look at his very fancy watch that lit up as he turned his wrist. "I like your smartwatch." Looked familiar too, but probably because she'd noticed it on his wrist without cataloging the information before. Maybe. Didn't sound right, but for now, she was going with it.

He held out his wrist for her to inspect it. "It's a handy thing. Mostly so I can push a button to find my phone. Terrible reception out here, so I've usually lost my phone in a drawer or coat pocket somewhere."

Both stalled in the middle of the cramped room before crawling into their separate beds, hesitating, avoiding eye contact. It was ridiculously obvious they'd be moving way too fast if they shared his bunk like they clearly both wanted. Although she seriously doubted she was a virgin, testing that out with a little fooling around would quickly and pleasantly answer that bit of information for her.

No. Bad idea all around.

For now.

Settling into her borrowed pillow, snuggled up in her borrowed blankets on the couch that was just a little too small to be comfortable, she closed her eyes and waited for sleep to hit her. Normally, sleep took her rather quickly and effectively.

"Ryan?"

"Yes, Quinn?"

"Can you tell me what we are?"

"Tomorrow."

"Ok."

8

THUNDER BELLOWED THROUGH THE ship, heralding the start of a long day. Footfalls of the busy crew resonated down the halls and overhead. Like with the sea monster at the whirlpools, Quinn was wrought with the compulsion to pitch in. However, she suspected the tightknit Coast Guard crew knew what they were doing in a storm.

She'd probably just be in the way. Pouting to herself, Quinn tried to do nothing, yet again. It was almost worse now, after the promise of entertainment.

Hours passed. Quinn tightened anything down that rattled. Even a little. She made Ryan's bed, folded loose blankets, cleaned the bathroom, scrubbed the toilet. None of it easy in the violent heaving of the ship, but she enjoyed the wee bit of challenge. She tried reading, but the ship was being thrown about by the storm too violently for her to hold the book still.

Bored to tears, she couldn't find anything else to do. So, she stood and waited, feet wide on the floor, arms extended, entertaining herself by pretending she was surfing as the ship rocked and reeled.

Bundled in Ryan's coziest fleece, boots tied snuggly, she was ready on the off chance she was needed. Not that she would be. This was one of the fiercer storms she could imagine, but she felt like she'd been through worse.

And laughed. She really was odd. Although, she did admire those that could laugh in the face of danger, so she guessed she was glad she was one of those.

Finally, when she was officially bored to the point of slap-happy, the door swung open. Soaked to the skin in his usual t-shirt and cargo pants, having skipped the rain gear as usual, Ryan stalked into the room and slammed the door shut behind him. He crossed the few feet of the room to get to her, stopping inches away.

"You ok?" his voice dripped with worry, his expression tense with concern.

Not even needing to fake it, she smiled pleasantly. "I'm fine. Just wish I could help. I'm really sensing this is not my first storm, and I hate feeling useless."

Pulling her close, throwing off her balance but righting her against him just as fast, he pressed his freezing lips to her forehead. He trembled against her, his voice gruff. "You're amazing, you know that?" For a seasoned sailor, he was sure a nervous wreck.

"Are you okay?" she asked, looking up, searching those dark eyes.

Pulling back, he looked down at her, and his expression eased into a smile, steel eyes melting into liquid silver. "Of course. I just don't like *not* being able to control the situation."

"And you can control most storms?" She chuckled and smiled up at him, expecting a joke.

He shrugged. "Sort of. Like the whirlpools. But this... this is pure mother nature at her finest. Came out of nowhere. We got word she was coming about an hour before that first crack of lightning. She's not showing any sign of relenting."

"Yeah, mother nature's a bitch sometimes. Do you need anything?" She smiled wide and shrugged her shoulders openly.

"Actually, no. We're pretty solid for the night. We'll keep patrolling for any nearby vessels that may need help, but luckily, everybody else had been able to make it safely out of this shit so far. Stable for now, I'm supposed to be resting for the next few hours. Galley's pretty limited, so I was going to go grab us some storm rations."

"How about you change into dry clothes, and I'll go get dinner?"

Realizing he'd drenched her in his hurry to ensure she was okay, he glanced down at her wet Ryan imprint and smiled sheepishly, his eyes crinkling in the corners. "Sorry."

"No worries. You change, I'll get food."

He was already sitting and taking his boots off as she left. Poor guy looked wiped out. The entire crew did. Ryan was right though. They didn't need her help. They were an above-average crew for sure.

She followed a few sleepy sailors to the galley and grabbed some packaged sandwiches. Harry appeared in the doorway, looking green as an unripe apple, then sprinted back out at full speed.

Leah nudged her and said, "You look like you're holding up ok. Seasickness can hit anyone, anytime. Glad it's not me this time."

"Me too. I'm envisioning barfing and missing my target as the boat crashes down off the waves." She stopped and thought for a moment. While she enjoyed the visual, she couldn't seem to imagine herself doing it, but maybe a friend. She had no idea what vomiting might feel like. You'd think that's the sort of revolting sensation that you'd remember.

Quinn didn't think she'd ever forget the sight that welcomed her when she returned to their room. Ryan was standing before her wearing nothing but his shiny black boxer briefs, his hair still wet from the rain and spiked up roguishly. Taking a slow, savoring breath, she stood in the doorway and appreciated those lickable abs for a bit.

Running a hand through his short hair, he flicked water in her direction and flashed her a devious grin. Still damp, his skin glistened in the low light, accenting every brilliantly defined muscle. And, perhaps, she had read too many romance novels from the ship's library.

"I'm so hungry. Thanks." Sadly, he pulled on a dry shirt before moving to the couch to eat.

After a relatively quiet, albeit wobbly dinner, they called it a night. Again, standing side by side, they brushed and flossed as they steadied themselves against the bathroom wall, swaying together with each tilt of the ship as it alternated between crest and trough.

This time, Ryan held out his hand before she settled onto the couch. "You'll be thrown to the floor in seconds. Come on, there's room for both of us in here."

Without arguing, she grabbed her pillow and climbed into his bunk. He followed her in, taking the outside for himself. Hardly bigger than a twin sized mattress, they somehow fit comfortably in the nook. Pulling her tight against him, his arms wrapped around her. She snuggled in, resting her head on his shoulder.

THE STORM STILL CRASHED and thrashed outside. Ryan blinked away the sleep from his eyes. Glancing at the clock on the wall, he cussed and tried to sit up. Quinn was still wrapped around him.

Fuck. He was due on deck in two minutes. He hadn't bothered to set an alarm because he never needed one. Apparently, his lack of sleep since Quinn came aboard was catching up to him. Having his arms around her all night hadn't necessitated light sleep, like when she'd slept on the couch.

Bullshit. He hadn't been sleeping the past two weeks because he couldn't clear his head of her. Not because he was a prison guard, but because he was a lovesick puppy. Definitely not a dynamic he'd imagined he would ever have to sort out.

Quietly sliding out of bed, cautious not to wake her, he grabbed dry cargos and a tee from the top of the stack in his closet and pulled them on in the near-dark room. With about the worst case of morning wood in living history, he pulled up the zipper with extra care. Moronic idea to have her sleep with him, but not much choice in this storm.

Swinging by the galley, he grabbed a quick bite of mess-free breakfast and made it to the bridge six minutes late.

"Sleep in a bit this morning, did you?" Willa goaded him from her perch by the weather station.

"Nothing like a storm to help me sleep." He checked the instruments, catching up on the comings and goings that had passed while he was out.

Leah came in just behind him. "Or a hot body tucked up against you."

"Watch it," he warned, shooting her the nastiest look he could muster.

Unintimidated, as the entire room seemed to be, Manuel not-so-subtly said to Leah as she settled in next to him, "He's clearly not getting any yet. Don't piss him off."

"Fuck off," Ryan sniped as he took over at the helm. He needed something to keep him occupied. Not much of an XO if his crew was so laissez-faire about his sex life. "Manuel, you're on cleanup for the next hour before you get any rack time. Grab Kyle to relieve you. Leah—"

"I got it. I'll go swab the deck or something." Rolling her eyes, she hopped to and sent up her relief.

Willa moved to stand next to him, staring out into the dark morning. He turned the wheel a quarter turn to take the next wave that was coming in from the north, then back again for a wave from another direction. Legs braced wide, he held steady against the stormy sea.

"Don't bite my head off, but, are you ok?" Her eyes heavy with fatigue, the steady captain still kept her crew in line, mentally, physically, emotionally. Pathetically sleepy, she smiled at him, knowing he wouldn't dare bite *her* head off. Casual as the ship may be, there was still a chain of command, and he'd be just as at risk to swab the damn decks.

"Yeah. I'm fine."

"I need an XO with his head on straight. What's eating at you?" Her voice was sharp, but he could hear the concern.

Pulling an extra draw of oxygen into his lungs before responding, he casually adjusted for the next wave. No fool, she'd see right through him if he tried to make any excuses. "They're not wrong. I'm trying to sort out everything with our guest."

"Does she know yet, what she is? At least if you can tell her that, it may help us to get her home again."

Her words choked him like he'd swallowed a damn gobstopper. "I keep planning to tell her, but..." He glanced around, finding the few others on the bridge excessively focused on their equipment. Undoubtedly eavesdropping, but he was having trouble giving a shit.

"You're afraid."

"Hell yeah. She's one of them, for sure. Not all of them are good. Right now, she's all sincerity and I can't help but think she's different." He shrugged, recognizing that might just be his dick doing all the thinking. Shifting his concerns back on his past, the reason he couldn't trust her as he wanted to, tension tightened across his shoulders. "I really don't think she's a threat to any of us. But what if she's got more blood on her hands than me?"

"You've scrubbed those hands pretty clean. You know her best. If she is what you fear, think she'll go back to that life after you've shown her the other side?"

"I—"

"You can show her the difference. She's got a good heart. I can feel it."

Yeah, he was terrified she was like the demon hunters he'd known, a bloodthirsty egomaniac. Unyielding hatred.

Not lacking in the brains department, he could admit he was in deep with her.

If she found out who she was and left him in the lurch...

Or discovered what he was and turned on him...

He focused on the incoming waves, the thrashing wind, pretending the sweat beading on his upper lip was from exertion, not panic.

Willa turned to leave him in peace. As she reached the steps, he heard her saying, "Hey Quinn. Go on up and check things out. Nothing like watching a well-oiled Coast Guard team in a storm."

Ignoring him at first, Quinn studied the actions of the other members of the crew, the radar, updates on storm activity. Finally, she came to stand next to him.

Completely at ease, she held on and moved her body with the waves like an experienced sailor. Whatever her life looked like before he'd found her, she was no stranger to life at sea.

⚓

QUINN STOOD A FEW feet from Ryan, enjoying watching him steer them safely through the storm. Unblinking, eyes sharp as a hawk, he adjusted the wheel with precision.

He reminded her of someone, she just couldn't place it. Gave her a peaceful sensation. Deep in her gut, she knew everything was going to be okay when he was driving.

"How's the storm looking?" he asked, genuinely interested in her thoughts. It felt nice, and didn't sound like he was mocking her. Not that she knew why he'd mock her, but she felt defensive for some reason.

"I'm no expert, but it looks like we're through the worst of it." She glanced over to Kyle. "That sound about right?"

Kyle nodded proudly. "Yeah, you got it. Ryan, you'll be feeling it soon if you aren't already. Wind at our backs, baby," he added with a whoop.

Ryan glanced away from the water only for a moment. His features fierce, he spared her an appreciative glance, before he returned to his task. He was so ridiculously sexy at the helm. Steady posture. Confident. Not a trace of hesitation.

"You want to take the wheel?" he offered, again, without a hint of sarcasm. Wow, she was really sensitive about this stuff.

"Bet your ass." She didn't wait for him to change his mind.

She could feel the stares from the few others in the room at her back. Supportive or concerned or curious, she couldn't tell. Didn't matter, she'd felt the need to get her hands on that wheel since the first gust of wind.

Stepping up to the helm, she steadied her feet, arms confidently gripping the wheel. As easily as breathing, she turned at precise angles across each wave, maintaining their trajectory to get out of the storm as quickly and safely as possible.

As soon as it became clear that she knew what she was doing, Ryan shifted to stand behind her with his feet planted wide. Softly, he rested his hands on her hips, thumbs grazing along her skin under the hem of her shirt. He didn't touch the wheel, didn't point where he thought she should go, just a steady presence behind her. "You look like you grew up doing this."

Beaming, she nodded, not taking her eyes off the tumultuous sea. "I kinda think I did. I can almost recall just barely being able to see over the wheel, a gentle voice above me, coaching me along."

"Whose voice is it?" His voice rumbled, his breath warm against her ear as he teased the memory to form.

The memory came clearer and clearer. Soothing, encouraging, kind. Smile growing wide across her face, Quinn felt the positive emotions flow through her. "My mother. She's a ship captain. Fiona." Memories, clear as day, flashed through her mind as she steered them through the storm. "Dad was usually out working, so I got to go along with Mom a lot. Quentin. I can picture their house. Somewhere on the coast. Not Alaska. California?"

Arms wrapping securely around her waist, she could feel Ryan smiling behind her, resting his cheek against her. It helped to concentrate on the water, on his presence behind her. The sense of peace the entire moment brought her. Remembering her parents was... incredible. Like a lifetime of their love washed over her, waking a dormant, critical part of her.

"Ryan?"

He leaned down and whispered into her ear, "Yes, Quinn?"

"Thank you. For trusting me." Completely at home, more so than she'd ever known, she felt strong, alive, with the storm wailing all around, Ryan's arms around her, and comforting memories of her family precipitating in her mind.

They stood together for hours as the wind slowed, the waves quieted, and the ship steadied on the vast, enduring ocean.

Coming to the windshield and looking out, Willa smiled and drank from her coffee, sans lid now that the storm was tapering and the risk for spills had declined. "We're going to have to put you on the payroll if you keep this up."

Quinn pulled away and relinquished the wheel to Ryan, ready to file that away as one of the better memories in her slightly less empty hippocampus. She leaned back against the side so she could watch Ryan and still check out the rest of the bridge. Exhausted faces filled the room as shift change approached. Still standing strong, Ryan looked more invigorated than he had in days.

"Apparently, I grew up with this. Not the Coast Guard. My mother, she owns a private charter line." Feeling Willa would appreciate the knowledge, Quinn shared her discovery, the memory of her mother teaching her to drive the boat.

"Feels good, doesn't it?" Willa grinned at her, her eyes twinkling with delight, acknowledging a fellow seadog.

"Taking on the storm or the fact that I remember something?"

"Both. Now, get out of here you two, I'm your relief. We have quite a few still green in the face. Now that things are calming, we're down to bare bones for the night and should fare just fine."

Ryan passed control of the wheel to Willa and offered his hand for Quinn to join him. Before they got to the door, Willa said, "Ryan, come see me in the morning. I've been tracking some activity off the Aleutians I want to go over with you."

His face scrunched with worry, but he didn't push for answers now. Acknowledging with a slight nod, he said, "Sure thing."

After grabbing a quick bite, Quinn was glad to crawl into bed. She was completely worn out from concentrating all day, from the swarm of memories that had flooded in, but in a great way. That was the most she'd used her brain in two weeks.

They brushed and flossed and took turns showering. Quinn grabbed her pillow and blanket and went to climb back on the couch. As much as she wanted to sleep tucked against Ryan again, she was still afraid of wearing out her welcome. Okay, so she was insecure, even after they'd been pinned together all day.

Before she could lie down, he grabbed the pillow and tossed it back on his bed. "Climb in." He gestured her ahead.

"Aye, aye XO Bossy Pants." She rolled her eyes at him, earning herself a pat on the rear and a sleepy grin as she climbed into his bed.

Ryan crawled in next to her, his voice heavy with sleep, he said, "Don't analyze, just sleep."

Good point. She had no wish to dwell on why she needed to be so close to him. They'd stood glued together at the helm for hours, and she still hadn't had enough of him.

Eyes drifting closed, she felt herself asking, "Ryan?"

"Yes, Quinn?"

"What are we?"

"I'll tell you tomorrow." His voice trailed off as he drifted into sleep.

9

RYAN SHOWERED AND DRESSED before Quinn even stirred. At the hint of morning and the increased activity that came with it, his eyes had popped open, not wanting to oversleep like yesterday. The crew had given him enough hell, and he really didn't want to hear it today. Especially knowing they were accurate in their taunts.

Not to mention, he *needed* a little distance. Didn't *want* it. Hell, the air in the two-foot radius around Quinn smelled sweeter than the crisp ocean air he reveled in, and he wanted to breathe her every moment of the day.

Bite my ass Lord Byron, he thought to himself as he stalked into the galley. He grabbed a cup of coffee, stuffed down a breakfast sandwich in four bites as he poured an extra cup, then dashed up to the bridge.

Whatever Willa had been hinting at last night, he didn't like it. Every time he felt like they were on top of things, they weren't. There was something stirring out there, but they hadn't been able to find anything tangible. Yet, with each passing month since the Valkyrie had set sail, the number of sightings doubled. Until now. There hadn't been as many the past weeks since Quinn splashed into his life. The relative quiet was not reassuring.

Toasty warm, the bridge was quiet. Now and again, Willa decided she wanted the bridge to herself. He understood. There was nothing quite like taking the helm alone, just you and the sea. She'd designed the ship to run on bare bones staff... for when things didn't go well.

"What's up?" he asked as he approached, handing her the spare cup of coffee he'd brought for her. She'd been taking the night shift way too much lately. When she got to her control-freakishness, something was up.

"Morning, Ryan. Sleep well?"

Okay, he could do small talk first. "Yeah. Sure did. Peaceful night?"

"Yeah. Not too bad." She paused, scanning the horizon before speaking. "Over the last few weeks, there have been scattered reports of a strange phenomenon. Huge whirlpools. Four ships have gone missing. A single creature or multiple, it's hard to say. Until recently, I'd been aware of vague, rare reports like these as long as the waters around Alaska have been traveled. Most are way out past St. Paul, but they're increasing in frequency and a lot closer to home."

"Huh. We'll need more information before we go walking into something like that. I really don't want to end up kraken food." He sat on the corner of a nearby desk, considering what she'd described. No one had actually seen a kraken, and he'd believed them to be one of those that humans had exaggerated to the point of hilarity, so they could say things like, *Release the kraken.* Massive whirlpools swallowing ships were not something he'd heard of happening in reality.

"I'm sure you realize the timing and location are remarkably co-incidental." Willa's eyes were wide with meaning, her narrow lips spread thinner with her grim smile. "Quinn may know something. If she can remember, it might help."

"That waterspout could easily have come from somewhere past St. Paul." Shit, Ryan didn't want to picture it. "Why would a monster throw her far away when it could just... swallow her like a minnow?"

Ryan cringed at the thought. Quinn had been a bit bruised and battered, but no sign she'd been vomited up by some massive creature.

No, she had been shot toward him for her own protection. By someone that knew who and what and where he was. Her landing on his doorstep was way more suspect than the kraken activity after her arrival. Was it him in particular? Or was he simply the nearest demon hunter?

"Have you told her yet?" Willa's voice was frighteningly, maternally authoritative. Not that his mother was at all authoritative, but he could imagine how a normal mother might lecture.

"No."

"I support you, Ryan. I trust you to make good decisions, or you wouldn't be my XO. But, I suspect we're going to need her. Before any other ships are taken. If this thing is half as big as I'm imagining, even two demon hunters may not be enough."

He tried to take the wheel and relieve her, but she nudged him out of the way.

"You've got homework. We'll search the area, question the locals about any unusual sightings. In the meantime, you're off regular duty until you figure out what this thing is. Figure out how to defeat it, make it go home, or take it out—whatever you can glean from its intentions. Make sure we're prepared. That includes pulling more memories out of Quinn."

QUINN SAT UP IN the narrow bunk, her head not quite touching the ceiling. She stretched out her limbs, warm and cozy from Ryan's heat that still lingered. He couldn't have been gone long, but she knew he would be working all day. Looks like she was back to reading and being bored again.

There was a soft knock on the door, and Ryan quietly entered. Cheeks heavy, eyes wary, he looked whipped, like he hadn't just had the same great night's sleep she had.

"Hey. You okay?" she asked.

"Yeah, I'm good."

"Cutting out on work today? Tough to play hooky on a boat," she teased, hoping to elicit a smile from him. Nothing. Looked like someone had died. Oh god, what if someone had? "You sure you're okay?"

"Really, I'm fine. I was looking for you, actually. Want to go on that tour now?" He mustered a smile, but the joy was missing from those stormy gray eyes. During the storm, he hadn't been able to shave, or maybe even a few days before that. He looked dangerous with the new growth of beard, topped off with whatever bee was in his bonnet.

"I lost. And, you already got your prize." She slid out of the bunk, just managing to not flash him.

Freezing in place, lips parting slightly, his eyes widened at the site of her in nothing but his shirt. At his heated expression, her imagination rushed back to the steamiest kiss she'd ever experienced. Well, she assumed it was. It sure felt like a record-breaker.

He finally seemed to find his smile, the corner of his mouth turning up seductively, that silver flickering in his eyes. "Not sure it counts if you let me win."

She cocked out her hip and bit her lower lip, scrunching her nose in a daring tease. "Then I want that kiss back."

"Mine, now." There he was. That arrogant grin was back in full force now. Lingering for a minute, she let the electricity zap and ping between them.

Finally, he seemed to remember what he'd come for. "Hurry and get changed. We'll start the tour in the galley. I'm starving." Dropping onto the couch, he leaned back and put his hands behind his head to wait for her to finish getting ready.

As a little revenge, hoping to bring back that roguish smile, she didn't pull the bathroom door closed all the way for her shower. She didn't have to see out the steamy faux glass to know he watched subtly with curious eyes, those lips slightly parted as he sought a gratifying glimpse. Didn't have to look out to know he was biting his knuckles as she leisurely ran the soap down her abdomen.

Yeah, she was a tease. But, just for Ryan. Hopefully. Ick, what if she was a tease around others?

Her brain flashed to a hazy image of a gorgeous woman with dark, wavy hair dancing on a table, surrounded by happy fishermen. Huh, friend of hers? Certainly not her up there. As quickly as the image had appeared, it was gone again.

Drying off as seductively as possible, knowing her silhouette was visible through the crack in the bathroom door, she heard his groan from the couch. Enjoying herself more than a little, she slowly pulled on a borrowed pair of jeans, sans underwear, again, her sole borrowed bra, and, thank goodness, a shirt that fit. A cute, feminine pink flannel that she tied at her waist.

Strolling out of the bathroom, she noted Ryan was still glassy eyed, wearing a dreamy expression on his face.

"Payback's a bitch," she said.

He shrugged, grinning that mischievous grin, eyebrow raised playfully, stirring that undeniable heat deep in her core. "Yeah, I did that on purpose."

"I knew it." She smiled, plopping next to him on the couch.

Before she even sank into the cushion, he abruptly stood and headed for the exit. "Come on, I can't handle being locked up in here with you."

"Ouch." She winced, knowing what he meant, but needing to rile him a bit first.

"Not what you'd be saying if we stayed sequestered in here all day." His rich, deep voice was gravelly.

He didn't need to be more specific. She knew exactly what would happen. Craved it so bad, every muscle in her body ached, every nerve on fire with anticipation.

She was rapidly becoming less terrified of never remembering her past, versus remembering everything and discovering something that made her give up what she'd found in the last few weeks. Fate could be that cruel, she had little doubt.

After the longest damn tour in history, or so she assumed, Ryan was finally done. Wow, that man could be boring when he wanted to be. He'd explained every last detail, including pointing out every movie in their inventory, book in the library, and lever in the control room.

Knowing he was an interesting person, she had little doubt that he was stalling. Time to answer the question he'd been dodging for weeks. She could wait a few more minutes.

The sun had already begun to set over the northern sky. Shades of purple, brilliant green, and pinks cast upon the sky in a cosmic light display, miraculously far south tonight. Waiting on the deck for Ryan, she marveled over the radiance of the night.

Appearing a few moments later, Ryan carried a blanket and mugs of piping hot tea for them both. Leaning against the slanted wall, they settled in so they could watch the night sky, snuggled up in the blanket.

Ryan finally broke the silence. Her patience had finally paid off. She nearly snorted at herself. Patience wasn't her thing. "Quinn?"

"Yes, Ryan?"

Shoulder to shoulder, she leaned further into him.

"Do you still want to know what we are?" Cautiously sipping the hot tea, he gazed off into the sky.

"Yeah. I need to." She sighed, waiting to hear what her gut was screaming at her so loudly it was indecipherable.

"Please, please... don't let it change you. I like you just as you are." She couldn't miss the heartache in his voice. Someone had hurt him, bad. Although he wouldn't say, she suspected that pain was the source of his distrust.

"But if it does change me, I'll still like you," Quinn added helpfully, hopefully.

"Maybe." He gulped a mouthful of burning hot tea. Wincing as it scorched his throat, he finally said it abruptly, like ripping off a Band-Aid. "Demon hunters."

Nodding, she returned her gaze to the cosmic light show above. "Yeah, that makes sense."

He looked at her like she was totally off. "In what world does that make sense?" Perhaps she was losing it. His eyes were as dark as the black sky in the distance, and just as mysterious. Maybe he was too.

She shrugged simply. "Well, something like it. We're ridiculously strong. I survived severe hypothermia, and I suspect you did too, as you mentioned swimming out to get me. That creature that you decapitated—nice moves, by the way. I guess the demon part is weird, but something magical."

"Fuck, not magical, but cursed." He spat out his words, boiling with hatred for what they were.

"I hadn't thought of it that way. How so?" She may not remember what she was, but she felt it. A calling, not a curse.

"Cursed to spend our exceptionally long lives killing monsters? How is that a gift?"

"I suppose that does sound rather violent. I... I was hoping this would help me remember the rest, but it's still a big blank. Whatever I was like before I met you, I *know* right from wrong. I know power when I see it. I was impressed the way you drove the rest of the whirlpool-creating monsters to their home. Wherever that is."

"That's why I'm afraid you'll change when you remember, honestly. In part. Most demon hunters don't look past the monster. They just kill without thinking of the repercussions. Some of these beasts are just lost. Like the grindylows. Defending themselves when they ended up on the wrong side of the veil."

Downing the last of her tea, she leaned across Ryan to set her mug next to his in the corner. The vivid lights overhead danced and formed new shapes, an intricate pattern, where nature meets magic. "Then why do I feel like we're so deeply, inherently trained to kill? When you took out that creature, my instincts cried out to dive into the sea and take out the rest. Awful as that sounds, I had a hard time fighting it. You're not wrong, that blood-thirst disturbed the hell out of me."

"My upbringing was probably a lot different from yours. My mom was awesome and doting like it sounds yours was. But you would have been raised to hunt demons. I didn't know what I was until I was nearly seventeen and didn't understand why I was different. My mother is still a card-carrying hippy, even if she wasn't born until the movement was fading."

He was stiff at her side, clearly uncomfortable with the things she'd said. With how little she had going for her right now, the least she could do is be honest—with them both. His gaze was lost in the light show above.

Shifting in the blanket, Quinn moved herself in between his legs, leaning against him to watch the night sky together. Although she could tell he was upset, he didn't hold the grudge and immediately wrapped his arms around her.

His breath warming her, he placed a slow kiss on the top of her head. "I'm sorry. I've had some bad run-ins with some pretty violent demon hunters and am jaded."

"I'm sorry." She hated hearing the pain in his voice. Maybe it was because he was one of the few people she knew, but he epitomized strength and character, and she hurt for him. "I don't know what sort of demon hunter I am, but after meeting you, I know I'll be forever changed."

"Demon hunters normally form teams, as many of the monsters we fight are too big for any of us to take alone. That's another of the ways I'm different. I don't have a team, and I don't want one." He held his voice steady, but his fury was palpable as his body shivered beneath hers.

"Somewhere, I must have a team then?"

"Yeah, I'm sure you do. We'll find them and get you home."

"What about you? Why don't you want to be on a team?"

She felt him stiffen behind her. "I think that's enough for tonight."

Letting it go, she turned, wrapping her arms and legs around him, on his lap, the cozy blanket draped around them. As the lights reflected down on the sea all around them, she pressed her lips to his in luminous contact, melting away the barriers that had weakly attempted to rise between them. Softly at first, growing stronger, she tasted him, entreating his lips to open for her.

Hungry, sweeping into her, he buried himself inside her, kissing her deeply, urging her to understand him as she silently pleaded for his acceptance.

Needing his touch, she guided his hands under her shirt. Eyes searching hers, he watched her reaction as he slid his hands under her bra. Grasping her breasts in his palms, his fingers gently squeezing her taut nipples, an electrifying thrill rocketed through her. Arching her back, she offered him more.

Groaning, he unhooked the top buttons of her shirt and opened the fabric, scooping her breasts out from the bra until he could see everything. Lips parted, gaze heavy as he studied her, he brushed his fingertips down her sternum.

Hot against the icy wind, no more curious exploration, his mouth covered a breast and he suckled. Hard. Blazing heat pumped through her veins, radiated from deep in her core as she instinctively moved against him.

Hands cupped around her breasts, he shifted his mouth and trailed his clever tongue over her breasts as he held them, massaging. Hands gripping in his short hair, she gasped at the delicious sensation and she soared above the clouds and he took her in his mouth again.

Aching, gripping him tight as the intensity and sweetness of his fevered touch brought her to a pinnacle, she bit her lips to silence a satisfied moan.

Smiling at her reaction as he touched lingering kisses to her chest, as she caught her breath.

He shifted her bra back over her and kissed her again, their mouths moving together in a sweetly sensual joining. Snapping like lightning in the center of a storm, their past, present, and futures shattered around them, held together only by the bond that was building between them.

Whatever her story before, it was so clearly written ahead of her. Like a question nagging in her mind before, she had her answer... Even though she couldn't remember what the question was.

Ending the moment long before they made love right there on the deck, she leaned her forehead against his, their synchronous breathing slowing together.

She felt him smiling against her, his hand cupping her cheek. "We really need to slow down. Let's figure out your last name first."

Chuckling as she nuzzled into him, she said, "Let's figure it out quick. I'm not sure I can wait much longer."

Looking up at her, he grinned playfully. "Impatient, aren't you?"

"Bet your ass. I can make something up. No one would know. Quinn Hanes. Quinn Klein. Quinn Jockey. Quinn Victoria's Secret."

"Those are all underwear brands."

"As much as I'm enjoying the freedom, jeans were not meant to be worn without a soft layer of cotton or satin underneath."

Nibbling along her neck, his rumbling laugh tickling down her spine, he tormented her. "When we go ashore, I'll buy you a hundred pair."

10

Ryan lay completely still, watching as Quinn's eyes slowly blinked open. Groaning adorably, she sealed her eyes shut and snuggled closer into him.

It was mornings like this that he struggled to recall why they weren't having sex. With him off official duty, they could be researching this creature in between fuck sessions. Grinning to himself, he imagined the fun that could be. Actually, with two demon hunters, they could go all day and all night without coming up for air.

And, Quinn was back out. For a demon hunter, she sure could sleep soundly. Call him crazy, maybe it was the deranged poet brewing within him, but he really liked watching her sleep. Her every thought played out in her expressions.

Before she'd stirred, she'd treated him to a secret, seductive grin. Now, a crease between her eyebrows was forming and her breathing accelerated. Another nightmare. She was so riddled with them. Clearly, her brain was protecting her from her unspeakable memories.

The dim light of the room cast a reflection off her damp eyelashes. "Bennett," she whimpered.

Rolling to his back, he gripped his hand in his hair as he was reminded of *exactly* why they weren't having sex. Bennett could easily have been just a member of her team that was hurt, or even killed, but the despondency in her voice... chances were, he was a hell of a lot more.

Her eyes finally fluttered open in wakeful finality. The haunted look had yet to leave her eyes. "Ack." She flopped onto her back next to him, the two of them just fitting side by side on the narrow mattress. "I wake up crying and can't even remember why."

He propped himself on his elbow and wiped away the tear that trailed down her cheek. "Maybe your brain is locked up tight for a reason. Whatever brought you to me... I'm willing to bet it wasn't something you want to remember."

She nodded, the corners of her mouth turned down.

He ought to tell her what she'd said in the dream. Serious ethical dilemma. If the name Bennett wakened her memories, she might collapse under the gravity of them, as her brain was probably locked up tight for a good reason. If the name triggered nothing, it would drive her mad trying to figure out who Bennett was and why she cried over him. Or, it could cure the amnesia comfortably, and she'd remember her mission, her life... and leave him forever.

His stomach roiled with indecision. Yeah, he was a serious asshole if he didn't say anything. For now, Ryan decided to keep it to himself and play it by ear. Bring it up when the time was right. Hating himself more than a little, he slid out of bed and took a quick shower.

After a light breakfast, they curled up on his couch to kick off yet another long day of memory-mining. "So, there are roughly five hundred demon hunters in existence today, and we all came from one demon, millennia ago?" She was an eager student and wanted to get it all correct.

He couldn't blame her, it was a lot of information. When he'd started, he assumed she would start to remember like she had with driving the Valkyrie. She seemed to know a bit, but not much more than an ordinary human. Yesterday, he'd spent all day telling her more about demon hunters. Yet, her amnesia hadn't budged.

"The Demon Mother, as she's often called, Deandra, took a human lover and began the hybrid race of demon hunters. Most descend from her, not all."

"So, where do those other demon hunters come from?" She looked adorable, cross-legged across from him on the couch, notepad in hand. Their empty breakfast dishes were stacked on his desk, and they'd already downed a carafe and a half of lukewarm coffee.

"That's a lesson for another day. You come from the demon mother." A much later date.

"Wait, if we began so long ago, why are there only five hundred of us?"

"First, it's exceptionally rare for a demon hunter to conceive more than one or two, maybe three children in their lifetime. And, when that child reaches adulthood, they make the decision to be human or demon hunter and there's a ritual to free them from their powers, if that's what they choose. Well, those from Deandra get to choose."

"I suppose that makes sense. Don't want anyone forced into the role, just those that are dedicated. Huh. Okay. What else? You mentioned earlier that we hunt in teams. Do you think I was with a team when I disappeared?"

"I have no doubt. No problem with other hybrids, like vampires or werewolves, or some of the smaller demons. But it's practically suicide to not have help against any of the bigger, more dangerous monsters. And, teams learn from each other."

"How do you establish a team?" Her scrawl was illegible on her notepad, already overfilled with blue ink. He doubted she'd forget a word of it, but she was determined to get it right.

"Like any friendship. Usually, it's quite organic. Perhaps the child of a teammate of your demon hunter parent. Maybe an old friend or even a coincidental meeting."

"And, do people keep these same teams for life?"

He nodded. "Usually."

Her brow scrunched again, and she tapped her pen against her notepad. "Why don't you have a team again? Sounds rather foolish not to, and unusual."

"I'm not like other hunters. I don't need or want a team." With most of this information so new for her, he really didn't want to explain why.

"Why?"

Dammit. "I did have a team. My mentor, Greg, was concerned that I was seventeen and hadn't ever even met another demon hunter. He meant well, but he sort of pulled me into his team. They'd recently lost a member and were grieving. He'd hoped new blood would help them approach things in a new, more positive light."

"Mentor? What about your demon hunter parent? How did you find out so late?"

He'd been afraid she'd catch those nuances. He stood from the couch and poured another cup of coffee from the carafe. Not that he needed more caffeine, but a brief distraction was necessary. "Left before I was born."

"I'm so sorry. You said earlier that he couldn't stay?"

Unable to make himself answer, he shook his head and sipped the lukewarm coffee, his face contorting at the unpleasant sensation. Damn carafe wasn't worth the stainless steel it was made of.

"What happened with your team?" she asked, setting her notebook down, her eyes heavy with copious sympathy. Gratefully, she changed the subject, but this one was even worse.

Gulping the entire mug of the crappy brew like the shot of whiskey it wasn't, he set the cup down and plopped back on the couch. Sighing heavily, he ran his hands over the beard that was becoming denser than stubble. He really needed to shave. Good thing Willa didn't seem to care. "I really don't want to go there today. Let's just say, it wasn't a good fit."

Easily reading his regret, she moved on as quickly as possible. "Okay. You mentioned demon hunters are the shoot first, ask questions later sort. Why do you think that is?"

Staring at the ceiling, its textured surface painted white like fresh snow, he considered how to answer her questions. He'd assumed this would be an easy Q&A. Not so. Why he had assumed that with Quinn, he had no idea. "Some is instinct, being half demon and half human. You get the idea. A lot of it probably comes from generations of seeing some truly awful demons tormenting their friends and families, and I think they just get jaded. Stopped teaching their children to read the situation beyond strategizing for the quickest kill. But, that's just my theory."

"But your hippy mother raised you for peace and love."

Gesturing to the photo of his mom, he smiled. "Yeah, that's Sunshine. I'd say half or more of the monsters we face are quite content to cause mayhem and annihilation on Earth, which is why we exist. However, some are just lost on the wrong side of the veil. They attack because they don't know better or are frightened."

Tossing her notebook down, she'd curled into him, wrapping her arms around his torso and resting her head on his shoulder. "This is why I like you so well."

Chuckling into her hair that tickled his nose, he asked, "Why?"

"You're different. Somehow, I know I've never met anyone quite like you."

❖

"W<small>HAT'S THE PLAN FOR</small> today?" Quinn was remarkably chipper the next morning. After another night of helplessly holding her through tearful dreams, Ryan dreaded discovering what was bouncing around in the amnesic brain of hers. Refreshingly, she had an optimism and humor that couldn't be suppressed.

"Next, we figure out what swallowed those ships. The first was near Zhemchug Canyon, the next closer to St. Paul, another near there again, then the fourth was close to Adak." Holding his hand out for her, he warmed her fingers in his and they walked out to the deck together.

The ocean wasn't quite as calm today. A few white caps topped the waves, but nothing the Valkyrie couldn't cut straight through with ease. Holding onto the back rail, he looked out over the water.

"That's where we're headed now?"

"Yep. There have been reports of massive whirlpools, way bigger than what we saw with the grindylow things. Entire ships have gone missing."

"How many people?"

"The latest was a crew of eleven. Trawl vessel. Was way off course. Rumor has it, they were chasing a big catch, tons of groundfish clustering outside of their normal grounds." Looking into the distance, he hated to think of how they were going to stop the massive thing.

"Kraken?"

Smiling proudly, he nudged her with his shoulder. "Nicely done. You've been paying attention. Or, remembering something. Human myths and legends are helpful. Generations of stories passed from person to person, so things get twisted a bit. But, yeah, sounds like a kraken."

"And we, in this relatively tiny boat, two demon hunters, one of which is terribly out of practice, and a human—although fierce—Coast Guard crew, are going to take on one of the most notorious sea monsters of all time?" Despite the uncertainty in her words, he couldn't mistake the thrill of adventure vibrating behind her words.

She may have forgotten what she is, but deep down, she clearly felt it. She stepped to the back of the ship next to him and scanned the choppy seas in their wake.

"Yeah, pretty much. We're better equipped than anyone else to take it on. A handful of others have been taken down in the last few centuries. Just none that I've specifically heard of," he muttered under his breath, not voicing his clarification clearly, for his sake or hers, he wasn't sure.

"I'm assuming this kraken isn't a little lost monster on the wrong side of the veil." She smiled innocently, imagining yelling at it like a neighbor dog digging up the roses in her backyard. Huh, what an odd memory to surface.

Stuttering in his amusement, he shook his head. "No... No. From what I hear, they really enjoy eating ships. Likely for the nutrition, but more, they like the crunch of the hull in their jaws. Or, again, so I hear. I've never met one."

"What if I don't remember any of my training? Because, well, I don't."

"That's why we're out here. We're going to practice. See how much is ingrained in those sweet muscles of yours." He raised his eyebrow and bit his lip in playful invitation, pinning her against the back of the ship between his arms.

A salty, wintry breeze kicked up off the water, blowing her hair straight into his mouth. Sputtering and spitting out the mouthful of hair, he teased her with theatrical annoyance.

"Sorry." She turned to face him and reached in her pocket but came up empty handed. "Huh. Think I normally keep hair ties in my right pocket, just for such an occasion. Now I feel naked without it. Didn't realize I was missing it until just now."

Grinning, he nudged her with his knee, still pinning her between his arms. "Say 'naked' again."

She blushed... he'd never seen her blush before. It was fucking hot, like she'd just had her way with him and was flushed from the effort. "No."

"Please?" He was absolutely not against begging.

"Fine. Naked," she blurted out flatly, leaning back defiantly against the rear wall of the ship.

"No, say it all sexy like you did a minute ago."

"That wasn't sexy."

"Fuck yeah it was. Come on. Please?"

"So needy." She ribbed him with a sly look in her twinkling midnight eyes. There was the ornery Quinn he knew and loved. Sensually gliding her tongue along her lip, she moved closer and stood on her toes. Murmuring in his ear, her voice was breathy and seductive. "*Naked.*"

Groaning, he pulled her close and brushed his hands underneath her shirt, striking over the smooth skin of her back, needing to feel her close against him, the skin to skin connection becoming more critical every time they touched. "Again," he begged.

She giggled, her delighted laugh echoing off the waves. If anything was to scare away the fiercest demons of the sea, it was the pleasure she found in the simplest things, in refreshing contrast to their taste for destruction.

"Okay, fine." He backed away and stood in the center of the deck. He beckoned her to follow. "Hit me."

"What?" Brow scrunched, she goggled at him like this idea was the worst thing she'd ever heard.

"You won't hurt me. Punch me right here." He tapped his finger on his cheek, waiting to either feel the gentle tap of someone that didn't know how to punch, or get his ass handed to him.

"I don't want to hurt you." She looked wary at the prospect, somehow not fearing for herself, but maybe for him, and stepped closer.

"Trust me."

Scowl fiercely uncertain, she didn't look so sure.

"You are awfully tiny." He stepped closer and lifted her arms, flopping her around like she was a rag-doll. "See? Look at these flimsy limbs. You couldn't hurt a fly."

His taunting got the desired reaction. Before he knew what hit him—and it was clearly Quinn—a solid roundhouse kick smashed into his face and slammed him to the ground.

Rolling around on the ground, he held his hand over his bruised jaw to hide his enjoyment. Although, it really did hurt like a son-of-a-bitch.

"I'm so sorry." She dove to the ground to check his injuries.

Taking advantage of her position, he flipped her over and pinned her beneath him. Thinking himself clever, he went to steal a premature victory kiss.

Before his lips could connect with hers, her legs swung up and flipped him over.

On impact, the hard, low-slip surface of the deck reverberated through his throbbing ribs.

He leaped to his feet as she sprang to hers. Beckoning her closer, she didn't take the bait this time. They circled, each waiting for the other to make the next move.

Kicking her legs in a chain of wind-milling spins, he was forced to step back to avoid another strike to the face. Watching her timing like he was jumping rope, he grabbed her foot on its next approach.

While she was still airborne, he spun her in a swift three-sixty.

Wrenching his wrist in mid-air, she slipped out of his grip, but crashed on the ground. Her cheekbone crunched against the floor.

Wincing, he almost felt guilty, until she brushed away the drip of blood from her lip, raised her mouth in a fierce grin, then dove at him in a frenzied attack.

Blasting his fist at her, she ducked and threw her elbow at his ribs. With a juke, he dodged the blow and spun out of her reach.

Fists and elbows flew.

Feet and knees bounced and cracked, a few hits landing, but most were skillfully evaded.

Finally, he caught her foot again and pulled her off her feet. Somersaulting backward over her shoulder, she was back up again and transitioned her momentum into a backflip, landing beyond his reach.

Feet barely planted, she seized a loaded harpoon gun from its hook and aimed right between his eyes.

Raising his arms, he immediately surrendered, triumphantly grinning at her victory over him. "See? You may not remember the how's or the why's, but you know all the right moves, and can improvise better than most." Leisurely, ignoring the weapon trained at his head, he closed the distance between them.

Mouth quirked up in an adorably arrogant smile, she returned the harpoon and met him halfway. Hand wrapping around the back of his neck, she rose to meet him. "I've got lots of other moves I don't need my memories for." Plunging, she dove into the kiss with the vigor she approached everything.

Confident, passionate, she seemed to funnel the lingering adrenaline from the fight into the kiss. Unable to resist, he met her stroke for stroke. The warmth of her tongue sparring with his sent lava pumping through his veins. Hands gripped at her hips, holding her pelvis snug against his, he hungered for more.

At the sound of hooting and hollering from the crew in their various positions around the ship, clearly having all skipped their normal duties to watch the show... he pulled away. With a sweeping bow, he moved back to the rail, stopping a few feet away from Quinn, tempted to haul her back to his bunk, disregarding his vow to himself.

He needed to tell her about Bennett first.

11

"ANYTHING YET?" WILLA CAME strolling onto the bridge. Ryan and Quinn stood on lookout, scanning the horizon.

He shrugged. "Nothing. Dull as a tepid bath out there."

Kyle leaned back in his chair at the nearby desk, rubbing the visual fatigue from his eyes after spending too many hours in front of the mind-numbing screen. "Nothing here. No reports of whirlpools or missing ships in well over a week now."

Scowling, Willa folded her arms across her chest. "Obviously, I'm glad there's been no activity. But I'd hate for us to get too far away, then have it attack again as soon as we're too far away to help."

"This is where the last ship went missing?" Quinn scanned the sea with intensity, her brow scrunched in deep concentration. Like she had a personal vendetta against this kraken. Ryan's gut roiled as he realized it may be *the reason* for her amnesia, or at least part of it.

"Yeah, about a mile south of us." Willa pointed beyond where they could see.

Darkness shrouded the periphery of the horizon as the sun descended behind them. "I think it's avoiding us," Quinn said eerily, almost mechanically. "Like it's on a tight leash."

His head whipped toward her, shifting his gaze from the empty sea. Thrilled she seemed to be tapping into the memories, but so much more fucking terrified. Of her hollow tone. Of what she implied.

Her midnight eyes grew clouded, her focus on an invisible, distant target. Fearing the answer, but needing more information, he asked gently, "Who's holding the leash?"

Her features flat, she continued, as if in a trance. "She has her own plans for... *us*." Tears marched down her cheeks, a gutting melancholy washing over her. Eyelashes fluttering, she slumped as her muscles gave way.

Before she hit the ground, Ryan scooped her up in his arms. As he had the night they met, he clutched her snugly against him. Barking to the bridge, he demanded, "Notify me of any changes."

His attention only on Quinn, he carried her down to their quarters and laid her on the bunk. She didn't stir, her limbs heavy as she fell into a viscous slumber. Wrapping her in his arms, he murmured that she was safe now.

Again, she cried in her sleep, whimpering for Bennett. Ryan ignored the constriction in his chest, recognizing it wasn't about him right now. If she really loved this Bennett, he'd get out of their way. Yeah, he was a selfish bastard and wanted to keep her for himself, but he wasn't a complete asshole.

Again, she cried softly, finally saying something other than the prick's name. Oops, he shouldn't think ill of someone he'd never met. That may be dead. Probably was dead, for how upset Quinn was about him. Someone that Quinn loved.

"It's ok." She seemed to be soothing him no. Although her eyes remained shut, she was still lost in memories that refused to surface into consciousness. A slow smile blossomed across her damp cheeks. "It's going to be okay. I found him."

Body relaxing against him, Quinn turned into him, clinging as if he were her lifeline. Gradually, her breathing slowed, and she drifted into restful sleep.

Unable to release his hold on her, Ryan trailed his fingers along the contours of her jaw, savoring the smoothness of her porcelain skin. Little did she know, she drove him mad each night, saying another man's name. Yet, tonight, she melted into him, reassuring him, someone, herself... that she'd "found him."

A glimmer of hope dared to flutter in his chest, that she might be referring to him. Bennett brought her sadness, but could Ryan be the *him* that brought her comfort and security. Even if she couldn't love him, at least he could bring her peace.

SHORTLY BEFORE NIGHT FADED into day, Quinn's eyes fluttered open. She knew she'd collapsed looking for the kraken. Knew she'd experienced the gamut of emotions while she was out, her heart still heavy with grief. Despite the density of it, a buoyant optimism outshined the darkness, filling her with the knowledge that she had everything she needed.

Encased in Ryan's arms, she felt glorious. His skin warm against hers, she snuggled closer. Amazing, she was physically as close as was humanly possible, yet it wasn't quite close enough.

"Quinn?" His raspy voice rumbled against the top of her head.

"Yes, Ryan?"

"Are you part boa constrictor?"

She laughed, the sound vibrating across his chest. Grazing her fingers along his skin, she watched as goosebumps formed in the wake of her touch. "I hate snakes."

His gruff morning chuckle boosted her higher. Her fingers trailed down his abdomen, triggering a sharp intake of his breath. "How is a demon hunter afraid of any creature?" he quickly said, poorly attempting to distract her. Or him. Or both.

"Phobia," she said casually. Ignoring his attempts at distracting her from her mission, she reached into his shorts.

This time, his breath hitched, his heart skipped a beat under her ear, and he withheld the air in his lungs for a moment as she ran her fingers skillfully along his rigid length that thickened in her hand. Riding on the thrill of his reaction, of the feel of his smooth skin under her fingertips, his rock hard shaft at full attention for her, she reveled gripped him tightly, stroking.

"Stop. Really, I..." Hissing a gasp, he bit his lip and his hips shifted ad he trusted into her hand. "Shit, Quinn, cut it out," he said with a laughing groan.

"Okay," she said, trailing her fingertips up his abdomen as she released him. Whatever her dreams had done to her, she craved him so damn bad. "If you're sure. We've got a lot of time to kill."

As she pulled her hand away, taunting him with a light touch in her retreat, he grinned and guided her hand right back down. "No, wait, I changed my mind. Keep going." Rolling his shoulders, he settled his head against the pillow and smiled.

Chuckling, she slipped her hand back down and continued her efforts. Watching his expressions, his dark eyes fluttering closed, his humor quickly dissipated as he reacted to her tightening grip, instinctively thrusting into her hand with a breathless groan.

Fuck, she needed so much more. Each time she kissed him, she felt something rising from deep inside her. Whatever her past, she knew he was her future. And she craved all of him.

As she increased her pace, he cussed again and shifted out of her reach.

He pulled her in for a deep, turbulent kiss. Exploring, he nibbled on her ear, tracing his hand along her hip as he lay facing her.

It wasn't enough. She rolled atop him. One hand on her hip, his other shifted under her shirt and grasped her breast. Pressing her body over his, she kissed him again, pressure building and no relief in sight. Hips tight together, he cupped her breast in his hand as she ground against his rigid cock. He groaned against her open mouth. Moaning at the sensation that lit through her, desire built higher and faster, uncontainable.

Only a thin layer of cotton separated her from the bliss of feeling him rubbing against her core. Breath coming faster, lost in the dizzying awareness of nothing but Ryan, she burned with an unbearable yearning to take him inside her.

"Dammit," he growled, pulling his lips away from hers, holding her hips and gently rolling her back to his side. Both panting, ridiculously sexually frustrated, she knew his scowl matched hers without even looking.

Unable to resist, dreams of him and how they could make each other feel rocking in her mind, she shifted back over him and nipped his lower lip. Playfully, but firm enough to let hook know she wasn't playing.

Before he could argue, she looked him in the eyes, seeing how severely his desire matched hers. She lowered her body down over his, flicking his nipple with her tongue on the way by, and slid down that damn slick fabric of his briefs that was always in her way.

Ravenous, she trailed her tongue up his hard shaft.

"No, fuck, Quinn—" he growled.

"I need all of you," she said before she nipped him gently, then licked the hurt away.

Groaning, he moved against her. His voice hoarse, he didn't refuse. "If you insist, but trust me, payback's going to happen, and you don't get to argue." He sighed theatrically, a throaty laugh escaping his lips.

Something told her it had been way too long since Ryan had been with anyone. Or, since she had enjoyed herself, or felt this confident, in a long, long time.

Slow at first, building, she savored the feel of him.

Surging, gasping in that sexy deep voice, his body stiffened as she pulled him over the edge.

When he settled, she moved back up him and rested her head on his chest, her leg draped over him.

"Fuck, Quinn, that was... surprising." He exhaled languidly. "You woke up awfully... playful."

She grinned against his skin. "Last night wrecked me, but I awoke with this incredible sensation that I have everything I need. That no matter what, we can tackle anything. Not to mention, overwhelming sexual frustration."

Wrapping his arms around her, he laughed and planted a kiss on the top of her head. "Understatement of the decade." He inhaled as if about to say something, then closed his mouth.

Instead, he traced his fingertips along her side, shifting her at his side and cupping her breast in his hand again. Igniting the sensation she'd tried to burn off on him, he lowered his hand and cupped her. Curious fingers explored her, slick and agile as he dipped under her panties.

Already nearing the tipping point, she bucked against his palm. Overwhelmed by his touch, her breath came fast and desperate.

"Fuck, we need a real bed," he cussed. "Come on. Let's move to the couch."

She covered his hand with hers and said, "Don't stop."

Had she said sexual frustration? So far and gone past that, she writhed against his hand.

Her eyes fluttered open, and she found him watching her. At first, he looked down at his handiwork as he rubbed, a heavy curiosity with lips parted and aroused focus entirely on her. As he upped the rhythm, she burned, slick and thrusting at his touch, and he shifted his gaze to meet hers, holding her in his dark eyes as he caressed her to her climax.

Breathless, stunned by the strength of her reaction to him, at how natural and fluid their connection was, she snuggled into him. Neither spoke for a while, breathing and thinking and savoring.

Finally, as reality grew thick around them, Quinn conceded. "We should get moving. We have a kraken to find."

His breath stilled, his heart pounded harder, echoing into her skull. "What all do you remember from last night?"

Her heart thundered in her chest, pulse firing erratically as she ventured back to the awful sensation of *knowing*, remembering, but not. "The fear before I passed out, the certainty that this creature is truly a kraken, and that its master is the real threat to our world."

"What if you pass out when we get closer? I can't beat it without you. Clearly, it has something to do with how you came to land in the water off my bow." His hand swept a stray lock from over her brow as he spoke, quietly reassuring her it was okay to run from the fight.

She sat up, her elbows on either side of him, their faces inches away. "It's not the kraken that haunts my subconscious, but whatever holds its leash. Let's draw it away. Take out the guard dog, and, when we find my team, we can take out whatever holds its leash."

His brow scrunched in surprise and concern. "How did you figure this out?"

"A lot is just guessing. I'm a good guesser. Really. But I think a little memory slipped through. Stormy skies, high seas, the whirlpool in the distance. If we can draw it away, far from the protection of its master, we can take it out where she can't reach." Although the vision came on stronger and stronger, the darkness, a heartbreak she couldn't identify, a sense of hope, the joking banter as they sailed into hell... she didn't resist it. Needed to feel it and dig deeper into her memory. Or more ships would be crushed, and more sailors lost at sea.

Sliding off of him, she sought solitude in the shower as she struggled to remember more. Something deep inside told her this was right. She was on the right track to solving the riddle that was Quinn, and how she came to be here, without a memory to her name.

Delivered exactly where she needed to be.

12

Valkyrie, Kiska Island, Offshore.

SLIPPING A USCG T-SHIRT over his head, buttoning up his sturdiest navy-blue cargos, fastening his sleekest boots, Ryan held his focus steady, despite the fluttering in this chest weakly attempting to tell him this was fucked. Quinn sounded so sure in her plan. When she'd passed out, limp and pale, uncharacteristically helpless for the second time in his arms... Ryan's heart had plummeted into the pit of his gut.

Powerless as she'd been, he'd felt unhinged. Nothing he could do but wait for her to get through it. And now she wanted to dive into the middle of it?

Sitting on the couch, as ready as he was ever going to be, he watched as she pulled on a pair of borrowed black athletic pants and a snug black shirt. Not that they needed the dark clothes, but it was habit, as the demon hunter often stalked its prey at night, as so many demons are nocturnal.

Not because of choice, but, like vampires, couldn't handle the realm's intense sunshine. Or so they said. For all his former team's fucked approach, they did know their demons.

Willa had thought Ryan deranged when Quinn and he had presented the scheme to her. Waiting in the old military harbor at Kiska Island, all fishing vessels warned off from the region, they were the only ship in its anticipated range. Drifting, they feigned engine failure. An irresistible meal.

Lifting the seat off his couch, Ryan revealed a hidden cache filled with pointy objects of all sorts. Like a kid in a damn candy store, Quinn rubbed her hands together and dove in. Carefully—again, pointy objects.

She held a sword up, only to decide the weight wasn't quite what she was looking for. Gripping his favorite shield, she held it in front and posed dramatically, only to return it to the trunk as well. Finally, she settled on a pair of matching short swords.

Strapping on her bulletproof vest, she slid the swords into the back à la Deadpool. "Nice." He nodded, admiring her badass presentation.

Beaming, she looked into the chest again. "Thanks. Any throwing knives, stars, something for longer range?"

"Nah, those are too easy to lose at sea. I had some, but they're all at the bottom of the Pacific. How about a harpoon gun, like the one you aimed at my skull?"

"I like it. Good idea."

Without much thought, he wrapped his hand around the worn handle of his favorite broadsword, for no other reason than it had good balance and he hadn't nipped it from his old team when he'd left. He turned and opened another drawer. Pulling out a pair of handguns, he checked them efficiently and offered one to Quinn.

Scowling, that crease formed between her eyebrows again. Her lip quirked up in a full sneer. "I hate guns."

Nodding, he huffed a subtle laugh, appreciating her honesty. "As do I. But they come in handy sometimes."

The air was crisp as they stepped into the light. Blindingly bright for mid-day Alaska in spring, golden rays cast a calm glow over the

Valkyrie, the sky a rare brilliant azure. Good. Far cry from the glimpse of a memory that Quinn had described.

Ryan strode out onto the deck, the bulk of the crew standing ready, awaiting his instruction. Quinn stood off to the side.

Every so often, she seemed to act like she felt unworthy or insecure, in such opposition to her character. Broke his heart to see her anything less than her brilliant, confident self. He wondered where she'd gotten it, as it was as unnatural for her as her feigned syrupy-sweet was.

He motioned her to join him up front. It was as much her plan as it was his, and the crew needed to know any command from her in the thick of this was to be followed as much as his.

Rolling her eyes with a big old grin, she came to stand at his side. The April morning was pleasantly cool without being unbearable, for demon hunters, anyway. Some of the other guys were letting their beards grow out to fight the cold.

"Listen up. This is bigger than anything we've taken down before. Kraken—whatever you want to call it—it's big, and it's hungry. Let's not let it eat us. If it cracks our hull, you know your emergency procedures."

He heard a few chuckles in the small crowd of misfits. "Dive over the side and hope you don't get caught in its wake?"

Burly, ornery, but eager... maybe a little overeager sometimes. Today, Willa stood behind and let him do his job. She ran the ship. He ran missions like this.

"Pretty much. Now, if legend holds true, which it does now and again, don't let its tentacles wrap around us. That's how it will pull us down. Modern interpretations suggest teeth, but if it's more of an octopus, we're not likely to see those shark-like teeth. From my research, I'm leaning more toward a squid-like beak."

Quinn nudged him in the side. He looked around and noticed the wide eyes of his companions. "Not much of a pep-talk," she muttered out of the corner of her mouth, flashing him a teasing grin.

"What I mean is, be prepared for anything. You all have faced about the scariest, most deadly creatures any human has dared face. We got this, but it's going to be tougher than anything we've come across. Divide up on repairs and defense. Willa, you'll be at the helm, ready to gun it if things are looking bleak?" His voice strong, he was completely at ease in front of the crew. Had joked around with them so much, they felt he was one of them. But, when it came down to it, every one of them looked to him to keep them safe.

Manuel hollered from the back, towering a good head above the rest, "And what will you two be doing?"

Scratching his stubbled jaw, Ryan laughed hoarsely under his breath. "Yeah, about that. This is why we exist. What we were born for. So, if it comes down to us or you... save yourself." He glanced at Quinn. "She may not have a clue who she is, but as most of you saw, or at least heard, she kicked my ass without breaking a sweat. When in doubt, get behind either of us."

In the distance, he saw a growing black inkiness in the water.

Quinn pointed and nudged him.

With a subtle nod, he tilted his head as the familiar thrill, the rush of adrenaline from instinct, experience, and demon blood surged through him. The corner of his mouth rose into a devious smile.

"It's time," she said. "Know your role. We need every last one of you to beat this thing. The missing fishermen... let's not let this thing get anyone else."

"Or us," Leah called from the crowd.

Ryan shrugged a mirthless laugh. "Or us."

A deep rumbling stirred beneath them. Waves started to form in a circular ripple around them.

Eight tentacles, thick as tree trunks, rose fluidly from the water. One by one, tentacles latched onto the Valkyrie.

Over the cacophony of waves crashing over them, the crew shouted back and forth, coordinating defensive maneuvers, as they'd practiced.

Pulling out his pistols, Ryan blasted testing shots into the serrated suctions on the tentacles.

A slight recoil. It felt it.

He fired again, again, unloading both cartridges focused at a single target.

Oozing blood and mangled flesh, the tentacle adjusted its hold.

It wasn't nearly enough.

QUINN HADN'T REALIZED HOW heavily armed the ship was, but she should have guessed. Still, none would be strong enough to penetrate the dense hide of the monster beneath. Like the bullets to the tentacle, mere flesh wounds.

Deafening explosions pounded into the tentacles in rapid succession as the crew targeted attacks. She ran to the side.

Hands gripped as she steadied herself against the lurching, she searched the depths below.

Like a damn fish in a tank, albeit hungry and fucking huge, it lurked beneath them. Big enough to swallow the ship in a bite or two. And in no rush to suck them under, it seemed to be playing with them.

Yep. Squid. Nothing like what Hollywood had created. It was tough to make out the details as its turbulence unsettled the quiet harbor, but it definitely had two eyes and likely a brain in between. Actually, it looked like a pretty typical Humboldt, but at least three times the size of the Valkyrie.

After barking a few orders here and there, Ryan ran up behind her to look down at the creature as well.

"What do you think, I'll go for the eyes while you scrounge up some dinner for our new friend?" she asked.

"I want its tentacles off my boat." Ryan studied the water as intensely as she did. "The plan is solid. Just... don't let it eat you." His heavy smile didn't reach his eyes.

"How long can you hold your breath for?"

He shrugged, pondering. Behind them, the crew battled intensely. "Maybe twenty minutes, fifteen if I'm exerting myself. You?"

"I think I could go at least twenty. Ready?"

"Showoff," he teased, then dove in before she had the chance.

Grabbing the harpoon, she followed him in. A tickle in the back of her mind reminded her of all the foolish banter in the midst of battle. Friends. Teammates. Finding strength in each other. Achingly familiar, but unreachable.

Kicking her legs so rapidly she couldn't tell if it was the friction or the freezing ocean against her goosebumps that burned, she caught up to Ryan. Above them, she could hear Willa firing up the engine, giving the kraken a run for its money as she rocked in its unbreakable grip.

The monster glanced lazily at them like they were seals, not identifying the difference. Most of the humans it would have seen close up were likely already drowning, she realized sadly. If this creature was as old as she suspected, it had killed hundreds, more likely thousands, in its lifetime.

She aimed the harpoon as she drew nearer.

It withdrew one of its tentacles from the boat.

The shadow descended behind her, growing as it approached.

Too late. She fired..

The harpoon pierced right into its sack-like eye and ruptured the membrane. Inky blood oozed out from the wound.

Lightheaded, the vision striking deep into her mind, she sealed her mouth shit as she recoiled. Darkness enveloped her, like a curtain lowering over her vision.

Blinking against the narrowing aperture of her vision, she struggled to keep her eyes open. Flashbacks threatened behind the curtain. Consciousness waned.

No, not here. She shook it off, swimming toward her next target. Focus. The mission. The crew. Ryan. She pushed the darkness behind her.

Ryan swam rapidly in her direction.

Reaching past the curtain, she lashed at another approaching tentacle. The darkness began to recede from her vision.

Go, she motioned to Ryan to continue with the plan.

Nodding, she forced a smile, needing him to trust her to keep focus. No other choice.

When he hesitated, she gave him a thumbs up, and added a snark to her smile.

His expression shifted toward relief. He turned back toward his objective and swam away, fading from sight.

Above, the engine wailed louder. Looking up, she saw the hull deeper in the water than it should be. Anything but a heavily reinforced Coast Guard Cutter would be taking on water.

Kicking full speed at the tentacle nearest, that looked to be pulling down on the bow, she slashed, gouging deeply with her twin swords.

Thick, oily blood leaked out and filled the water around her.

Kicking fast, her legs aching as heated muscle burned against the cold of the sea, she swam to the opposite end of the ship to destabilize the creature's grip further.

A tentacle splashed into the water near the bow as the Valkyrie crew took out another.

Slashing again with her swords, this time gouging down the length of a tentacle, the kraken's grip weakened further.

The engine hummed smoother, a little lighter in the water.

Moving to the next, she felt the rumble of a massive explosion. A mutilated tentacle splashed like dead weight back into the water. Nicely done crew.

Like plucking fingers of its nasty grip, the crew knocked off another.

The damn kraken was stubborn, angry or hungry or simply stupid, continue its efforts, rather than running.

As she took on another tentacle, one of its feeding tentacles snaked around her foot. It yanked her downward. Nowhere to go but beak.

She rotated her body in its grip.

Steady, she waited.

As it drew her in, a light snack toward its unbreakable beak, she aimed her sword.

Darkness surrounded him as he propelled deeper into eerily waters. Like a damn graveyard Scattered in front of him were hovering, spiky sea mines, massive maces dotting the harbor.

Not many in the general public knew just how active the North Pacific had been in World War II. Luckily, the mine cleanup force hadn't been able to remove them all yet.

This had better work. They didn't exactly have a backup plan, unless one considered running and trying again another day to be a decent Plan B. But he knew they weren't going to get another shot at this.

Driving his heavy broadsword into one of the links, he twisted and broke apart the chain. Grabbing hold of the sea mine by the attached chain like a kid with a cheerful red balloon, he kicked toward the kraken.

In the distance, he saw Quinn ensnared in a feeding tentacle. She waited, trusting.

Glancing his way, she flashed him a watery grin as he approached. And she got sucked in closer to death.

The creature's feeding tentacles held firm on her ankle. Pulling her downward, Quinn wriggled in its solid grip, slowing its progress to give him enough time.

As she neared its face, she aimed and launching one of her twin swords.

They'd debated how to get the creature to open its mouth without endangering the Valkyrie and her crew.

Beak wide open, it readied for its snack.

The sword nailed the eye. Inky blood flooded the sea.

Quinn held on for the wild ride as it thrashed wildly to pull in one last bite before rushing off to recover from its injuries.

Ryan kicked faster. Cutting it pretty fucking close, but no other choice.

As captive Quinn neared the beak, Ryan flipped his body and kicked the mine into its open mouth ahead of her.

Sword firm in her hand, she slashed through the feeding tentacle, severing its limb and freed herself from its grip.

Quinn swiftly swam away from the closing beak.

Furious it had lost its tasty morsel, the creature gripped with its remaining tentacles onto the Valkyrie for dear life. Pulling, pushing, he could hear the Valkyrie's engine screaming on high, explosives blasting above.

Ryan rushed for Quinn and linked hands. Together, they kicked rapidly towards the surface.

The kraken locked down its beak as the mine drifted into its gullet.

The force of the explosion radiated in all directions.

Massive bubbles shot toward the surface. With the blast, they surged toward the surface, rocketing out of the water and launching into the air.

AFTER A DEAFENING FLIGHT above the ocean, they splashed back down again into the rough sea. Its body shredded below in a mass of haze and blood, the kraken's remaining tentacles, lifelessly heavy, crashed down. Dodging the falling limbs as she swam back to the surface again, Quinn searched for Ryan in the chaos.

A gasp of breath rushing into his lungs, he surfaced and whipped his head from side to side as he looked for her.

The moment he spotted her, he flicked water from his hair and brandished a roguish grin.

Freezing, goosebumps prickling her skin, she could hardly feel the barely supra-zero temperatures for the thrill of the adrenaline pumping through her as he swam toward her.

Cheers resounded from the Valkyrie. Below them, dust from the sea floor mushroomed around the kraken's limp body as it collapsed into its watery grave.

In the far distance, lightning lit up the sky, but nothing more. Mourning the loss of her pet, but not avenging, the faceless threat in her mind quieted. For now. Quinn shook it off and swam for Ryan.

Pumping a fist in the air with the crew, Ryan whooped victoriously.

As they reached each other, Quinn wrapped her limbs around him. Ryan pulled her close, his mouth covering hers.

Kissing him right back with everything she had, heavy, wet, breathless, they treaded in the thrashing waves.

From the loudspeaker, Willa's voice echoed over the water. "Get your asses in here before you scare all the fish away." The joy in her voice radiated across the water, traveling miles further than the words themselves.

Sopping wet, freezing, Quinn didn't feel a thing as the crew tossed her about from hug to hug. Hand linked with hers, Ryan wasn't letting go, even as he was pulled in for enthusiastic embraces.

Willa fired up the engines and got the hell out of there, while the deck was still overloaded with celebratory hoots and hollers. Good. Quinn had an uneasy feeling, being so close to that lightning. The further away, the better.

"Whoo. Got that monster good," Kyle roared and pumped his fist in the air.

Ryan shook his head. "Actually, I think that was a local."

Stepping closer, Leah threw her arm around Quinn and gave her a squeeze on the shoulder. "Local? That wasn't normal."

Nodding, Quinn followed his thinking. "I don't think that was from the other side. It was a pretty ordinary squid, aside from its massive size."

Looking at them like they were nuts, the surrounding crew pondered the statement. Edging his way closer, Dean shrugged. "A fricking *massive* squid. Does that mean we can talk about it?"

Shaking his head, Ryan flicked water at the eager beaver. "Fuck no. Let some scientist find one someday."

As soon as the chest bumps, airborne hugs, and squeals started to slow, Quinn felt Ryan gently pulling her out of the crowd. She was wiped out from the battle, but the adrenaline still sounded through her like overcharged electrical sparks.

Determined, walking with deliberate strides, he led her into the ship and straight to their quarters.

As soon as the door closed, his mouth was back on hers. As thrilling as the battle had been, it wasn't anything compared to the ecstasy that coursed through her in a frantic rush as he kissed her, ignoring all the reasons they shouldn't. Because there were infinitely more reasons they should. Lines crossed, lives entwined, she knew he was hers.

The velvety warmth of his tongue rubbed over hers, his hands wrapped around her, fingers gripping her hips.

Peeling off his soaking shirt, she tossed it aside, the wet fabric slapping against the hard ground. Running her hands over his spectacularly ripped abs, her mouth trailed along his collarbone.

Impatiently, he peeled off her vest and shirt, then quickly pulled off his wet boots. Finally, every last sopping layer forming a mini lake on the floor, he scooped her up, wet and naked, and backed her against the door. Skin to skin, his heat radiated into her.

His strong arms holding her like she was light as air, he balanced her against the door and trailed his mouth down. Running his tongue over her breast, taking her in his mouth, he devoured and sucked until she cried out.

Frantic, buzzing with sensation, she cried out at the thrill of their connection.

Balancing her easily in one arm, he reached between them and teased at her core, rubbing and igniting the explosion that was brewing just under the surface, bringing her feverishly to blissful climax. Breaths coming faster, her heart thundered against her ribs as victory surged through her.

"Ryan, now." she gasped, needing more of him. All of him.

Pressing her against the door, holding her so his hardness rubbed over her slick heat, his eyes laced silvery with desire as he met her gaze. Unable to speak, she nodded, digging her fingers into his shoulders.

Eyes locked together, he drove into her in a swift, penetrating thrust.

Sensation rocketed through her as he filled her, so thick, smooth as she tightened around him, she knew he was built only for her. Her every nerve vibrated with each motion as he plunged into her again and again. Hands tight around her hips, eyes locked onto hers, his hips rocked in rhythm with hers.

The door firm and cold against her back, she wrapped her hands around his shoulders, tracing up and entwining her fingers in his hair. Her breath came fast, her pulse faster.

Skin slick from sweat and the ocean, their bodies moved together. Harder, faster. She took him deeper with each thrust, contracting around him as heat stoked more intensely from each point of contact to deep in her core. As she tightened around him, boiling past the point of no return, he accelerated with her and they came together in fevered climax.

Both frozen in orgasmic tetany, breath uncatchable, he buried his head against her, still holding her against the door.

His laugh rumbled against her neck. "Holy shit, we should have done that sooner."

Running her hands along his damp skin and his sculpted arms as he held her, she was overcome with an incredibly new, delicious sense of wonder. "Let's not dwell on the past. Instead, let's aim to do *that* as often as possible from here on out."

Still buried inside her, he pulsed with a testing thrust. An exhilarating zing rushed through her as he hardened again. "Actually, I think I could go again right now."

Delighted, her laughter quickly evolved into sighs of ecstasy as he drove her out of her mind.

13

Astrid, Sitka.

"I'M SICK OF SITTING here, waiting for her to walk in the door. Let's cruise down the coast, see if there's any sign of her." Bennett ran a hand through his untidy hair, his beard unshaven since healing from his injuries.

Astrid snapped, losing her deliberately unshakable composure. "We are searching. With logical clues—far more effective than blindly searching the entire Alaskan coast." They were a great team, having never had major spats... before now. A few disagreements, but nothing irreparable. The loss of Quinn was getting to all of them.

Upstairs in Bennett and Quinn's apartment, Astrid had claimed the seat by the window. She was sick of the place after spending so many hours in this same spot, tending to Bennett as his body slowly re-accepted his abdominal organs that had completely extruded, thanks to one foul lash from Typha's razor-sharp arm. Once he'd been stabilized, they'd flown him by charter back to Sitka to recover.

Honestly, she was shocked he was alive. Demon hunters had died for lesser injuries. Yeah, he was stubborn. Back to full health, he still preferred to watch the harbor from the window of his apartment, where he could watch the ships come and go. As if Quinn might stroll off one by happenstance, cheerfully waving and saying she's healthy and hale.

Typha had been so furious when that waterspout had rushed Quinn out of the room, that they'd been able to move the last of the boulders and get out of there. Quinn could be anywhere. Halfway across Russia, for all they knew. She'd been right. They should have focused on their exit to get out of there quicker rather than attempting a stand. They might all still be together.

As soon as they'd cleared a big enough gap in the boulders, Vann had shaken off his concussion, scooped up Bennett, and they all sprinted out of there. On board the boat, Astrid had them through the graveyard and full speed toward medical care. Rarely did a demon hunter need formal medical care, but this was more than they could handle.

It had taken a huge chunk of change to keep the doctor quiet about what she had seen, via a sizeable donation to the small clinic. Dutch Harbor didn't have a hospital, but they pulled together to stabilize Bennett. Leaving the Circinus in Dutch, they'd chartered a plane and flown him back to Sitka to recover while they began the search for Quinn.

Finally, after a solid week of painful waiting, his body pale and clammy, he'd stirred. Eventually, he came to full awareness. Furious when he realized how badly they'd lost, that they hadn't stood a chance.

"What, we're going to find her current location in books that were written before she was born?" He demanded, tossing down the ancient text to the floor. Back to full strength, his fury... and something else... Sadness? Regret? Regardless, he was not good company these days. There was something he wasn't telling them.

Picking up the discarded book, she neatly set the stray pages back into place. Astrid shook her head. "Yes. Vann and Lana are out there looking for her as we speak. It's our turn to hold down the fort in case she comes back on her own. These books may hold the answer to defeating Typha, which may lead us to Quinn."

He stood staring out the window at her side, leaned on his forearm against the glass, just as he had so many times since their return. "Sorry, Astrid. I know you're as upset as I am."

"I miss her, too." She returned to her book, sitting quietly with him in the hope he may open up about whatever was bothering him.

"I... I'm starting to doubt." He didn't look away from the boats in the harbor, studying for any sign of her from afar.

"What do you mean?"

That was a first. Bennett was so sure of everything, she often wished she could be half as self-assured. At least he was talking sensibly again.

"I love Quinn. I really do. But, maybe Lana's right. I don't miss Quinn in the way I should. I... she... the night before we left for... she wanted to have sex." He closed his eyes, regretful, his cheeks heavy with insecurity.

"And?" Cringing, Astrid really wanted to inform him this was TMI. But she didn't say stupid things like TMI.

"I said no. Told her I want in mood. Was too caught up in the mission. If I'd loved her like the prophecy said, she would have been more important." Sliding his fingertips down the window, he backed up and dropped onto the bed.

"I'm not disagreeing, but even in the most loving relationships, sex is important, but not the number one priority. Everyone gears up for a mission differently."

"You're right. I don't know. I'm just doubting everything right now. Maybe I'll know when I see her again."

A cheerful pattern of knocks on the hotel room door interrupted the melancholy that had draped over the room. Lana came dancing in. "Well, we didn't find her, but we found information. There's a rumor among the fisherman about a *kraken*." She jumped and clapped at her vague news.

Eyebrows halfway to his forehead, Bennett raised his hands in exasperation. "I don't see how that's helpful. We really don't have time for a kraken right now. I'm not even sure how we'd... no, we have other priorities right now."

Plopping onto the foot of the bed, she rolled her eyes at him and smiled. "No, there was a kraken in the Aleutians. *Was*. As in, rumor has it, a Coast Guard ship took it down."

"Again, not helping."

"Come on, how would a bunch of civilians know how to take down a kraken? Quinn was a little obsessed with them. Remember the whirlpool off Typha's island? Quinn spotted it from miles out and thought it was no big thing. What a coincidence, right?"

"You're saying Quinn took down a kraken? Alone?"

Astrid tried to reign in the distracted banter. "Actually, if Quinn is aboard a Coast Guard ship, she's not alone. Maybe she found Six, and he or she helped her defeat the kraken."

"Tada." Lana held her hands out, twinkling her fingers in dramatic jazz hands.

Bennett sunk back onto the bed. "That's pretty thin. You're trusting a flimsy rumor that has traveled across the Alaskan coast from drunken fisherman to drunken fisherman."

"Nobody said they were drunk." Lana rolled her eyes.

Arms crossed, Vann stood a few feet away. Astrid jumped at the sound of his voice, forgetting that he'd arrived with Lana. Not much was visible outside of vibrant Lana when she entered a room, and he was so sneaky.

Vann didn't seem to mind. Actually, he didn't seem to mind much of anything. "Thin, yeah. But, awfully coincidental. We're resting our entire plan of attack on one of the world's most formidable monsters, that already handed our asses to us on a silver platter... on an ages-old, mysterious prophecy. At least the word of the fishermen is a bit fresher."

Pulling his feet up onto the bed and leaning against the headboard, Bennett crossed his arms over his chest and scowled. "Do we have any idea how to find this Coast Guard ship?"

Lana leaned back, her head bumping his knee. "Still working on that. But, on the bright side, if it signifies that Quinn is alive, I have no doubt she'll come find us."

Astrid couldn't seem to find the same sense of optimism the rest were savoring. "This is a whole lot of what-ifs. Assuming Quinn was somehow picked up by the Coast Guard and is making her way here, maybe she found and is bringing Six. And, if she is, what makes Six so special? What about the elusive Seven? If all of our assumptions pan out, we have a long way to go to defeating Typha."

Bennett shrugged. "We'll know more when we see her. Maybe... maybe we'll confirm that we aren't the team to take down Typha."

Valkyrie, Unimak Pass.

ARMS DRAPED ACROSS RYAN'S supine form, Quinn snuggled tightly into the crook of his arm. His fingertips mindlessly grazed along her arm, the wheels in his brain cranking even more loudly than hers. Despite her dry eyes this morning, she felt emotionally drained.

The nightmares of her past had rared up a few times during the night. When they did, Ryan was there for her. On the times she awoke, they took each other again, washing away the darkness with love.

Smooth sailing today. The ship was silent as the crew had finally crashed, catching a wink of rack time before any more monster sightings. Quinn was surprised at how much demon activity they'd been managing, just day-to-day life around here. According to Willa, they were indirectly headed back for Kodiak for resupply and for official meetings, although a bit delayed after chasing down the kraken. The crew would continue to stay busy gathering intel from other vessels, locals, and whatever data they could compile from their equipment.

Activity in the region was incredible. From the sounds of things, the Valkyrie was probably the busiest ship in the fleet, and no one would ever know it. After Kodiak, they'd continue to gather intel and hunt monsters, making their way toward Sitka. Then, a much-needed break for an exhausted crew on a long deployment.

She wasn't sure she wanted a break.

For weeks, she'd felt so desperate to find her past. To hunt the demons that haunted her. Now, she wasn't so sure. Progress, truth... these weren't always good things. What if her past was a wedge that would drive Ryan away?

At least the memories of her parents grew stronger each day. Underwater, when she'd felt memories pull her under in the blackness exuded by the beast, images of her father had wafted over her like a familiar scent. *Never doubt yourself... You're small but strong... I know one day you will find someone you love as much as I love your mother...*

"Ryan?"

"Yes, Quinn?"

"My last name is Fischer."

Although she couldn't see his face, she could feel his wide smile as he squeezed her tight against him, those pearly whites showing the joy that grew more and more steady each day. "Quinn Fischer. I like that."

Propping herself up on her elbow, she grinned down at him. "Was your mom's last name Hunt?"

His eyes flickering to a deep gunmetal gray, his smile wavering, he looked away for a moment, pointedly returning his gaze. "Doesn't exactly suit her. Sunshine Hunt. She chose Sunshine at age seventeen in a declaration that she would bring warmth to the world. Hunt was a compromise. Inspired by my father."

"What was Sunshine doing with a demon hunter?"

Darker, his eyes morphed to onyx, and he suddenly was intent on staring at the poster of the California coast he'd hung at the foot of the bunk in lieu of a window. "He wasn't a demon hunter."

"Then, how...?"

Blowing out a long breath of pent-up air, he rubbed his free hand in his hair. "He was a demon."

His words shook her, writhing a panic that rattled her to the core. Logic fought back, knowing exactly who and what he was no matter his DNA. That's why he hadn't trusted her. No memories to guide her, and she'd instinctively felt a snarl rise in her throat, crushing her reaction as quickly as it had begun.

"Do you know the story between the mother of all demon hunters and her lover?"

A gnawing, wrenching stone formed in her gut as she ached in sympathy. His distaste for demon hunting was becoming painfully more understandable. The brief alarm that flickered in her gut before she quickly extinguished it... she could imagine others wouldn't stop to see the amazing man he is. Like her response to the grindylows, demon hunter instincts could be violently reactive. Born to protect *humans*.

"It's ok. You probably hadn't anyway. Not many would know of it. The demon mother, Deandra, is your ancestor. Not mine."

"Who's yours then?"

Again, he blew out a heavy breath before speaking. "I'd better start with why she's yours. Deandra loved our realm, would watch humans like we might watch a sitcom. Not everything on the other side is dark and violent like so many of the monsters that cross. Deandra was kind and beautiful, and Bain, the king of the realm of demons, was fascinated by her. A kindhearted warrior of the realm, she was loved by many. Bain was selfish and arrogant, but for her, he was willing to change."

Reflections swelled in Quinn's imagination, almost like a memory, but not her own. A graceful, warrior-turned-benevolent humanoid demon exploring a silvery world. A dark, devastatingly handsome titan pursuing her with flowers and gifts. It wasn't his gifts, but his roguish smile and humble devotion that drew her in.

Ryan's words painted the picture more vividly. "Somehow, despite his many faults, she fell in love with him as deeply as he did her. As an engagement gift, foolishly, he attempted to create a doorway so she may travel openly between our worlds and explore the land she loved so well. There have always been areas where the veil is thin, like damaged ozone, that demons use to cross over. But, once a demon crosses, it easily becomes disoriented on this side and it's not easy to cross back over."

Ryan paused, considering his next words carefully. Not wanting him to stop, Quinn remained quiet at his side. "In his arrogance, because of his attempt to make a two-way door for her alone, blocking any others from accessing our world so freely, he didn't consider the repercussions. Their combined power too unpredictable, he inadvertently generated a massive rift. He hadn't listened when she said it was like a snow globe for her, beautiful, but she could never live inside. His overestimation in his ability to manipulate the veil resulted in thousands of human deaths when some of the realm's more vicious demons flooded across. Determined to right the wrong, Deandra crossed over to protect our world from what he had done. As the king, couldn't risk leaving an unstable situation and risk making things even worse by leaving the realm."

Already troubleshooting, Quinn parked her tongue between her teeth as she considered the solution. "He'd built the door for her alone. He wouldn't be able to repair it while she remained on this side, would he?"

Shaking his head, Ryan's brow scrunched in darker gravity. "No. And she refused to leave humanity unprotected against the creatures that had already crossed. They say the original vampire sire was among them."

"Hence, demon hunters?"

"Exactly. She took a human lover to create offspring to fight in her stead. Creatures that were strong enough to protect our world. However, on her way home, she was intercepted at the portal. No one has seen or heard from her in millennia."

This felt eerily familiar. Like a dense mist encapsulating her, Quinn couldn't grasp the knowledge she sought from her memories. The answer was there but covered in fog so dense it would make even a San Francisco native wary. "Your father is Deandra's lover, on the other side, the king of the demon realm, isn't he?"

"Yeah." Ryan sighed, fisting his fingers in his short hair.

"Why did he wait all this time, before having you?"

"Initially, he gave her time to help right the wrong, trusting in her strength. Bain was heartbroken when Deandra took the human lover. Silently, he accepted that she had moved on from him and had chosen the human for her mate. Once he realized she'd gone missing trying to return to him, he searched tirelessly, but he couldn't risk crossing and getting trapped on this side, as she had. After what he'd done, the chaos he'd created, his realm needed him more than ever. So, he bided his time. He carefully chose a human woman to bear his child, one filled with love and brightness to raise his own child, that would be strong enough to find his lover and repair the rift."

Shaking her head with a baffled smile, Quinn teased, "This is getting awfully Greek."

Chuckling softly, he raised his head and brushed his lips across hers, then dropped back to the pillow. "The Greeks had a better view behind the veil than most."

"So, you're more than a demon hunter. You were born to find Deandra. How are you going to accomplish this?"

"Honestly, I'm not sure. In his limited time here, he taught my mother all of this, whatever he could do to prepare me. As he and I have never spoken, I have no idea how I'm to find his lover on this side, and somehow help her cross back over. When I do, supposedly I'll be able to repair the damage he did from this side while he repairs from the other side. From what I understand, the veil is unstable, and any botched attempt to repair it could cause a catastrophic collapse."

Something, a memory, a gut feeling, swelled in her mind, her ears ringing as the dizziness returned. "If it was made using his power *and* hers, and he needs you to close it on this side, wouldn't one of hers be needed to close it from this side?"

"I hadn't thought of that. But, yeah." He paused, meeting her gaze, holding, the answer simmering in his dark eyes. "That's why you were sent to me."

Lightheaded, a dark curtain shaded her vision. She pushed past, needing to stay here with Ryan. "That's a pretty big burden to carry. No wonder Sunshine didn't tell you until you were older."

Trailing his hand down her cheek, his silvery eyes searched hers, a sweet smile forming. "I don't think it's mine to carry alone anymore." He brushed his lips across hers, lightly at first. Warmth building, both adrift in memories that were not their own.

14

Valkyrie, Near Kodiak Island.

INTERRUPTING THE RIOTOUS LAUGHTER of the room as Quinn handed his ass to him in poker, yet again, this time with a damn straight flush, Ryan snatched her cards and tossed them on the table. He tossed her over his shoulder, tears of laughter rolling down her cheeks, and the off-duty crew cheered as their stiff competition was carted away so indelicately.

"Wait, I need to collect my winnings," she said between laughs.

He gave her a slap on the ass as he carted her out of the room. "That was my money, anyway."

She hollered to Kyle from over Ryan's shoulder, "I'll let you handle my winnings. Nobody else. I don't trust those thieves."

Tossing her on the bunk back in their quarters, he quickly followed and pounced on her, pulling their clothes out of the way as quickly as possible, kissing away the laughter as desperate need surged through him. As she wrapped her legs around his hips, he plunged into her in one smooth motion.

As they had every night... days too... since defeating the kraken, they made love. Against the door, in the bunk, one very awkward attempt in the cramped bathroom, regularly on the sofa, and even the engine room.

With each passing day, each kiss, each look, the bond between them grew more powerful, more unbreakable. The damn poet in him seemed to come out more often than he cared to admit.

Sated, yet somehow craving more of her with each passing moment, he rolled off of her and pulled her into his arms. Their hearts pounded against each other as he held her close. He watched as her eyes drifted shut.

Hours later, as the sun was rising outside, her soft whimpers began again. Eyelashes moist, tears trickling down her cheeks, she was lost in yet another memory he couldn't rescue her from. "Bennett." She sobbed as she said the name.

He was such an ass. Every day, he'd been putting off telling her. Had always come up with some lame excuse why today wasn't a good day. The deeper he fell for her, the worse it got. Buried too thick, it was getting harder and harder to tell her the truth that had been eating him up inside.

Now, he had no doubt she was falling as hard for him as he was for her. If she'd loved someone else, and he didn't stop things from progressing between them... it would tear her apart. And, she'd never forgive him.

"No... no," she cried. "Seven?"

Seven?

"It's him. I found Six." She almost seemed to be talking to someone now. No longer weeping, she looked almost peaceful.

Her lashes slowly fluttered open, her breathing returned to normal. Watching her come to, Ryan brushed away the lingering tears from her cheek with his thumb. A small smile was pasted on her lips as she looked up at him. So trusting. She'd hate him, but it was time.

Rolling to his side to face her, hating that he was about to shatter the adorable, loving smile she wore, he knew it was passed time. "Quinn?"

"Yes, Ryan?"

Closing his eyes, he didn't even want to see her reaction to his betrayal. Kicking himself in the ass, he forced himself to be straight with her. "Do you know you talk in your sleep?"

Her smile was so sweet, half expecting him to say something teasing, but she must have sensed the dire tone in his voice.

"You... I'm really sorry. I should have told you sooner. Since a few days before the kraken... do you recognize the name Bennett?"

Brow scrunched in deep concentration, she aimlessly searched the room fruitlessly. "No. why?"

"You've said his name a few times in your dreams, always crying... I think he... means something to you, the way you say it. I was afraid to tell you sooner." Her expression grew grave, her brow low. He pushed on, "At first, I feared it would trigger the terrible memory that had caused the amnesia to begin with. Then... then I didn't want to tell you because I knew you loved him."

She closed her eyes, and he could see her searching the ether behind her eyelids. Disappointment dripping from her words, she said, "Yeah, you should have told me sooner."

He rolled out of bed to give her the space she needed to process. Every muscle in his body throbbed, taut and exhausted like he'd run a damn marathon and couldn't push himself one more mile. He flipped the shower on straight to ice-cold water, needing the shock to keep him from slumping to the floor.

Cringing, he forced himself to keep going and let her think. Dressing as quickly as possible, he was out of there. They'd be docking in Kodiak for a resupply and meetings in a few hours. At least he'd have plenty to do to distract himself.

WORKING THE SHAMPOO VIGOROUSLY into a lather, Quinn struggled to make sense of what just happened. Her heart and soul, all the intangible, poet mutterings screamed he was it for her. There had never been nor would ever be anyone else. No memories to rely on, she followed her instincts.

But there was a shred of something else, screaming that Ryan wasn't wrong. That Bennett had meant something to her.

Furious, she gave up on the inadequately soothing power of the brief shower and flicked off the faucet. Storming out of the bathroom, she tossed on a borrowed uniform and threw herself onto the couch. Closing her eyes, she whispered, *Bennett*, over and over, desperate to remember something.

Forcing a memory hadn't worked before, so she didn't know why it should this time. She pulled on her borrowed boots and stalked to the mess for coffee. Grabbing the tallest mug of the bunch, she took the steamy brew to the deck and stood out of the way as they docked in Kodiak.

By the time she reached the bottom of the cup, a voice interrupted her torturous thoughts. "Tough, not knowing who you are, isn't it?" Willa walked up next to her, casually watching as the crew efficiently docked and began their routine resupply.

Staring out to sea instead, her unfocused gaze resting on the hazy line where shadowy sea met thick gray clouds, Quinn nodded. "At times, it's almost like a vacation, not having anything to worry about. Other times, it's terrifying to think I'm missing something critical."

"When you speak, eat, drive the boat, fight... you use what you've learned in the past, right?"

"I suppose so. A lot of its muscle memory. It's the facts, the personal parts that don't seem to surface as easily."

"Mind you, I don't have any medical training, but the heart is a muscle, isn't it?" Willa didn't miss a thing, from her crew each methodically seeing to their duties, to Quinn's unsettled gut.

Nodding, Quinn closed her eyes, inhaling slowly and carefully.

"Tell me, does your heart have a clue what it's doing right now, or is this an entirely new sensation?"

Biting her lip softly, Quinn opened her eyes and looked at the insightful captain. "I know what you're getting at, and it makes no sense biologically... But, yeah, my heart is beating in a very new, very scary, very amazing rhythm it has most certainly never experienced before."

With a mysterious smile, Willa left her to her thoughts and strode across the ship, up the dock, and out of sight. Quinn stared out into the water, the clouds, the setting afternoon sun... nothing. No memories would come.

Each time they'd actually emerged, she'd had Ryan nearby to draw them out. It would be torture for them both, but maybe he could help her find Bennett... and find out what he means to her. Loving Ryan encompassed every part of her. She couldn't imagine sharing that with anyone else.

Heading back to their quarters, Quinn tidied to keep busy while she waited for Ryan to come back from his meeting with Willa and some of the other boats that were docked. From the galley, she collected an assortment of snacks. Satisfied, she curled up on the couch, waiting the final six minutes until Ryan came home.

As he stepped into the room, exactly on time, thrill rushed through her. He flashed her a sweet, regretful grin. Keeping Bennett from her must have been excruciating, the lie of it. There wouldn't have been a good time before the kraken, and after... she wished they could both un-hear it and go back to the way they felt last night.

Carefree.

Eventually, they'd need to face reality, and with it, came the possibility that the meeting of her old life and her new would be catastrophic. She could hear Egon warning her to not cross the streams or it would be *very bad*. Ridiculous. Her memories were evolving enough that she could recite *Ghostbusters* backwards and forwards, but anything relevant was a total blank.

Sitting next to her on the couch, momentarily ignoring the cleverly arranged food tray, Ryan gave her space. She saw his inner struggle, his hand flexing as he held it back from reaching for her.

"I really need those memories back. Ryan... whatever Bennett was... is... I love *you*."

Staring at the ceiling, he looked to be breaking into tiny pieces. "I don't know that I can share you."

"You fill my heart so intensely, fill my veins... I can't imagine there was anything before that could have left me so open, waiting for you to complete me." She reached across the chasm between them and slid her hand into his.

Bolts of silver danced in those dark eyes, seeking acceptance. "And here I thought I was the damn poet around here. Maybe I'll stop keeping those corny thoughts to myself."

She chuckled softly, still hurting, but needing to hear him say the words.

Closing the distance between them, Ryan brushed his lips over hers. He didn't pressure, just offered. "I love you so much, Quinn. I have no doubt you were sent to me for a reason. That you are what Bain was waiting for." Pausing, he cleared his throat. "But... when we put your past together, and find this Bennett, I'm stepping back. I love you enough to let you decide what you need. Know that I will always be here for you. Whatever you need me to be."

Kissing him back, hungry, they melted into each other. Sliding onto his lap, she pulled off her shirt and bra, tossing them aside. Taking his hands, she guided him, placing his palms over her breasts. Aching, heavy with need, she pressed into him.

Locking eyes with each other, he watched her reactions, anticipating exactly what she wanted. Slowly, tenderly, they made love unlike any joining before. Somewhere in between goodbye and holding on forever, she showed him what he meant to her. No matter what the future held, they had today.

USCG Base Kodiak.

WAKING THE NEXT MORNING, Quinn's mind raced again, wondering what to do. Whatever she'd had with Bennett, and she didn't doubt it was something romantic... if she loved him with even half the depth she felt for Ryan...

No, she shook her head. She couldn't imagine anything feeling so right as what she had with Ryan. But, was there someone out there looking for her? Loving her? Breaking hearts wasn't really her thing.

Across the small room, Ryan pulled his shirt over his sculpted abs. That was a sight she didn't want to go without on a daily basis.

"Ryan?" She grinned up at him.

He ran a hand through his hair, the military fade getting a little scruffy. Smiling over at her, his deviously sexy quicksilver eyes nearly setting off another orgasm just with the once-over he gave her, he said, "Yes, Quinn?"

Distracted, she propped herself onto her elbows and found herself saying, "I could cut your hair for you."

"Do you know how to cut hair?" He looked a bit... put off by the idea.

"I think so. Let's give it a try." She nodded for extra enthusiasm.

"Maybe later," he said, avoiding eye contact.

Rolling out of bed, she pulled on one of his too-big t-shirts and stepped up close to him, running her fingers along his biceps mindlessly. Finally, she worked up the courage to ask him what she'd intended in the first place. "What else do I say in my sleep? Nothing about giving back alley blow jobs or storing dead bodies in my garage, right?"

Chuckling, he raised his eyebrows suggestively at her and slid his hands up her shirt and around her waist, pulling her against him. "Nothing like that. Mostly just how much you want to suck me off every morning."

She pinched him in the arm, and none too gently, either. "You have a one-track mind."

Grabbing his arm, he grimaced. "Isn't that a pretty big part of what you love about me? Although," he said as he backed out of her reach. A massive, smartass grin sprouted across his face. "If you want to swing the other way, I'll be happy to watch. Maybe help you out, offer a few pointers."

"Wow, you have watched too much tacky porn for your own good."

"Sorry, they were fresh out of classy porn last time I downloaded anything." He pulled her back to him again and tried to peel her shirt over her head.

Squealing, she wriggled her way out of his arms and headed for the bathroom. "Seriously, it's time I figured out who I am. Maybe when you get back from work today? Do you have another meeting?"

Ryan paused with his hand on the door. "Yeah. We should be done and the Valkyrie underway by noon. I'll convince Willa to give me the afternoon off. She'll want answers before we get to Sitka. She'll be meeting with her superior and the few who know what we're up to. They'll want to know our plan for calming things down around here." With a melancholy smile, he slipped out of the room.

Great. Five hours to kill. Needing the coziness, she curled up in Ryan's USCG hoodie and attempted to read a yellowed copy of a regency romance from Willa's collection.

While she had hoped for a distraction, it was painfully close to home as the heroine was torn between marrying her childhood friend and giving up everything for the dashing rogue. Well, at least the heroine had knowingly gotten herself into the pickle.

Miraculously, Ryan's phone chirped from his desk drawer. Leaping from the couch, she saw Sunshine's face pop up on the screen. She really shouldn't. But, she couldn't resist.

"Hello?"

A puzzled, husky voice chuckled on the other end. "Well, hello. Ryan, your voice has certainly changed since we spoke last."

Wow, Quinn liked her already. Snarky and a good sport. "Hi. Sorry. Ryan's in a meeting. Is this Sunshine?"

Voice warm and enriching as her namesake, she said, "This sure is. I hate to sound like one of those mothers... but am I speaking to a romantic friend of my son?"

Plopping down on the sofa, Quinn curled her feet up under her and leaned into the armrest. "Wow, I have no idea how to respond to that. I'm Quinn. And... yes, I am in love with your son." Might as well dive right in and be honest. She was hoping Sunshine could shed a little light on a few things for her.

"Well. Wait—isn't he only in port for a few days? Are you a new crew member?"

"Not exactly. I'm... Ryan fished me out of the Arctic. I, uh... I'm like him."

Long pause. Was she crying? Throat clearing. Confident voice back online, Sunshine responded finally, hiding the wetness in her voice, "About damn time. I've been waiting for him to find you. It's a hard thing for a mother to know her son carries the weight of the world on his shoulders."

Curling tighter into a ball on the couch, Quinn asked, "How did you know about me?"

"His father. He promised me Ryan wouldn't be alone, that he'd have a partner, someone who loved him, when the time came."

Quinn waited patiently for more, but Sunshine didn't expound. "Did he tell you anything more about what was to come?"

"Sort of. Honestly, he was vague, and I doubt he was certain this would work. But he was desperate to repair the damage he had done and bring his lover home."

"Can you tell me about his father?" Quinn accepted she wasn't going to learn more about the future. But maybe the past would help.

"That man... well, demon, I guess, took the phrase tall, dark, and handsome to a whole new level. Had a confidence, embodying the warrior king he was, yet had gentleness to him, or I never would have agreed to bear his child. Ryan wouldn't want to hear it, but he is a lot like his father."

"I suspect he's at least half you." Quinn smiled into the phone. "He's fierce but a total softie."

"Yes, that he is. I'm so glad you can see that. Tell me about yourself."

Quinn explained her unusual arrival, what little she knew of herself. "I'm hopeful Ryan can help me dig up enough memories to learn what sent me to him. Which, I'm suspecting has to do with repairing the veil."

"I have no doubt it is connected."

"Do you know anything more that can help? I'm sure you would have told Ryan, but if there is anything more that Bain told you?"

"I have told Ryan everything I know. Well, except about you. You can't tell someone, especially your stubborn, distrustful son that the fate of the world rests on his shoulders, and that he'll find his soulmate to help him right the wrongs of his father."

Smiling, Quinn could picture Ryan's initial distrust of her, and how daunting it would have been to know more about his future. And, she was beginning to suspect that her own amnesia was more by design than by accident. They chatted quite a while longer, sharing stories about Ryan and promises to meet once things calmed down. The time passed enjoyably as they visited.

"Quinn, please take good care of my son. He's had more heartbreak in his life than his fair share."

Cringing, Quinn pictured their current predicament. What if learning the truth would break his heart, make him lose trust in her, or drive them apart? "I will do everything I can to keep him safe and happy. Whatever happens, I love him so much."

"I can't guarantee this will all work out. I am terrified of losing my son as he cleans up his father's mess. But I have complete faith in him to do the right thing. And, I'm a pretty good judge of character. Whatever happens, you two will work out whatever it is that's bothering you."

After switching to a more pleasant conversation topic, they eventually disconnected the call. Quinn plugged his phone back into the charger. She changed into a borrowed uniform, in case anyone other than the crew that knew her was around, and wandered out on deck.

She'd planned to let her conversation with Sunshine settle as she took in the late morning air. But, strolling down the docks with a serious swagger, Ryan came into view. He'd gotten a trim while ashore. Clearly, he didn't trust her enough to let her cut his hair. Chuckling to herself, she plotted how she'd convince him to let her try sometime.

He stopped a few feet in front of her, hands deep in his pockets, rocking back on his heels. Biting his lower lip to hide his grin, he kept an appropriate distance in sight of non-Valkyrie personnel. "Hey," he said.

Heart trotting eagerly in her chest, she struggled to subdue her own smile. "Hey. Your mom called."

Ryan raised his eyebrow at her curiously. "Did you answer?"

"I like her."

"She's pretty awesome. She didn't tell you about the incident in fifth grade, did she?" He cringed.

"Maybe."

"Nah, she didn't tell you."

"You'll never know."

With a nod of his head, he gestured to their quarters. "I'll grab us some lunch, then let's see if we can't chip away at that amnesia. We've got a few stops to make before we get to Sitka. Won't be much time for memory lane. Quite a few stories pointing to a cluster of sirens at the mouth of the Copper River."

"Sounds fun." She raised her eyebrows before they separated outside his room.

In the room, she ditched the formal Coast Guard uniform and curled up in a pair of jeans and one of Ryan's t-shirts. He wasn't gone more than ten minutes, just enough for her to fester with apprehension. Passing her a ham and cheese sandwich and a hot cup of coffee, he stuffed his own in his mouth.

Swallowing a massive bite, he gulped down his own coffee and took a deep breath. "'It's okay, I found him.' That was one of the other things. You've also said something about finding six, asking something about seven. Mostly gibberish."

"Who did I find?" She took the last tasteless bite of sandwich, needing the food but unable to focus on anything but the fear that she'd said anything else that might turn her world upside down.

"Six, I think. Whatever that means. Honestly?" he asked.

Dumbass. Of course she wanted his honesty.

He leaned back into the couch, stretching his legs out in front of him. "I've sort of been hoping you meant me."

Downing the last of her coffee, she bit her lower lip in a hopeful smile and nodded. "I like that. Let's assume you're Six." She leaned back on the couch next to him and laced her fingers with his.

Raising their joined hands, he kissed the back of her hand and raised his eyebrows playfully. "Let's start digging into your beautiful brain."

"That paints a disgusting and painful image."

"Thought you'd like it." He flashed her a wicked grin, the side of his mouth turned up in pure orneriness.

She had no doubt he loved her enough to withstand most anything, but... "What if neither of us likes what we find?"

"I know you cry out for some other guy in your sleep, so some of my worst fears have already been realized. It's more you getting crushed under the weight of your memories that concerns me."

Quinn had downed way too much coffee today for sanity. She couldn't seem to get her head on straight. Couldn't seem to focus.

Tough to dig up memories you were afraid to discover. Maybe, just maybe, before she'd realized her memories could change things between them, she might have been less afraid of what was bouncing around in her thick skull. The two of them had taken down a kraken together. They were a damn good team. She didn't want a different team.

"You've got to concentrate. Let's start with the beginning. What's the most recent thing you remember with your parents?"

Laying back on the couch as he'd insisted was necessary, her eyes closed and her head on a pillow, feet resting on his lap, she felt like she was working with Sigmund Freud. Not exactly the relationship she wanted with Ryan. "I've never had any penis envy. I'm quite fond of them but prefer them on my partners. Certainly, no complexes about my parents."

"Shut up and pay attention. How old are you?" He pinched her leg, his voice clearly amused.

"Okay, I'm focusing. Let's see. I'm thirty-two." She opened her eyes and sat up. "How old are you? I'm not a cougar, am I?" Aging slowly, neither had aged past their mid-twenties. As much as she enjoyed not having to worry about wrinkles and gray hair, she'd like to be respected for her maturity a bit more.

"Ha. I'm thirty-six." He grinned at her, biting his lower lip. "Now shut up and focus again."

Closing her eyes, she settled back on her pillow, enjoying not being the older one. Didn't matter, her father was seventy years older than her mother, but, still, it made her smile. Sadly, she tried to block his sexy face. "Hey, I went to college. UCSF so I could stay close to home. I have an apartment. Tiny, but I love it. I've lived there for years."

"In San Francisco?"

"Yep."

Something about the casual, easy moment settled her mind. Open and honest with each other, she felt the barrier lighten.

She studied every detail she could in her apartment, like walking through a dream. A huge wall of books took up a big chunk of space, a set of comfy chairs in front of it, a plush white slipcover couch opposite. There was a person she couldn't quite make out in one of the chairs, but she liked her. Long, sleek blond hair.

No matter how hard she strained, she just couldn't make out the face. Or the name.

A voice hollered from the closet-sized kitchen, *"Yo, Quinn, when does the pizza get here?"* She couldn't place the voice, but she knew she liked her, too.

Maybe she could handle having some of her team back. Good feelings flooded into her as she thought of these people.

A rumbling voice, smooth as ice but rich as chocolate, announced the arrival of said pizza as he strode in the front door. Tall, but equally faceless. Everything moved slowly, in flickering images, like a strange dream where she wasn't quite there.

Behind him, someone more tangible slipped in. Not quite so tall, but solid, confident. Button-up shirt, open in front over a crisp white t-shirt. Khaki cargos. No face. Shit, this must be Bennett. Walking over to her, he placed a chaste kiss on her cheek and sat on the chair across from the blond. She couldn't help but feel the disappointment in the lack of enthusiasm at his greeting.

Hating that she couldn't make out the faces, she strained to immerse herself deeper.

The blond read from the dusty leather book on her lap. "*You guys are going to love this one. Typha, that awful creature that was said to be set on flooding our realm with demons took Deandra, our demon mother...*" Quinn couldn't quite make sense of rest of what she said, until she said, "*There will be six. Wait, seven. No, six. Anyway, there's also something about love between demon hunters that this whole prophecy hinges on.*"

Bennett sat up in his chair, his tone excited as he said, "*It's me and Quinn.*"

She felt herself roll her eyes in the flashback. "*That's awfully presumptuous. I don't see myself embodying any prophecies. No offense, but we're pretty ordinary and I'd like to stay that way. I'd rather fate stay out of my life.*"

"Quinn, what do you see?"

"Shut up. I'm onto something." She squeezed his hand in hers to let him know she didn't actually mean shut up harshly, just that he needed to shut up if she were to make any progress.

Trying to lose herself in the conversation about a prophecy, feeling that had something to do with her prior sleep talk of "*I found him,*" she focused on Bennett, knowing it must be connected.

Crushing pressure fell over her body, her ribs constricting as she struggled to pull air in. Bodies flying, swords swinging, a lilting voice in her head. Pulling herself back to the image she'd almost found of Bennett... his face slowly appeared.

As soon as she grasped his face in her mind, struggling to hold on, a razor-sharp... arm?... Something, it sliced through his gut. His intestines poured out of the open wound. Furious, she wanted to scream at him for refusing to wear armor. Running to him, she was abruptly thrown from the scene, blasting across the sky, and everything went black.

Jerking up on the couch, she felt air passing into her lungs more freely. Her cheeks were soaked, and her gut was knotted in coils of dread.

Before she could figure out where she was and where she'd been, she was enveloped in comforting arms. Ryan pulled her onto his lap and wrapped her snugly against him. "It's ok. I'm here."

"Oh god, Ryan. I saw them."

"Who?"

"My team. Not in detail but I got a good feel for them. I like them. There were really happy memories at first. But... Bennett... I could see him so clearly. He's dead. Whatever we were fighting, right before I was sent to you... I watched him die." She sniffled, reliving the awful image over and over in her mind.

"Are you sure?"

"Yeah. He was... it was awful. Eviscerated? Disemboweled? It was so graphic. No wonder my brain shut that memory out."

"I'm so sorry." Ryan held her quietly for minutes, hours, who knew.

Finally, as she processed the image that had been driving her subconscious to despair each night, she was glad she at least had her answer.

Still holding her close, Ryan asked, "Were you and he...?"

"I hate even saying it, but... yeah, I loved him. But it felt different. Not how I love you. Ack, I feel guilty even saying it, but I know it's true."

Both sat in silence again. She nuzzled against his neck, needing the physical connection. Softly, she described the prophecy from what she could decipher from her broken memories. "There was talk of a prophecy. Six are needed, and love between demon hunters. It's so strange, that I can picture it like a faded home movie, feel what I felt, but can't truly remember it."

"You will. Soon, I hope. How many were in your team?"

"There were five of us in my apartment in San Francisco, then the same five in... I think it was a cave. I couldn't see any of them clearly, aside from Bennett. I think you'll like them."

He sighed, not commenting on that one. "Five? Then, yeah, I'm thinking I'm Six."

"I agree. It's you I found. Six are needed for the prophecy, or seven, but that might have been wrong. And, the key seemed to be the love between two demon hunters."

Pressing his lips to her temple, he lingered. "Yeah, I have no doubt that you were sent to me for a reason. Bain wasn't taking that long to think it over, he was waiting for all of this to come together. You, me, your team. Although, with Bennett gone, that brings it back down to five. Finding another to make it six again, I can't help you with that, and definitely not with seven."

"Maybe they'll have found one or two more? If we can even find them. I'll keep working on it. Worst case, I can find my way home to San Francisco. Or, maybe I could find my parents. Shit, they're at sea, too. South America. No idea how I know that. Some of this stuff just comes to me before I realize I know it."

Ryan inhaled deliberately and held his breath, slowly releasing a pent-up concern. "This is going to sound weird. But... were you, you know, you?"

"As in...?"

"Like, your personality. Did you feel like a different person or like you feel now? You said you liked your team, so you must have felt yourself a bit."

She pulled back to look at him. His face was riddled with heartache, his eyes tired, cheeks heavy. Grazing her thumb along his strong jaw, she smiled. "Even via flashback, I could feel my smartass comments, and my sense of right and wrong. Whatever damaged by memories has not affected my personality."

Features softening in relief, he found his smile and wrapped his arms around her.

15

Vann, Sitka.

THEY'D BEEN AT IT for hours. Days. Weeks. Vann ran a hand through his coiled brown hair. He needed a damn trim. Quinn always cut it for him. Too many months they'd spent too busy to worry about basic needs.

Not Quinn. She always kept them from getting too focused on the mission. They needed a dose of her right now.

Astrid shifted in her seat in their nook at the tavern, her nose shoved in a book, as usual. From over the dusty pages, she sighed heavily. "I know you don't want to hear it, Bennett, but I'm beginning to doubt that we have anything to do with this prophecy. We should start looking for the ones who meet the description, maybe teach them what we've learned."

Taking up the entire couch to himself, Bennett opened his fingers to look through his hand that covered his face. "Not this again. I get it. Quinn and I aren't lovers that were foretold generations ago."

Lana snorted at Astrid, gulping a swig of her beer. "I think she has something new. Other than a sour attitude." If Lana weren't a sculpted, highly trained demon hunter with some damn good DNA, plus a few hours of exercise every day, she'd be a bloated couch potato with the way she ate and drank.

Closing the book he'd been pouring over all night, not getting any more out of it once the words started swimming around the page, Vann tossed it on the battered coffee table. "What did you find?" he asked Astrid.

"I'm going to back pedal a bit here. Deandra didn't fall in love with the human that impregnated her. She had a demon lover."

"Ooh, now this is getting more interesting." Lana flipped sideways in her chair, her bare legs dangling over the side. How that woman thought wearing a miniskirt in the middle of Alaska was even close to discreet, he'd never understand.

"When I started researching Deandra's history rather than digging into anything written about Typha, I stumbled upon her lover. Her demon lover. We've always been taught she loved our realm, and became trapped here, then fell in love with a human. Not the case. She was engaged to a demon. The king of the demon realm, actually." Eyes glowing with knowledge, Astrid pulled her hair into a knot at the back of her neck and continued her lesson to her captivated audience. Even Bennett seemed to be paying attention. "Bain. He sounds to be a good sort, maybe even more peace-loving than she was. He loved her so much, he tried to break down the barrier between heaven and earth. That's a rough translation. I think they're saying he tried to create a portal in the veil to give her convenient access to our world. As a gift."

Bennett crossed and uncrossed his feet that were stretched across the couch, his hands now behind his head as he leaned back on the opposite armrest. "Didn't exactly go his way, did it? His folly is the reason she created us, right? I think I'd heard that once."

Astrid nodded enthusiastically. "Exactly. This is where I'm running into even more unanswered questions. Typha needs Bain's blood. She is Bain's blood. No, she needs his blood." She glared at the book in her hands. "Dang, this isn't making sense. Anyway, I think if she got a hold of him, she could fully break down the barrier, letting the demon and human worlds unite. That's why he couldn't cross to find Deandra."

Sitting back on his perch in the corner, Vann didn't interrupt. Didn't need being said. Oil and water, fire and ice, boot and ant... the worlds should not be united, or this world would be flattened.

She continued when she realized no one had a wise crack. "That's why she's holding Deandra. With Deandra on this side, Bain cannot close the tear he made. If he tries to come for Deandra, Typha can feed off his energy and maybe even expand the rift. But I think the same holds true for healing the veil. We need his blood to heal it. Although, I think we actually need both Bain and Deandra's blood to repair the veil. It gets pretty vague on the details. Lots of poetic metaphors about blood and strength and destruction and healing."

"Let's just pick up a pint of demon king blood from the local market and see how it goes." Bennett rolled his eyes.

Picking up his own barely touched beer, Vann took a long pull before speaking. "First, Bennett, you've been spending way too much time with vampires. Second, I'll bet it's not quite so literal as a pint of blood. Third, this doesn't mean we're not part of the prophecy."

Leaning forward, resting her elbows on her knees, Lana sighed in heavy frustration. "Bain is on the other side of the veil. How would we get his blood? If we did, how could we be sure Typha didn't use it against us? Deandra's been imprisoned for millennia, and he hasn't come for her."

Considering, Astrid looked up from her pages. "The portal was designed by Bain for Deandra, so she could always go back home to him. From what I understand, their blood would need to be on both sides simultaneously to repair the veil, as it was designed as a two-way door."

"Like a double demon smoothie? Yum," Bennett added. He'd become rather snarky since that awful night. Not that Vann didn't appreciate seeing Bennett coming down to earth a bit, but he'd fallen a bit too far, from his high horse down to a muddy face plant.

Clearly just as irritated with Bennett's attitude, Astrid scowled. "Not quite. I'm still working on it."

Rising from her chair, trailing her hand along the back of it, Lana grinned, always finding the positive. "I think we're on to something. Even if we haven't nailed down what that something is. Yet." She stopped in her tracks and leaned forward, resting her elbows on the back of the empty chair.

Before she snuck off for the night, Bennett stopped her. "Hang on." He sighed deeply and sat up, rubbing his hand over his jaw. He pulled out a heavily creased map from his back pocket. "Quinn wasn't aboard the Coast Guard ship that arrived yesterday, obviously. So, I pestered the crew until one took pity on me after I gave him my sob story. I had him mark down the locations of all the other vessels in the region and their anticipated routes."

As Bennett laid the map over the table, smoothing as he went, Vann restrained the beast inside him that blew smoke out his nostrils. "Didn't think you ought to share this with us sooner?"

Biting his cheek firmly between his teeth, Bennett grouched, "Of course I was planning to share. I... Cut me some slack, okay? Things... this... I'm in a weird spot." He looked to them all, daring them to question him when it came to Quinn.

Yeah, Bennett had been through a hell of a roller coaster with Quinn, but something was eating at him. He'd been so convinced he'd been the stuff of legends, only to find out he wasn't and had paid a steep price for his vanity. To top it off, he awoke to have his heart broken thinking his girlfriend was dead. Disrupting his healing again, she probably wasn't really dead but lost. Still, Bennett was unpredictable in his thinking when it came to Quinn these days.

"It's not just the map, is it?" Astrid lips were turned down in sorrow. She reached across and put her hand over Bennett's knee.

"Come on Astrid. If anyone were to figure it out, it'd be you. We are the fucking prophecy. Not me and Quinn, but our team."

Raising an eyebrow at him, Lana beamed with a toothy grin. "Now you're talking. A whole team of demon hunters in this prophecy. Not just star-crossed lovers."

"I've been doing a lot of thinking the past few weeks. Things Quinn was saying just before we left..." He trailed off, a weary sigh escaped his lips. His gaze scanned the rowdy Coasties across the tavern, a thick cluster of testosterone and flirtation. "Doesn't take a rocket scientist to figure out why Quinn was the one blasted out of there, and where she was landed. Pretty fucking obvious who's involved in the love-of-the-ages part of the prophecy, and it doesn't involve me." He snorted, glancing again to the mass of sailors that had been cooped up too long. "Fucking Coasties."

Vann took it all in. About damn time Bennett was calming his ego a bit. "Our timing wasn't wrong. We all knew we needed to go there. How else would we have found Six? Regardless, however this goes down, we're all needed. Demon hunters work in teams."

"Here, here," Lana cheered.

He could see Bennett chewing his cheek as he studied the map again. Hell of a thing, to find out your girlfriend of two years was getting it on with some other guy while you were on your death bed. "Sorry, man. You doing okay?"

Lips pursed tight, Bennett nodded in subtle acknowledgement.

Astrid set down her book and moved next to Bennett on the couch. Pouring over the map, she shook her head as the corners of her lips turned up in a smile of relief. "You made a good friend. If Quinn's on her way here, she's probably on one of these ships." She sketched her calculations on the map. "She's probably only a few days out."

Abruptly folding up the map, Bennett shoved it back in his pocket. Something was eating at him, and it was more than heartbreak.

Valkyrie, Sitka Sound.

As THE SUN SET behind them, stars slowly brightening against the darkening sky, Quinn leaned into Ryan. He'd taken the wheel for their final entry to Sitka. The town glowed brightly ahead, a growing beacon on the horizon.

Fighting side by side with Ryan, making love, talking all night, downright giggling... Quinn was reluctant for this chapter of her life to come to an end. Knowing what she did, she needed to catch the next flight out. Home to San Francisco so she could find her team.

Two months of living and breathing Ryan, surrounded by vast ocean and good people. It had been a long, busy journey. Grindylows, sirens, the kraken, what may have been a vicious mermaid... how had the region survived before the Valkyrie? Another month of their intense deployment still ahead, the crew was eager for a few days of shore leave.

Obviously, none would reveal the reason for their celebratory demeanor, as even these rowdies could keep a secret, or they wouldn't be on this crew. And, quite frankly, anyone else would think them crazy as the sailors of old, returning to shore with demented tales of sea monsters. Easy to keep secrets like demon hunting, as anyone that blabbed sounded totally nuts.

Willa had agreed to a few days shore leave in Sitka. Apparently, it was a regular stop for their ship. They had a few contacts in the Sitka air division that reported in on unusual occurrences throughout the region, as well as her superior.

"Take a lot of women to this place we're going for dinner tonight?" Quinn knocked her elbow into his ribs. Gently this time.

"Maybe one or two." He winked at her, then turned his gaze back at the water.

"Will I have time to go shopping first?" She pictured wearing her typical jeans and oversized tee to the fancy restaurant.

"Crap. Sorry. I don't think we'll get in on time. Our reservation's for seven, and we'll be cutting it close as it is." He winced with guilt.

Quinn had forgotten there was extra crew up top today to set anchor and secure everything, as the crew would be bare bones. They'd rotate so everyone got shore leave, but a few were still needed aboard. Without looking up from her computer, Leah said, "I've got a dress you can borrow. *Borrow.* Tomorrow, I expect you to do some serious shopping. I want my pants back." Her teasing smile told Quinn she was actually being sweet. A bit unpredictable, and possessive of her clothes, but Quinn was grateful.

Sitka.

Brushing the nonexistent lint from his nicest slacks, Ryan was suddenly nervous. Quinn had never seen him out of uniform. Well, he still had his combat boots on. He didn't own nice shoes. Loafers weren't exactly Alaska-friendly, anyway. And, he really wasn't a nice outfit sort of guy, but he really wanted to impress her with a fancy date.

Thanks to long lives and rather unusual sources of income and investments, demon hunters tended to be well off. He suspected Quinn came from money, even if she didn't act like it.

Wow, he was really nervous all of a sudden. Maybe it was that reality was about to flood over them and wash away the honeymoon they'd been living.

Tonight, he wanted to do something normal with her. Show her that he was more than a demon hunter and sailor, but a man she could spend the rest of her life with. He had no doubt they'd enjoy each other no matter what the circumstances, but with her leaving, rejoining her old life...

He was thrilled she'd be able to see her family and friends again. Would she have room in her life for a jaded demon hunter that spent half his time at sea, and the other half in his mother's basement?

Quinn had gone ahead with Leah, while he ensured the others on the Valkyrie were all set. Rarely were he and Willa both off-ship, but Manuel was beyond ready to start taking more of a leadership role.

Pulling his phone off the charger, he turned it on and shoved it in his pocket. Felt weird to carry it, as it was usually rattling around in his drawer when at sea. His watch buzzed on his wrist as the Bluetooth connected.

Leah promised she would drop Quinn at the restaurant right at seven. Not that he worried she would forget everything again, but he hated being away from her until her life was sorted out.

Dashing down the street to Anchor's Away, he headed inside. Five minutes early. Perfect. Against a chill gust, he pulled open the door to the arctic entry. As he stepped inside, a foursome was passing the other way.

A pretty boy with a trendy shag cut, although solid muscle, rammed right into him as they passed each other through the narrow path. What the hell? His head whipped around and glared at the egotistical ass.

With a cavalier smirk, the other man said with an unapologetic shrug, "Sorry."

The tiny, dark haired woman next to him clocked her friend in the ribs with her elbow. Chuckling, he immediately thought of Quinn. The woman hung back as her friends left the restaurant. "Really, sorry. His girlfriend left him for some Coast Guard guy. He's a little bitter."

"No worries," Ryan offered affably. He ran his hand through his military short hair and recalled his clean-shaven face. Yeah, his occupation was probably pretty obvious compared to the fishermen and locals.

"Enjoy your night." She winked before joining her friends outside. Something about her really reminded him of Quinn. It must be that falling in love thing and seeing her traits in everyone else.

Quinn wasn't here yet. The host led him through the classy restaurant. Amber lights glowed softly above, and hip music offered background noise for extra privacy among the guests. On the deep green tablecloth, a trio of white candles floating in water bobbed and cast a twinkling radiance in the secluded corner.

He had no idea what Quinn drank, or what she ate, really. Not wanting to be presumptuous, he just ordered waters until she arrived. At seven sharp, she strutted in wearing a short, slim satin navy-blue dress with strappy heels. Her hair was straight aside from a few playful curls that danced above her shoulders, luminous against the dim light of the restaurant. She'd even added some smoky eye make-up and a natural gloss on her lips.

Breathless, he rose from the table as she approached, showing his best manners—his mama taught him right. Meeting her at her chair, he kissed her on the cheek, not wanting to mess her stunning appearance. "You look incredible." As he pulled her chair back for her, she straightened her dress and sat gracefully.

The server appeared seconds later to take their drink orders. "I'd love an IPA."

"Great, we have a local brew from just down the street you will love," he responded in a thick Russian accent.

"Same." Ryan nodded when the server asked after his.

"Would you care to start with an order of calamari?"

"No." They said simultaneously, panic in each of their voices. By the twinkle in her eyes, he knew she was picturing the kraken's tentacle on their table like he was. He added, "I'll just start with a salad."

Quinn said, "Same, and a cup of chowder."

Chuckling as the poor server left, he finally started to relax.

Looking around, ensuring no one was looking, she adjusted her boobs in the dress. "Sorry. I hate push-up bras."

"You know, I don't mind them so much. You have great breasts, but now I feel like the girls are on display just for me."

"I'd consider being offended if I hadn't enjoyed your jaw hanging open when I walked in."

"You're gorgeous in a baggy t-shirt, ponytail, and lack of make-up. But you look amazing tonight."

"You clean up pretty nice yourself." She shifted again. "Something tells me I really don't dress up much. As much as I'm enjoying feeling pretty, I miss my jeans."

"Did she at least let you borrow some underwear this time?" His eyebrows raised up and down as he tried to guess.

"You'll have to wait and find out."

He exhaled a slow sigh as their food arrived. Knowing she was still *her*, still normal off-ship, was a massive relief.

16

"I HAVE CLOTHES," QUINN cheered as she danced into the room ahead of him the following evening.

Ryan slumped into a side chair while she dumped out the shopping bags on the bed, she laid out her ten pair of underwear, a bra, two pair of jeans, two t-shirts, a baker's dozen package of thick socks, and an amazingly cozy wool sweater. She sat and extended her fancy new hiking boots to admire her feet before pulling off her shoes.

Vision blurry from a day of overstimulation, Ryan turned the cushy club chair to face Quinn. "You know, you had full use of my credit card. You can get more clothes." Propping his feet up on the bed, he rested his arms behind his head, catching a much-needed rest after the long day. Shopping sucked. Exhausting as fuck.

They'd been up all night, then all morning, testing out every last square inch of the hotel room, as planned. Splurging on room service for naked breakfast, then shopping, lunch at a local seafood bar... Not a bad day, but a serious change of pace. More draining than battling a kraken, that was for damn sure.

Twirling the short distance between them, she landed on his lap and curled into him. Wrapping his arms around her, he scooted her to a comfy position and inhaled her fresh scent.

"I didn't need much. Something tells me that even when we get home..." She trailed off. "I mean, once I get my stuff, I don't think there's much more than this in my entire apartment." She closed her eyes for a moment. "Yep, my closet at home is about the same size as yours on the Valkyrie."

"We need to make a plan. I've been putting it off. But, it's time."

"I know. I'm all for procrastinating when it makes me happy. But, time to be serious." Her groan rumbled through her chest and into his.

"Actually, I was just thinking, I might be able to claim a family emergency to go back with you to get your things. See if I can get you to your team." Why didn't he think of that before? This clearly qualified. Sort of. Maybe.

Leaning back a bit, she looked at him with soft eyes, immensely relieved. "That would be spectacular. I'll be fine if you can't, but you know. I'd rather have you with me. Then... after that?"

That familiar ache, that began when Quinn had come into his life, throbbed under his ribs. "I have no idea. I've got a little more than a year's commitment left in active duty. You can be my sexy stateside wife, or I'm sure Willa won't mind if I smuggle another demon hunter on board as we've been doing. Whatever you want." He brushed his lips over her temple, silently begging for her acceptance.

Her grin so wide she must have strained muscles in her cheeks, an elated giggle bubbled from deep in her belly. "You just said wife."

Biting his lip, he couldn't hide his matching grin. "Yeah, yeah I did. Slip of the tongue."

"You can slip your tongue in me anytime you'd like." She raised her eyebrows suggestively. "That was a great plan. Why didn't you come up with this days ago?"

Smile still plastered to his face, he was thrilled she was on his same page. Still, she hadn't been reunited with her team. Once she saw them, remembered them truly, would she feel the same?

"Dinner ideas?" She leaned into him, pressing her lips to his neck, nipping at his ear. It didn't matter how many times they made love, he couldn't get enough.

"Keep this up, and you'll be dinner." Scooping her up, he tossed her on the bed next to her new wardrobe. "Burger, fries, and a pint. There's an awesome fisherman's tavern as old as Sitka a few blocks away."

Rising to her knees, she pulled his t-shirt off over her head and rubbed her palm over her bare tummy. "Yum, that sounds like my kind of place."

"Then why are you undressing? Not helping." He glanced down at the erection already tenting his jeans.

Flashing him a come-hither grin, she looked down at her new bra. Lacy, not much to it, she'd invested in a few pieces just to drive him wild. Teasing the edges as she looked down to check out her own appearance, she finally unhooked it and sent it flying across the room. Naked from the waist up, wearing nothing but unbuttoned jeans, she was so fucking hot.

"Dammit. Now we're going to miss happy hour," he grumbled as he pulled her legs out from under her. Crashing onto the bed, she laughed as he dove on top of her and nibbled along her neck.

Four minutes later, they sat side by side on the bed, tying their boots. "See? We can be efficient," she said. "Still in time for happy hour."

Attired in her new fitted t-shirt, sexy as fuck lace bra and panties, and some new jeans—oddly full of holes considering how much he'd paid for them, she twirled in front of the door. "It's great to wear clothes that are all mine. I'll bring the rest back to Leah tomorrow."

Holding his hand out, he clasped hers as she joined him. "Let's go. Really. I'm starving. Big. Fat. Juicy. Cheeseburger."

Bennett.

BITING INTO THE FISH and chips, best place in the state to get them, Bennett savored the juicy bite.

Lana nudged him under the table. "How can you order the same thing *every* time? We're here like, at least four days a week."

Lana should know it was the best. It was her family's joint. Which was why they always got the big table. Her mom, dad, sister, or whoever was working, always reserved their couch area when they were in town, and, if they arrived early enough, didn't argue when they monopolized the biggest table all night.

Although the place was old, it was neat and clean. Creaky floorboards in a homey way, leather and wood dark and cracked from use, all added to the ambience. Well maintained, the antiquated dining tables all had smooth sheens of fresh shellac.

"Your family makes a mean fish and chips. Almost as good as the ones in BC."

"True. I don't question you when we're just here for a week or two, but we've been here a long time this go around, and you're still eating the same thing." She stabbed her fork into her smoked salmon caesar, more smoked salmon than romaine, to drive the point home.

They needed an evening to just be normal. Every damn night for the past two months, well, since his intestines had healed back in his abdomen, they'd searched. He needed nights like this to forget about Quinn.

He'd grieved. He'd accepted. He'd been ready to move on. Hell, he'd been grieving and accepting before Typha. Since even before Quinn dumped him.

He could be pissed at her, but he wasn't. Not anymore, anyway. She wasn't wrong. They weren't some foretold love that had the power to repair the veil. That last night in their hotel room, he hadn't wanted to hear it. Now, he knew she was right. They *were* boring.

He hadn't told the team about the break-up. A rather moot point when she was dead, anyway, so why taint the memory?

Then, they'd figured out that she was alive. Still, he couldn't bring himself to admit it was his fault, that he hadn't pulled the plug sooner.

Then, what do you know, someone took down a kraken. Could be any group of demon hunters. But, no, it's probably Quinn and her frigging soulmate.

The bite of halibut swelled in his throat as his mouth went dry. Dammit, this isn't how this mission was supposed to go. When he'd heard about the prophecy, when Vann had heard whispers of Typha's location... Bennett knew they would be the ones to take her down. To free their distant demon mother, if the legends were true.

And, what a coincidence? He happened to have just started dating Quinn. She'd taken some convincing when he'd first asked her out. They'd known each other since they were kids, her father and his mother on the same team. They'd developed an easy rhythm, friends to lovers.

Wiping his hands clean on the napkin, he tossed it in the basket, cleared the other empty dishes from the table, and carried them to the busser's tray. They were here often enough that he never wanted to wear out their welcome, so he often pitched in. On crazy, restless nights, he'd gained some serious muscle waiting and bussing tables.

Stepping up to the bar, he caught Missy's eye. While Lana decided to be a full-time demon hunter, her sister gave up her powers and chose an ordinary life. Since her big decision, she ran the family tavern when their dad was off hunting demons. Content in her life, she always had a genuine smile for him. Well, let's be honest, a few years ago it had been more than a smile. What the hell, may as well see if she was still interested.

"You look like you need a drink." She leaned over the bar, giving him a spectacular view down her v-neck top.

"Yeah, I really do."

"Scotch?" Her eyes lingered on his, her shoulders gently rolling to draw his eyes downward to her exposed cleavage.

"Please," he responded weakly, his veins flushing with the most desire he'd felt in too long. For a lot longer than the last two months, before Quinn had disappeared, he begrudgingly admitted to himself.

As she poured his drink, she greeted the incoming customers. "Grab any table you'd like. Ollie will be right with you." She slid the glass carefully across the bar. He let his fingers linger over hers, letting her know he was definitely interested.

"Bennett," she said. "I... Want to, catch up later? I'm off at ten—shit, no, I'm off at midnight. Another Coast Guard ship is in the harbor, so we're primed for an influx. Not too bad last night, but they got in late—"

Jerking back, he realized what that meant. Whipping his head around, he knew she'd walked in the door before he even saw her.

Laughing like the world was rosy and great, Quinn looked amazing. Smiling, relaxed, gorgeous. Happy. Her red hair slightly tousled and wavy today, a new, tighter than she normally wore t-shirt...

Throat parched, he grabbed the aged scotch and drained it in a mindless gulp, his eyes frozen on the jamb-packed doorway. Behind her, moving synchronously with her through the crowd, a Captain America sort of muscled giant had his hands all over her. He whispered something in her ear and grazed her temple with an adoring kiss. Grinning up at him, she blushed and leaned into him.

What? Quinn didn't blush.

The Coasties that had just settled at one of the high-top tables flagged them down. "About time you two show up. Quinn, you gotta let that man out of his bunk now and again for food and beer," one of the rowdier ones taunted in a liquored voice.

Throwing her head back in delight, she laughed out loud in her lilting soprano voice. Captain America guy grinned even wider and slipped his hand under the hem of her top, his fingers splayed over the bare skin of her belly.

She hollered back, "Kyle, I'm surprised you can lift that drink. Your jerking off hand must be awfully tired from those lonely nights at sea."

Quinn? She'd gone all sailor. What the hell?

Well, Bennett had to admit to himself, she'd always been uninhibited. Fool that he was, he'd always tried to quiet her when she got carried away. Now, here she was, shouting about jerking off across a crowded bar, and the guy behind her was laughing with her, loving every minute of it.

Absorbed in her new world, she didn't seem to realize her team was here. Her friends. Not looking for them in their favorite strategizing nook, not even glancing at their regular dining table... Huh. Weird.

Suspicious, he needed to see what the hell was going on. As Bennett moved closer, big muscled dude saw him approaching and halted. Ha, it was the guy from the restaurant. Blind luck, he'd taken his anger out on the right Coastie after all.

Studying Bennett with a calculating gaze, the guy's mouth opened slightly, forming a surprised, *Oh*. His gaze narrowed in acute recognition. Quinn glanced up at her lover. Reading him, she turned in the direction her lover was looking.

Bennett felt the moment her eyes landed on him like an elbow to the throat. Her face scrunched in despairing confusion.

Sadness. Relief. Joy.

Head whipping around, she found their friends finishing their meals at the big table. Chest rising and falling rapidly, her eyelashes fluttered.

He moved to soothe her.

No need. Rather than sinking to the floor as her eyes rolled back in her head, her lover scooped her up and held her tightly against him, preciously cradled in his arms.

With a nod to Bennett, he gestured silently to meet outside.

Bennett didn't hesitate. Catching the attention of the team, he waved them after him.

Stepping out the front door, he saw her lover pressing his lips to her forehead, whispering softly to her. Looking up as Bennett approached, he asked, his eyebrow quirked up in question, "Bennett?"

Nodding, Bennett hardly knew where to begin. No idea what to say.

"The Sleeping Sailor, room 412," the other man said, turning to leave.

The rest of the team filtered out behind him. "We're coming. Now," he replied. They'd been missing her for nearly two months. He wasn't about to let her out of his sight now.

Already on the move, not waiting for anyone, her lover carried her wilted body as swiftly as he dared, not risking jostling her. Over his shoulder, he nodded. "Fine."

17

RYAN WAS READY TO kick the damn door down. Fucking electronic locks. As soon as the absurdly slow green light flashed and the lock clicked, he adjusted Quinn in his arms to open it.

Didn't need to. A giant of a man, even taller than he was, grabbed the handle and had the door open wide in half a second. Grateful, he carried her in and laid her carefully on their bed. Not wanting to leave her side, he sat with her, pulling her feet over him so he could stay connected.

A bubbly sort, with a mop of black hair on her head, bounded across the room and sat on the bed next to Quinn. The woman from the restaurant. Running her fingers over Quinn's forehead, she shifted a stray red lock out of her eyes. "I knew it. I knew you would come." Unrestrained tears flooded down the tiny woman's cheeks.

Taller, more sedate, a willowy blond sat next to the other woman on the bed. "Hush, Lana. She's lost in the labyrinth of her thoughts." Smart woman.

The tall guy, with his rumbling bass voice, asked softly, "Are you Six?"

Raising an eyebrow in question, Ryan shrugged. "So it seems."

Growling, Bennett stood a few feet away, arms folded over his chest. "What did you do to her?"

Keeping his voice calm, not wanting to push Quinn further into the nightmare, he pulled his eyes away from her and looked at Quinn's boyfriend. "Amnesia."

He'd had trouble believing Bennett was dead. Something inside him knew better and had from the start. Still, he'd fallen so hard and so fast for Quinn, he'd ignored the nagging voice in his head. And, he knew winning over Bennett would be his biggest hurdle, the biggest risk to losing Quinn.

Voice raised, Bennett looked ready to tear him limb from limb. "Bullshit. My intestines fell out in that battle, and I recovered within days. You can't tell me her brain's been dysfunctional for two fucking months."

Ryan shot him a vicious glare. "Keep your voice down," he said as calmly as possible. "She's got a lot of memories surfacing right now. It's a lot to process."

The blond nodded. "Bennett, you're not wrong. Amnesia's not the right word. I... I'm not sure, but I suspect Deandra blocked her memories. Only a powerful spell could be affecting Quinn so severely."

Lana watched Quinn's pale, motionless form nearly as intently as he did. "Why? Look what it's done to her."

Smiling in the corner, the tall guy answered where the rest could not, or would not, out of respect for Bennett. "If she'd remembered, she wouldn't have given herself to Six, and she would have rushed back to us."

Nodding, finally understanding, Ryan added, "Some memories have been trickling back." He looked to Bennett. "She dreamed of you, whispered your name in her sleep. A few weeks ago, she was able to fish out some memories. Vague, but enough. She thought you were dead. She mourned. Seeing you in the tavern, alive, recognizing all of you... it was enough to send her over the edge."

Bennett started to lighten up. "Yeah, I thought she was dead, too. I mourned her." He moved to get closer, but his legs stiffened, his feet frozen in place.

Poor guy. What an awful spot to be in. Ryan was miserable for him. He'd said he'd step away if this happened. Now that it was here, he couldn't seem to tear himself away from Quinn. Her brow furrowed, and he imagined memory after memory flashing back for her.

The blond reached out and rested her hand on his forearm. "I'm Astrid. I've known Quinn since college. We found each other quite fortuitously. A god's-gift sort of jerk at a party tried to drug me and take me to a back room. Quinn jumped in and knocked him out with a light tap of a punch." She smiled sweetly, looking down at her friend. "A bit of a temper back then, I nearly punched her right back, telling her I'd planned to break his penis the moment he whipped it out. We've been friends ever since."

The tall guy spoke next. "Vann. Neighbor in San Francisco. She caught me cutting the head off a werewolf in the alley behind our building. Told me I was joining her team. There went my solo days." He grinned, letting Ryan know, as Astrid had, that he wouldn't turn him away.

The petite woman, still snuggled up next to Quinn, spoke next. "I'm Lana. She's my cousin. No one gets my quirky humor but her."

Ryan found himself smiling for the first time since Quinn went limp in his arms. "I think we'll get along just fine."

They all looked to Bennett. "Fuck. Fine." He paced, walking to the window and staring down at the traffic on the street. "My mom and her dad are on the same team."

Lana flashed him a nasty glare. "And?"

"Not relevant."

Her glare intensified.

"Fine. Until two months ago, she was my girlfriend. Shit changed. Not the love-of-the-ages, so I'm gathering." He looked to Ryan, hatred glowing in his eyes. "Who the fuck are you?"

Vann walked closer, standing close enough to stop a fight, should there be a need. "Bennett, cool it. He didn't ask for any of this."

Watching Quinn, seeing her eyes shifting rapidly beneath her closed lids, he ached to kick them all out and hold her in his arms. "Ryan Hunt. I'm XO of a top-secret Coast Guard crew, patrolling the Pacific Coast. Hunting, scaring off monsters of all sorts. A great crew, but I'm the only demon hunter." He paused, hoping they wouldn't ask the questions he'd refuse to answer.

He stuck to what he knew about Quinn. "Two months ago, a gigantic, comet of a waterspout from the sky splashed into the water off our starboard bow." Finding himself smiling again, he remembered their meeting. Her feisty attitude from the first moment she'd seen him. "I fished out this smartass. She spent the night in the medical bay, recovering miraculously easily. Without a doubt, I knew what she was. When she woke, she didn't remember anything. We found her name written in her bulletproof vest, with a smiley face."

Chuckling at his side, Vann uncrossed his arms, slipped his hands into his pockets and rocked back on his heels. Lana and Astrid smiled. Bennett's scowl hadn't lessened in the least.

"It took a few weeks, but gradually some of her memories came back. Not many. Her parents, some flashes of you all. Often like this, but less intense. This is the longest she's been out." He hated watching the torment tearing her apart.

Predictably, Bennett looked ready to sock him. "Did you start fucking her while she didn't even know her full name, or did you take advantage while she was grieving her dead boyfriend?"

Astrid hissed an admonishment. "Cool it. You remember your reactions the last two months? The things we've learned? Then, if you still want to, you and Ryan can hash it out. When Quinn's not in such a fragile state."

"He's not wrong. I messed up. Big time." He moved his gaze to Bennett, letting him see his genuine regret. "Before anything even happened between us, I convinced myself I'd give her up if she wasn't mine to have. Then, when I heard her saying your name in her dreams, I swore I'd walk away." Chest heavy, a leaden pressure constricting his lungs, he knew that was now impossible. "I love her so much. I'll be whatever she needs. If she wants me to walk away, I will." Again, the fucking poet was coming out, but he knew, from the depths of his soul, they would always be at each other's side.

Lana and Astrid patted him on the shoulder as they rose from the bed. Vann gave him a subtle nod. Bennett turned on his heel and stalked towards the door.

Buzzing in his pocket, his phone caught his attention. "Hang on guys," he asked. "Hunt," he said into the receiver.

From the other end, Willa's voice sounded apologetic. "I need you on board. Quick mission. Should be done in the morning and on our way back. Sorry to interrupt your shore leave, but it can't wait. This one requires your expertise. Not something I've heard of."

Running a hand over his short hair, he cringed, knowing he was going to have to leave Quinn. Sounded like he'd be back, maybe even before she woke up, but he hated the thought of it. Still, he trusted her team would put their own lives on the line to keep her safe. "Roger. I can be aboard in ten minutes."

"Wait, are you bringing Quinn?"

"No. She's... we found her friends."

"Damn. I mean, I'm glad she's with her friends, but we could have used her help. That's ok, nothing we can't handle."

He hung up the phone and shoved it back in his pocket. Addressing Quinn's team, he knew he had to ask a massive favor. "Look, I've gotta work. Should be back tomorrow sometime."

Vann flexed his arms and pecs. It seemed to be an unconscious move, but the message was clear, he didn't even need to vocalize the offered, "Need a hand?"

Grinning, thinking he might just be able to make friends with at least this one, Ryan shook his head. "Nah, we got this. Thanks, though."

"Man, I haven't had a decent fight in weeks." He flashed him a brilliant grin.

Relieved, Ryan almost felt secure leaving Quinn. Almost. "Lana, can you stay with her?" He'd considered asking if any of them could stay with her, but he couldn't bear the thought of Bennett snuggled up with her all night.

She took her coat back off. "Of course."

The rest filtered out of the room. Astrid glanced back. "If you're in by tomorrow evening, meet us back at the tavern around six. Five if you want dinner."

His stomach grumbled so loud he was surprised no one commented. "I never did get my burger. Yeah, dinner would be great."

She smiled softly. "We'll save you a seat."

Bennett cleared his throat. "Her stuff's at the Weeping Mermaid." Turning on his heel, he stalked out. Was that an offer or a challenge?

The room clear, Lana moved back to her sentry position next to Quinn. Reassured, he knew she'd be okay for the night. Slipping his watch off his wrist, he fastened it around Quinn's. Not that she'd have reception, but he knew she'd appreciate the gesture.

18

TEAR-ENCRUSTED EYELASHES FLUTTERING OPEN, Quinn was surprised when the memories didn't dissipate into a blinding fog when she awoke. Not that she was relieved. The piercing howl of Typha as she was blasted through the sky was deafening as it echoed in her mind.

Vision clearing, she was more than a little shocked by her surroundings as she woke. Rather than Ryan's handsome face, Lana lay sprawled out next to her, hair in a dark mass covering her eyes, mouth gaping wide open. Good thing she'd looked around before groping her bed partner.

Sliding out from the sheets, she tiptoed into the bathroom. She wasn't quite ready to chat yet. While her brain processed her bizarre situation, she needed to brush her teeth and take a shower first. The water from the shower blasted out with brilliantly heavy pressure, unlike the Valkyrie's miniscule trickle of a spray.

Before she stepped in, she realized a watch lay heavy on her arm. On its face was a photo of she and Ryan cheek to cheek, grinning like an absurdly happy duo. He'd snapped it during their shopping spree yesterday and texted it to Sunshine. A barrage of tearful happy faces and thumbs up had been her response.

Pulling on one of her new outfits after her shower, she tried not to worry about her rather odd change in situation. Although her memories had all come flooding back in the most intense barrage of dreams and nightmares, she had no idea what had happened over the past twelve hours. Ryan had insisted he'd step back and let her decide what she wanted and needed from him when her memories came back. Asshole better not have *stepped back*. If so, he certainly wasn't playing fair, leaving the photo of them on the watch.

Good. She'd be crushed if he didn't fight for her, as she had every intention of fighting for him.

Coffee pot huffing and sputtering like an old smoker as it finished brewing from the single-cup brewer, she grabbed the steamy mug and walked to the window. A heavy, sinking sensation pooled in her gut when she looked in the harbor and realized the Valkyrie wasn't there. Something must have called Ryan away. Checking the watch, she realized the Bluetooth was disconnected.

Ignoring the potent, lonely ache in the pit of her stomach, fiercer than her lack of dinner last night, she sipped her coffee cautiously. Lowering herself onto the edge of the bed, she nudged the double mountains of Lana's feet under the blankets. Groaning in protest, her cousin pulled the covers over her head.

She nudged her again. "Wake your ass up." Despite the gnawing constriction in her gut at Ryan's absence, listening to Lana grumbling at her, a sense of normal settled over her like her grandmother's hand-made quilt on a snowy day.

How overcome had Ryan been by the invasion of her loyal team? She really hoped they hadn't been too hard on him.

Oh god. Bennett. He was alive. In the mountain, he'd been so... no way he could have survived that. Deandra must have some incredible power, despite her cage.

How had Bennett and Ryan responded to each other?

She hadn't exactly had decent closure with Bennett. They'd left their relationship a fuzzy mess with an unsatisfying conclusion. She'd been trying to end it. He'd been trying to hold on but had begrudgingly accepted it was over. Part of her felt bad for moving on so fast, even though she didn't remember him, but still.

After another growling protest, Lana seemed to realize who was waking her. Jerking out of bed, she flung her arms around Quinn. "You're alive and well and happy and I missed you so much."

Swinging her coffee out of the way, Quinn held onto her cousin tightly, absorbing the warmth and love that she hadn't realized she'd been missing. "Nice to finally remember you." She managed a weak, apologetic smile.

"Astrid thinks Deandra blocked your memories so you and Six would get it on without you worrying about Bennett."

"Six?" She smiled at the affectionately spoken nickname, grateful her team hadn't been resentful of him. Well, Lana anyway. Not that Lana was capable of such negativity.

Lana waggled her eyebrows and bit her lip in a knowing smile. "Your handsome boyfriend. Ryan."

Quinn shifted to the chair and sipped her coffee, not bothering to mask her smitten grin. "That's quite a nickname you've adopted for him."

"Where's my coffee?" Lana looked around, glaring at Quinn's steamy cup.

"Fine," she muttered. Setting the pot to brew another cup, she moved back to her spot to hear more.

"We didn't know what to call him. Rumor had spread that a boatload of Coasties had taken out a kraken. Fishermen enjoy their tall tales. Anyway, we sort of assumed that was you. You've always had a fondness for gigantic sea monsters, hence your sexy new boyfriend, I suppose. Anyway, although I have little doubt you could take down a kraken alone... not that I've ever seen one, but we jumped to the conclusion that the sixth in the prophecy must be with you."

"Pretty big jump, but right on target."

"We'd even hypothesized you and Six may be getting it on. Speaking of, he's gorgeous. Nicely done."

Blushing, Quinn moved to grab the coffee as the instant brewer sputtered out the last drops.

"Aw, I've never seen you blush. Must be pretty spectacular." Lana winked theatrically and accepted her coffee, sitting crisscross-apple-sauce under the blankets.

Quinn's cheeks heated in a fiery red inferno. Wow, he really did make her blush. "He's... incredible. I do have to admit, guilt is biting me pretty hard in the ass right now. What kind of person starts sleeping around when she doesn't know if she has a boyfriend? I mean, I did check for evidence of kids or a wedding ring, but... you know." She sank into the chair looking out at the harbor.

Lana nodded, solemnly taking her first cautious sip. "I get it. De-andra had a little something to do with it. You and Bennett were a lovely couple, but you lasted longer than you should have. You... you were like... friends, but not even best friends. Actually, he was a little rigid and overbearing for you and as much as I love him like a buddy, sometimes I want to smack him upside the head and say, 'chill out.'"

Quinn shook her head softly, considering as she took another slow sip. Yep, that might explain some of her sensitivity about being bossed around.

"When I saw you with Ryan last night at the tavern—before you fainted—I've never seen you lit up like that. That's the kind of love they write sonnets about."

"Yeah, I know now that Ryan's my sappy romance. But Bennett looked livid last night. Before I fainted. I don't know how to fix that." Shifting in her chair, she longingly watched the harbor as the sun rose above, casting a hopeful glow on the scattering of anchored boats.

With her memories came the weight of responsibility. Part of her still yearned to sail off into the sunset with Ryan, letting everything else go.

"Why don't I call Bennett to bring your things over. You and he can hash it out and see where you end up?"

Exhaling out her nostrils, her lips pulled tight in unpleasant anticipation, she agreed. "But, if it doesn't go well, I'm blaming you."

"Ha, good luck with that. You're the one that slept with somebody else." Lana dove out of the way as Quinn chucked a pillow at her. "Hey, don't spill my coffee."

HALF AN HOUR LATER, Lana ducked out the door as Bennett arrived. Along with Quinn's belongings packed in her well-worn backpack, he brought a pair of coffees from the café across the street. Quinn rose from her chair and accepted the peace-offering.

"Lana informed me I need to 'hash it out with you.' Said you're 'drowning with misplaced guilt.'" He tossed her backpack on the foot of the bed and dropped himself into one of the chairs that faced the harbor.

She poured her coffee into the ceramic hotel mug she'd emptied only moments before and sat in the chair opposite him. Quietly, she nodded in agreement.

Pulling off the plastic lid of his cup, he set it on the windowsill. Looking around the room, he said, "Nice hotel. Ryan buttering you up for something?"

"Bennett, I'm not going there with you. If you want to bring him down or make me feel worse, you can go." She cradled her coffee cup in her hands and pulled her feet up onto the chair. Maybe this wasn't such a good idea, while things were still so raw for both of them. Bennett had two months to adjust to the break-up and mourn. She'd had about twelve hours, preceded by weeks of utter confusion and grief and guilt.

Sighing, he leaned back into the chair and looked aimlessly out the window. "I was miserable. Worrying after you. Convinced you were dead."

"I'm sorry. If I could have—"

He waved her off. "No. No apologies. I grieved, then... What I'm trying to get at here is, it's not your fault. And, you were right. After a few weeks, once my insides were officially my insides again, and I had no more excuses to wallow in self-pity, I started to move on. Not that I let anyone know where my thoughts were heading, not wanting to tarnish your memory, but moving on was easier than it should have been. Yeah, I missed you like crazy. Hell, we've been friends since we were in diapers. But it wasn't so hard for my eyes to wander."

Focusing her eyes on her coffee, she listened. She thought about that conversation before they'd faced Typha. Terrible timing. She'd known it then, but she'd hoped her honesty, finally, would have stopped things before they faced certain death on blind optimism, following an only partially satisfied prophecy.

"I felt insanely guilty for even considering moving on so quickly. As much as things had been uncertain between us in the end... well, on my end of things, I felt like I'd betrayed you when I should still be grieving.

So, you know me, I overcompensated and tried to convince myself and the rest of the team that we'd loved each other beyond reason, and that we were destined to fulfill the prophecy." Methodically, he blew the steam across the mouth of the coffee cup before taking a testing sip.

"You were right all along. You are part of the prophecy." She'd been so hesitant about the prophecy before, she hadn't seen the rest of it.

"Yeah, just not the part I wanted. Like getting cast as a supporting actor when you've got your eye on the lead role."

"You'll get your starring role one day."

He grunted, rolling his eyes. "Not so sure I want it anymore. Typha's going to aim straight for you and Ryan, you know that, don't you?"

An unfamiliar wave of nausea washed over her. This was why she wasn't fond of being at the center of a prophecy. It was vague and didn't guarantee the outcome... and put a big-ass bullseye right on Ryan's forehead. "I know."

"You really love him, don't you? I mean, of course you do. But, it's just hard to wrap my head around all this. Last time I saw you, you had just dumped me. For you to disappear for two damn months and return head over heels for some guy I've never met... It's disconcerting."

Staring out at the harbor, she breathed slowly in and out, silently willing Ryan home to her. "Yeah, I do love him. A lot." Shifting her gaze to Bennett, she knew he needed her reassurance more than Ryan right now. Ryan knew how she felt. Bennett had suffered months of uncertainty, since before she'd disappeared. "I love you, too, you know. Just not the same way."

He nodded, his brow low and gaze lost in his rapidly cooling coffee. "A few weeks ago, it finally dawned on me that, if you and I were destined to save the world, as lovers, we would have had stronger feelings for each other."

"We were good together." She smiled at him. They had been a good team.

"We were okay. Seeing you come in the tavern, Ryan's arms around you last night, the two of you moving together through the crowd like an inseparable unit... we were never like that. Part of me was insanely jealous—"

She cringed. Not exactly the best way to greet your old boyfriend.

He shook his head. "No, not like you're thinking. Jealous that we never had that, that we never couldn't keep our hands off each other. Exactly how you were trying to tell me it should be. I knew, as soon as the two of you came in, the air crackling like fireworks over your heads. I knew the prophecy was true. Don't get me wrong, I really didn't enjoy seeing that, watching some movie-star-muscled-badass with his hands all over my it's-complicated-ex-girlfriend. Affection, lust, yeah, those were obvious. But, then... man, that guy was a monster last night. The moment you weren't doing ok, he had you scooped up and out of there so fast, snapped at any of us that even considered disturbing you. Protective as hell."

Quinn smiled softly against the rim of her coffee mug, imagining Ryan watching over her, growling at anyone that got close.

"What I'm trying to say, very circuitously, is that I'm okay. Better than I should be, considering. You know I've been obsessed with this whole prophecy thing. It's unflattering at best, that not only am I not some chosen one like I'd imagined, but the runner up. No silver medal, either."

"You deserve so much more."

"Damn right I do. But, today's not my day. Maybe tomorrow. I've gotta say, clichéd as it sounds, he hurts you and I kick his ass."

"Yeah, total cliché. But I appreciate the sentiment."

19

No sign of the Valkyrie yet. Quinn was, admittedly, going a little nuts. Okay, more than a little. She'd lived and breathed Ryan when she had nothing else. It was fine. She wasn't clingy or codependent or anything, it just felt... weird. Like a critical part of her was missing.

She checked the borrowed watch again. Had he added the picture on the watch face for her, knowing she'd be terrified of forgetting everything again? Or, had he been worried she'd actually forget him?

Foolish man. Quinn was officially convinced that Deandra had been behind her bout of amnesia. Clever demon woman.

Dressed in her new holey skinny jeans that Ryan had found amusingly grunge, hiking boots, slim white v-neck, plus her favorite leather jacket that her mom had gotten her for her twenty-second birthday, she and Lana walked arm in arm to the tavern. Astrid had her nose in a book and was snacking on peanuts at their favorite dining table. Bennett sat across from her, his nose shoved in another ancient text.

A resonant voice startled her from behind. "Hope you brought your reading glasses. Astrid has us down for intensive research tonight," Vann said.

Grumbling at her side, Lana pouted, "But look at all these tasty fishermen and Coasties. I haven't had a night off in months."

Quinn smiled as she rolled her eyes and lightly punched her cousin in the arm. "You are such a slut."

"I don't sleep with all of them. I just enjoy making new friends." She shrugged, winking at a handsome fisherman at the bar as they passed.

Missy came running out from behind the bar as they entered and threw her arms around her cousin. "Quinn, I'm so glad you're okay."

"Thanks. Me too. Things okay around here?"

Nodding, Missy pulled away and returned to her post. "Same old, same old, just the way I like it. The usual tonight?"

"Yes. Please. I'd love a stout, too."

"Anything for that sexy new boyfriend of yours?" Missy waggled her dark eyebrows.

Checking her watch, she lingered on the photo before answering, heart lurching in her chest as she basked in the memory. Five on the nose. "Yes. He'll need the best burger in the house and an IPA as soon as he gets here."

"Sure thing. Ollie will bring them out to you shortly." She passed Quinn the stout she'd expertly built. Sliding it to her, she hesitated. "It's good to have you back."

"Good to be back."

Missy tapped her fingers on the bar. Quinn hesitated before turning around to go sit down. Finally, Missy's expression scrunched with guilt. "You, uh, don't mind if I ask out Bennett?"

Where Missy felt guilt, Quinn felt sixty pounds of regret floating off her shoulders. "Of course not. I know you two had a thing a few years back." See? Things were going to be just fine.

Quinn sipped the head off her perfectly poured stout before risking a frothy spill, then joined her friends at the massive wooden table. Mostly quiet, all researching intently. Mostly.

Lana stole Bennett's beer and downed it in one massive chug. Setting it down with a resounding thud, sending a fine crack through the glass, she pouted, "I just... I'm all for saving the world and all that shit. But we got trampled. Yeah, Ryan looks like he could pummel a monster into submission without batting an eye. But I don't think Typha will be defeated with brute force."

Looking up from her book, Astrid shrugged lightly. "No. We'll need more than muscle."

Elbows on the table, hands folded, index fingers tapping his upper lip, Bennett shook his head in puzzlement. "I still say we splash her with a vat of blood like *Carrie*."

"Demon blood, not pig," Lana said helpfully.

Bennett chuckled impishly. "Good point. Maybe she's like the Wicked Witch of the West and we'll just melt her. Or was it the East?" He leaned back in his chair and brought his empty glass to his lips. Shooting Lana an eye-rolling glower over the cracked, empty glass, he waved down Ollie as he passed by with a tray for the next table. Nodding, the server acknowledged the silent refill request.

Leaning back in the rickety wooden chair in the corner, Quinn watched her friends. She would have missed them terribly if she'd remembered them. Probably a good thing she hadn't, or she would have tried to rush back to them. Even now, she retrospectively missed their never-give-up Goonie attitude.

It was tempting to give up. Had Typha not been gradually expanding her sphere, attracting more and more demons to this side of the veil, she'd say they should leave well enough alone. If her ancestor, the one that saved them from certain death and sent her across the sky to Ryan, hadn't still been imprisoned, she'd say it wasn't their problem. Not much of a demon hunter attitude, but there was so much more to life than killing demons.

Buzzing on her wrist startled her. Bluetooth connected. *Ryan*.

Leaping up from the table, she pushed through the crowded tavern to get to him. As if by magic, the crowd filtered out right as he walked in.

Grinning as he spotted her, the corners of his mouth turned up in a full, wicked smile.

She jumped into his arms, wrapping her legs around him, their lips meeting fluidly, hungrily.

RYAN NEEDED THE FRIENDLY chaos of the tavern, Quinn's humor and warmth, more than ever. It had been a long, bizarre, disgusting day. As they neared Sitka, he closed his eyes in a futile attempt to block the memory of the last few hours.

Even Willa had been horrified by what they'd seen. "What. Was. That?" she'd said. Her hands trembled at the helm, her wide-eyed expression frozen like Otzi the Iceman's mummified corpse. Ryan had never seen her look surprised before, so the stunned speechlessness wasn't reassuring.

Inhaling deeply to buy himself an extra moment before responding, the excess oxygen got trapped in his lungs until he nearly choked on it. "No idea," he sputtered out, his voice startlingly high pitched. He wiped yet another glob of oily monster bodily fluid from his hair.

Damn thing had splattered all over him. Part hydra, part lung fish, but mostly what-the-fuck-is-that... nothing he'd ever seen before. Not that he was any expert, but he guessed it was something new.

It seemed to have been following them. One of the helicopters patrolling the area had seen it taking a stroll across a rocky beach a few miles north of Sitka before it slipped into the water. The pilot had tried to follow it, wanting to give the Valkyrie as precise a location as possible.

Oddly, they hadn't had to look very hard to find it. Well, more accurately, it found them. A few miles offshore, nearing its last known location, they'd stopped to conduct a detailed search. Not a trace of it to follow.

Then, from behind, the strangest looking creature barreled straight for them and slammed into them with its three heads, like a trio of battering rams.

The Valkyrie had rocked pretty hard at the impact, but, for a three-brained creature, it was pretty stupid to think it could take down a reinforced Coast Guard ship with the blunt impact. Not a friendly critter on the wrong side of the veil, it was out for blood.

Bashing into them a few more times, it finally got the point. Heaving itself over the water line, it wrapped one of its heads and a flippery fin over the side of the boat and flopped its bloated body on the deck. Initially, they'd laughed at its pathetic entrance.

Until it rose on its hind fin-like limbs, standing more than twice Ryan's height, and bared three sets of vicious looking teeth. Snarling and hissing, it rapped its tail on the deck in a cacophonous, hasty rhythm that reverberated through the ship.

Ryan waved off help, not wanting to risk anyone to the creature's razor-sharp arms or shark-like teeth. A few stayed near him to be on backup, and the others were on lookout in case it had brought friends.

Ryan went straight for the heads, slicing off the nearest. Bad decision. Hydra-style, it rapidly regrew a replacement, plus a fuck-you spare.

Swinging again, he shaved a pretty decent chunk off of its arm-like fin, but it howled and lashed back, biting Ryan on the shoulder. Twice as painful as the injury should have been, the wound burned, and his vision darkened around the edges, lucky to stay on his feet.

Tenacious little fucker. Pissed off and bleeding like a stuck pig, it wasn't backing down.

Ryan dodged the next swipe and pulled out his gun. Ricocheting off the creature's armor-like ribs, he narrowly missed the damn thing as the bullet whizzed past him and embedded in the wall of the ship. Trying again on a weaker spot, the second bullet embedded in its neck, black ooze seeping from the wound. He fired a few more into the necks until it wavered.

In comically slow motion, the thing fell forward, holding itself up by its awkward flippers.

In a low slide tackle, Ryan skimmed underneath and drove his sword into the belly, aiming upward into its chest.

Black, viscous slime gushed out, pouring over Ryan like an oil spill.

The creature spasmed and tried to wriggle away. Ryan gripped the crook of its rigid arm and held it in place. His sword slippery from the creature's gooey blood, he managed to tighten his grasp and dig the blade deeper in its chest cavity and twisted. Finally, he must have hit something major, as the beast shuddered violently and crashed down on top of him.

Groaning, lying flat and almost not caring that he couldn't catch a full breath from the pressure of the beast over him, he was just glad it was dead.

Within half a second, Manuel and Kyle were dragging him out from under its leaden carcass. He narrowly missed another gash from its sharp teeth as it twitched the last dregs of life from its dying muscles.

"Ah, god, that's so gross." Ryan griped and grumbled as he lay flat on the deck, reluctant to even move, his body heavy from the nasty goo. Demon hunting was not as glamorous as it sounded. He'd ended up covered in disgusting, other-worldly guts too many times.

Incredibly freezing, high-pressured spray blasted from the deck hose, washing him clean like a painful, ice-cold shower. Turning his head towards the bearer of the hose, he saw Kyle grinning from ear to ear in impish satisfaction. "You love telling me to clean the deck. Just anticipating your orders, Sir."

Mouth quirked up in a half smile, he appreciated the smartass's helpfulness for once. "Try this when I'm not covered in this shit, and you'll be swabbing decks every night for the rest of your career."

Dripping with water and his own blood, he dragged himself to his feet and kicked off as many clothes as he dared without flashing the crew.

He'd leave the investigation and disposal of the discovery to Harry. The medic's fascination with forensics came in handy at times like this.

First, however, Harry tried to bandage the gash in his shoulder. Brushing him off, he growled, "Don't bother. It'll be fine in a few hours." He probably could have used it, but they could clean up his trail of blood easier than the thick nastiness from the mystery creature.

Not exactly what he'd envisioned for their quick mission. Having secured the area, they didn't hesitate before heading back for Sitka. He wasn't the only one weirded out by the whole ordeal.

After giving report to Willa, he took a selfishly long, hot shower until he was sure none of that gluey shit was left in any nooks or crannies. By the time he was feeling clean and presentable, his own wound nearly done bleeding, they were just pulling into the harbor.

Almost five o'clock. Perfect. He needed that burger now more than ever. And the cozy company.

THE SCENT OF SMOKY, flame-broiled beef wafted out from the tavern. Stomach grumbling loudly, Ryan could almost taste the burger from a few blocks away. A buzzing in his pocket told him he'd connected to his watch... and Quinn. Wired, his crewmates were bouncing around him, eager to celebrate another victory.

Barely managing to not knock down the door to get to Quinn and his burger, he strode into the crowded tavern. She was already running full speed toward him, nearly knocking him over from the eager leap.

Ready for her, he hadn't realized just how much he'd needed the certainty of her affection, unmistakable as she launched into his arms. He gripped her agile body against him, hands clenched around her hips, letting the foulness of the day melt away.

Slanting, he deepened the kiss, stroking his tongue across hers.

Cradling his face in her hands, she breathlessly pulled away and rested her forehead against his. "Love you."

Catching their breath from the intensity of the kiss, the adrenaline rush of their connection, they stood like that until the surrounding whoops and whistles sounded out the deafening thunder of their hearts pounding synchronously. "Love you, too," he said as he lowered her to the floor. "Wasn't sure what I was coming back to."

Arms wrapped snuggly around him, she chuckled softly against his chest. "For a moment this morning, I thought you were trying to give me space. I'd considered hunting you down and kicking your ass for pure stupidity."

Leah nudged him from behind. "It hasn't even been twenty-four hours. Get a room."

"I can cancel shore leave anytime," he fired back, his tone far too cheerful for any of the impatiently waiting crew behind him to take the threat seriously.

Lacing their fingers together, they walked through the crowded tavern to the big table. As he sat next to Quinn in the corner, a basket with a massive, loaded cheeseburger and an IPA were promptly delivered. Kissing her loudly on her cheek, Ryan shifted his complete, devoted focus onto his first decent burger in months. And it tasted so good. Double cheese, double patties, fresh baked bun, and a special sauce with a kick that redefined a tavern burger. Groaning as he took a satisfying bite, he closed his eyes to savor.

"Take out any feisty monsters today?" Lana cheerfully inquired as she stuffed in the last bite of her seafood stew.

Glaring over his rapidly disappearing burger, he wiped the corner of his mouth. Thinking about today's monstrosity was not good for the appetite. He held up a finger to stall her and shoved in the last few bites. Chewing, savoring, he finally swallowed and then took a long swig of beer, draining it by half. "Just one nasty beast."

Sitting cross-legged in her chair next to him, Quinn asked hopefully, "Not a lost soul on the wrong side of the veil?"

Bennett interrupted before he could answer, his elevated cheeks half covering his scrunched eyes thanks to his baffled expression. "What?"

Quinn answered for him as he devoured a handful of fries. "I have a little theory."

Clearly still feeling a bit aggressive, despite his appearance of acceptance, Bennett pushed. "You have a wittle theory about the wee wittle
monstuhs?" Dickhead.

"Yeah. I do," Quinn fired back at her ex in a well-practiced argument. Clearly, not the first time they'd quarreled. Looking around to
the rest of the team, their ears all focused on her, Quinn continued.
"Ryan was raised differently than we were. He wasn't told what he was
until he was out of high school. His mother is unique, and not your
typical demon hunter parent. Sunshine is exactly as her name sounds,
pure love and brightness."

Ryan watched as the curious looks grew wider around the table.
"Look. I'm a demon hunter, like you are. But I've been raised to see,
and quickly learned on my own, that not all monsters need to die.
Some just wandered through thin rips in the veil. Of those, many find
they enjoy being bullies over here and don't want to go back. They
need to be taken care of in order to maintain the balance of our world.
But others are just lost, maybe scared. In their fear, they might hurt
people or destroy property as they don't know the rules around here,
but with a push, gentle or not, they can be sent back across."

Thankfully, Vann seemed to get it right away. "We are a bloodthirsty bunch, bred to kill monsters without question. But, you're
right. I've had a few sleepless nights, wondering if I'm always doing
the right thing."

On point, Astrid routed the conversation back. "Not today's monster? What was it?"

Rubbing his hand over the gash on his shoulder, healing more
slowly than usual, Ryan leaned back in the sturdy dining chair.
"Nothing I'd ever seen before. Double my size, three hydra heads,
almost lungfish-like in its limbs and how it moved. Filled with the
most revolting, tarry black blood." Shivering internally, he refused to

let the image rattle him. Took out a kraken bigger than the Valkyrie, yet this new creature scared him.

"Where did it come from?" she asked again.

"That's part of what freaks me out so much. It was hovering around the coast, slipped back into the water, then, I don't know, maybe I'm being paranoid, but it seemed to be waiting for us."

"Some kind of sentinel?" Vann asked no one in particular.

Nodding, Astrid's calculating eyes lit up her expression. "With the hydra heads, unlike anything we've ever seen or read about... too coincidental. Typha must be behind it."

Quinn leaned against him and brought her knees up to her chest. "The kraken. The sentinel. Both practically beckoning the Valkyrie."

Ryan wrapped his arm around her and scooted her chair closer.

STRETCHING HIS LEGS OUT as he reclined in the worn leather sofa, Ryan glared at the antiquated book he'd been assigned to read. He had no idea teamwork involved so much reading. His head was pounded, and his eyelids grew heavy.

Yeah, research was an important part of the job, but he was toast from the long day. Well after ten o'clock. They'd been at it for hours.

Bennett rubbed a hand over his face, mussing his hair as the fatigue began to show. "Nothing in here about that sentinel. I think Typha's been experimenting, creating her own minions, creatures with arms like hers and that are able to move through the veil."

"Think she's getting it on with a lungfish?" Lana waggled her eyebrows.

Vann nodded. "Actually, she might be. Worked for Deandra, creating hybrids to carry on her mission. Making her own blood experiment."

Lana looked over at Bennett. "Sorry Bennett, but I don't think we get to throw vats of demon blood at her," she said with a playful shrug. "Ryan was drenched in Typha's monster's blood and it did little more than annoy him."

Snorting, Ryan muttered, "Annoyed. More like grossed me the fuck out."

Ignoring him, stretched out in the chair to the left, Bennett shrugged, his face turned down in feigned disappointment. "Let's just try throwing some of Ryan's blood on her, for good measure."

Without looking up from his book, Ryan flipped him off. Before he could re-focus on the ancient text, a lightbulb flickered on in his brain. "Actually, I do think you're on to something."

Grinning, Bennett looked a little too chipper. "See? Even peace-loving Coastie's on my side. Blood's the answer."

Sitting up with even more erect posture than she had been, Astrid crossed and re-crossed her legs. Finally closing her book, she focused her gaze on Ryan. "You're not of Deandra."

He leaned forward and rested his elbows on his knees to still the rapid vibration. "Nope," he said bluntly.

Vann remained silent on his perch.

Lana's head whipped back and forth between Ryan and Astrid.

Bennett rolled his eyes but seemed unimpressed. "You're the spawn of Deandra's demon lover. That's why we need you."

Astrid still looked puzzled. "How did he cross, to create to?"

Ryan shrugged. "The same way lots of monsters cross. Snuck through one of the many smaller tears in the veil, to avoid attracting attention."

"Why now? Why did he wait?"

Well, at least they weren't flogging him. Not that he expected them to, but no one seemed horrified at his revelation. He described his history, as he'd told Quinn.

"*You* make sense," Vann said, frowning. "But, why Quinn? She's no different from the rest of us." He nodded to Quinn. "No offense, but there's nothing unique about you compared to he rest of us."

Holding her beer up for a toast and smiling sweetly, Quinn calmly said, "I think we all know I'm awesome. 'Nuff said."

Air-toasting her, Lana nodded in agreement. "That you are. But, Deandra could talk to you. Like, inside your head. You must have some fancy genetic piece of her, like something that is dormant in all of us."

Bennett rubbed his hands over his face, his voice hoarse as he said, "She is special. I mean, not genetically. She's one of the most effective, dedicated hunters ever born, has an open mind, and is clever. But, aside from Quinn as a hunter, the real significance is that she's Ryan's fucking soulmate."

Nodding her head in vigorous agreement, Astrid could hardly contain herself. "It's like the next best thing to Deandra and Bain. He used his power over the veil, intending to create a two-way door for her alone, so he must have incorporated her attributes in the spell."

Nodding, Ryan added, "We've been thinking on that. Both need to be on both sides simultaneously to repair it. Deandra and Bain on one side, Quinn and me on the other. Not that either of us have a fucking clue how, but I'm assuming we'll figure it out when the time comes. As easy as it sounds, Bain fucked it up when he made the door."

Astrid scowled, taking a long pull on her beer before setting the glass on her knee. "Combining the power of two powerful demons to create the door could have been what set off the explosion that created the tear. Attempts to repair it could be equally dangerous, maybe more so with two full demons on one side, and just their offspring on this side. It wouldn't be balanced."

His rolling voice softly delivered, yet thunderously loud for the impact his words carried, Vann said, "Getting back to that blood theory..." He bit his cheek, looking Quinn over closely before continuing. "*Mixing* their blood might stabilize things. A hybrid, one that carries both of their traits, to balance out their power. As they haven't seen each other in a few millennia to accomplish that themselves, but seem to enjoy sharing their genetic material via humans, their proxies could accomplish that for them... by creating Seven."

Quinn set her beer back on the coffee table and opened her mouth to speak, then closed it again. "I—" She choked on her words, then began again. "As in... Ryan and I... create... a... hybrid... person. Like... a... baby person."

The words hung heavily in the air. Ryan could feel the blood drain from his face and the room close in around him. "I... huh... whuh..." Wow, his inner poet was tragically failing him now.

Laughing out loud, Bennett leaned forward and smacked Ryan on the back with a resounding slap. Sarcasm dripping from his words, Bennett was clearly enjoying himself. "And here I was considering making a Ryan and Quinn blood smoothie. This is way better. Congratulations, man."

Picking up Quinn's beer, Ryan chugged it to moisten the desert of his parched mouth. Defensively, his voice awkwardly higher pitched than he'd ever heard escape his own lips, he protested, "But, generally demon hunters know when things are..." He cleared his throat and tried again. "I... I know when my swimmers are locked and loaded and on a mission, and obviously avoid deploying until the threat is over."

Her lower lip pushed out in a pathetic pout, Quinn nodded slowly, "Uh-huh. I can feel when the girls are surfing the fallopian tubes, and nobody's been misbehaving lately."

Ryan couldn't fight the chuckle, his chest silently shuddering with restrained laughter. He whispered in her ear, "Somebody's been misbehaving, hence the predicament." Quinn squeezed her eyes shut, shuddering with a half-laugh, half-cry.

Plopping his feet up on the coffee table, Bennett sank more comfortably into his chair. He was clearly enjoying himself at Ryan's expense. "That Deandra is a clever one. Bet she rendered that little warning system dysfunctional like Quinn's brain."

Lana added with an unhelpful, delighted snicker, "I'll bet something in Ryan's genetics, or perhaps something more lustful and less scientific, hacked his missile launch codes without his knowledge."

Snorting, Ryan muttered under his breath, "Or consent."

He felt Quinn drooping at his side. Time to call it a night. Weirdest damn day of his life as of a few hours ago, now it was... fubared.

Dizzy from the ridiculous day, the lead that filled his limbs was starting to saturate his brain. Rising from the deep sofa, Quinn stood in front of him and gently placed her hand on his stubbled jaw. Looking up, he saw her face was as drained of color as his felt. Lacing her fingers with his, she dragged him up and led him back to their hotel.

After only four or five tries with the damn electronic lock, he got the green light to flash and pushed into their room. Each got ready for bed, performing their bedtime ritual side by side, stripping down, and sliding between the sheets. As the light was on her side, Quinn flicked off the switch.

A soft, blue glow from the full moon lit up her face just enough that he could tell she was awake. Pulling her into his arms, he gently kissed her temple.

"Ryan?"

"Yes, Quinn?"

At home in the midnight-blue of the room, Quinn's eyes shined with a brilliance he'd never seen. "I'm freaked out. Obviously, I'm taking a pregnancy test in the morning to confirm, even though I have no doubt they're right. But... I'm also a little excited."

His heart fluttered in his chest, not the rush that Quinn normally aroused in him, but an unfamiliar thrill. "Me too. I love you."

She curled into him, smiling as she burrowed into his neck. "I love you, too."

Depleted of coherent thought from emotional overload, he melted into her, grateful for her soothing touch. Focusing on her fingers trailing along his arm, he fell into dreamless sleep.

20

BLINDING RAYS OF SUN streamed in through the open curtains. Limbs entangled with Ryan's, she smiled softly at the serene expression on his face. For the craziness of last night, Quinn would have thought he'd still be scowling, tossing and turning, or awake and brooding. Yet, here he was, exactly what she needed to calm her own freak-out.

Her phone chirped on the bedside table. Huh, she hadn't heard that sound in months. She really hadn't missed its nagging.

Open your door, the message read, with a clever thumbs-up GIF dancing across the screen. She'd find the request suspicious if it wasn't from Lana.

Sliding out of bed, careful to not wake Ryan just yet, she pulled on the hotel bathrobe and opened the door. Hooked to the doorknob was a grocery bag filled with at least a dozen pregnancy tests. Goof. But, totally psychic.

Tiptoeing to the bathroom, she first checked that Ryan was still asleep. Perfect, out cold. Taking it three at a time, using both the pee-on and dip methods, Quinn ran every damn test. She didn't think she could pee that much, but, go figure, she made it happen.

All the tests lined up on the counter, she stared at all with the clock ticking ominously behind her. What kind of ancestor got you knocked up without your permission? Yeah, it might just save the world, but come on. Not cool.

First the blue plus sign appeared. Then a pink one. Then an equal sign. Then the fancy digital readout.

Son of a bitch, she was as pregnant as pregnant could be. With the timing... fucking shit, it must have been the first time they'd even done it.

Standing helplessly in front of the meticulously aligned, traitorous tests, she felt weepy. Yeah, she wanted to be a mom. But, come on. A little input on the timing would have been nice.

She jumped as the bathroom door swung open. Ryan bit his lip to hide his chuckle, brushed past her, flipped up the toilet seat, and emptied his bladder. Why was he so calm?

While she remained rooted in place, staring at the row of positive tests that confirmed her fate, Ryan flipped on the shower to steamy warm. Steadily, his lips hinting a sweet smile, he reached around her and untied her robe, sliding it down her shoulders. Letting it drop to the floor in a pile, she pitifully stepped in with him.

Working the shampoo into a lather, he massaged her scalp. Feeling the sudsy water flow over her, she felt her brain start to thaw, her muscles slacken. With gentle ministrations, he continued, working the conditioner through her hair, trailing the soap over her body, not seducing or asking or talking, just being what she needed.

Nearly human again, lids heavy and muscles loose like she'd just finished an hour-long Swedish massage, she turned and watched as he started his own hygiene routine. He still had the same sweet, faraway smile he'd worn all night. Yeah, he was *exactly* what she needed.

"Quinn?" he asked as he finished rinsing the shampoo out of his short hair, flicking the excess drips with a sweep of his hand.

"Yes, Ryan?" She stepped closer and wrapped her arms around him, letting the river wash over them both, closing her eyes while she absorbed the moist heat from his skin.

Rotating them sideways to share the warm mist, he nudged her chin until she looked up at him. "I'm not going to say I'm surprised by the baby. I'm not shocked at the whole destiny thing, that we came together by design. But..." The corner of his mouth turned up in that wicked smile she adored as his hands traced over her skin. "I don't care what efforts Deandra and Bain took to bring us together. Erase all of that, say we were two normal people that met at the tavern as strangers, you visiting your family and me on shore leave. I have no doubt I would have been drawn to you."

Scorchingly hot blood pumped in her chest, sending pulses of fire to the most distal of her extremities as she drifted into him. "Just drawn? What if I was there with my boyfriend? Ignoring you rowdy Coasties? Say you only had a few hours of shore leave."

Shaking his head in amusement, his grin grew wider. "First, I would have been polite. Watched you from across the crowd, but respected your space, your relationship. Then, you'd have flipped someone the bird and made some wisecrack. You'd notice me across the room and meet my gaze longer than was appropriate."

He paused, trailing his fingers down the stream of water that flowed between her breasts, sending prickling goosebumps in the wake of his touch. "And?" she asked, breathless.

"One look at me, and you'd ditch that guy you were with."

"So quickly?" She stilled, letting him find his own path.

His hands continued their exploration, his silvery gaze following his trail. "Hell, yeah. One look is all you'd need. All you did need."

Without looking up at her, he grazed his hands up her sides, settling with his hands teasing across her breasts.

On a sharp inhale, she almost forgot what he'd asked. She managed a lilting, "I remember finding you aggravating."

"You didn't have a memory to your name, blank slate. But you knew you wanted me."

A husky chuckle escaped her lips. "That ego is unstoppable."

Pausing, he drew his tongue along the stream he'd traced before. She felt his smile against her skin, his lips pressed across her breast. "Stop interrupting." He flicked her erect nipple with the tip of his tongue. She couldn't speak to interrupt anyway. "You'd head up to the bar and lean forward, waggling that very fine ass while you ordered a beer. After an impressive guzzle, you'd turn away from the bar, and I'd already be heading your way, on the guise of getting another drink."

Taking the tight bud into his mouth, he pulled. Breath shallow, she craved more. "Then?"

"I'd ask you to dance," he murmured, his breath hot over her skin.

Arching against him, she taunted him. "I don't dance."

Between caresses, he said, "Yeah, that's what you'd tell me. I'd say, 'neither do I,' wink at you and hold out my hand. Unable to resist, of course, you'd come with me and let me hold you against me as we swayed to the music." Lowering himself to his knees, he gripped her hips and looked up at her, driving her mad with anticipation.

Voice thready, she managed to ask, "What if there's no music?"

"Doesn't matter." He pressed his lips to her center. "We'd find our own rhythm."

"And?" She was panting as he held his mouth inches from her core.

"I'd ask your name, then tell you I wanted you more than any woman I'd ever met." He traced his tongue along her slick folds, then pulled away again. "You'd suggest we go for a walk." She could feel the heat of his breath brush over her as he spoke between tender licks. "Once near my hotel, I'd tell you I only had eight hours before I'd be gone forever. You'd tell me that you wanted me, that you'd take every moment we could have together."

Pressing his tongue against her clit, he circled.

He pulled away only briefly, and she almost cried at the injustice as she throbbed in anticipation. "And when dawn came?" she asked, breathless.

"I'd beg you to wait for me, knowing I need you in my life forever."

Hands clutching her hips as he steadied them both, he drank deeply, laving his tongue along her core, into her tight center. She gasped and gripped his shoulders, pulsing with need against his hot mouth.

Each touch drove her higher, anchoring her to him. Sweet and tender, he laved. A thick haze encased them in the heat of the shower, the warm flow of water streaming over her skin. Harder, aggressive, he flicked her with his tongue, then closed his mouth over her and sucked. On his knees, his big hands wrapped around her hips, his mouth covered her. The sight alone was enough to send her soaring. Surging, molten heat licked from her core, radiating through her until her body tensed and melted in an encompassing, dizzying response.

Orgasm quivering through her, every nerve-ending was awash with sensation. She gripped her hand s in his hair, crying out his name as she climaxed.

Mouth soft and gentle over her, he slowed his movements, tenderly bringing her back down from the pinnacle. Rising to stand, he lifted her and pressed her back against the shower wall, the warm spray streaming down their joined bodies.

She wrapped her arms around his shoulders, the back of his neck. Grinding her hips against him, she craved all of him. His expression heavy, no sweet flirtation this time, he met her gaze, silver laced in his dark irises, a loving ache shared as he held her.

Smoothly, he lowered her onto his slick cock. Taking him in deeply, sensitized and still vibrating from his mouth on her, she tightened around him. Kissing her jaw, her neck, her temple, then her mouth, the heady taste of her still on his tongue, he achingly, lovingly, rocked inside of her until they shattered together.

WHATEVER FATE, WHATEVER CRAP was written in the stars that he'd create a demon hybrid with Quinn, destined to save the world... he knew they had something extraordinarily ordinary too. Knew they were just a normal pair of people that wanted life and laughter and love. Whatever divine intervention may have written that they should be together couldn't possibly have written how well they'd actually *like* each other.

Quinn finally relented in letting him chuck the many pregnancy tests in the garbage. After she'd snapped a pic to send to Lana. Although her team had wanted to plot some more, Quinn had asked for a day to chill, to accept. He'd been grateful.

They'd enjoyed room service again and talked about nothing in particular all morning. Just the two of them. Things were going to be okay.

"Things went terribly last time with Typha. Horrendously nightmarish. I don't want to chance losing you. We're perfectly capable of protecting humanity as things stand now. Without risking... anything more." Quinn sat across from him in the other of the comfy chairs, her feet stretched across the gap and resting on his lap.

Leaned back in his own chair, he loosely held her feet and power-lessly brainstormed with her. "I can go with that. Not going to be easy, but I'm all for running and hiding. I'm not risking you or Seven."

Her foot pushed against his cheek before settling back in his lap. Her scowl matched her cranky foot. "We're not naming it Seven."

"Well, that's better than It." He shrugged, rolling his wakeful but exhausted eyes.

"How about Destiny?" She waggled her eyebrows and almost looked satisfied.

"No."

"Veil?"

"No."

"Not Ryan Junior?"

"Fuck, no."

"Ryan?"

"Yes, Quinn?" He kissed the sole of her foot. Grinning, he won-dered what he was turning into. Normally, not a foot guy. But they'd gone from the shower to bed, back to the shower, then back to bed again and back in the shower again. He wasn't sure her foot had even touched the floor yet today.

"What?" she asked, clearly wondering about his devious grin.

"Nothing. Just thinking about when you might want to go again. I don't think I've gotten a blow job in days."

Whacking him in the jaw with her foot, much less gently this time, she exhaled noisily. "Maybe I'll surprise you with one when you're not expecting it."

He was ready with a smartass remark when his phone buzzed. Willa. Dammit. She'd extended his shore leave after the sentinel, so anything she might need now wouldn't be good.

"Hunt," he said into the receiver.

"Ryan, we've got it under control, but I just wanted to let you know what's going on. One of those monsters crawled on board during the night."

Sitting bolt upright in his chair, he strained to listen closer. "Another? That's—"

"Impossible? Improbable? Worse. It headed straight for your bunk. Manuel, Leah, and Dean got it before it got in. Manuel is in the infirmary with a laceration on his back, filled with venom or something. He'll be okay, but it'll be a few days before he's up and around. I worry there are more. That they're looking for you."

Quinn sat up across from him. He rose and walked to the window. The Valkyrie looked to be peacefully moored in the harbor. "Agreed. I'll come back on board tonight and we should get out of here."

"I don't disagree, but I want more intel about these things in case we run into more. What about Quinn or her friends? Have they found anything more yet?"

"It... they, seem to be hybrids of some sort. It's bigger than just the sentinels."

"The kraken?"

"Bigger. Why don't we meet in an hour? I'll bring you up to speed on what we know. Quinn will hang here and update her team." He looked knowingly at Quinn. She was already nodding in agreement. "Then, if I can convince her team to come aboard, we'll head for the source."

Ending the call, he sat back in his chair. Not exactly helpful. His knee vibrated a mile a minute. Things were changing, fast.

Quinn scowled in frustration. "There goes our run and hide plan. They're after you. Get on the Valkyrie and just go."

"Are you crazy? As I told Willa, you go check in with your team, and I'll prep the crew. The time is now. We go for Typha. All of us, together. I'm not a fan of that damn prophecy, but there's no turning back now."

Mouth turned down in the corners, Quinn shook her head, more troubled than he'd ever seen her. "I'm not watching you and my team get killed."

He reached the short distance between them and cradled her face in his hands. "Not this time. Typha said before, you only had part of what you needed to defeat her. Now, we've got everything we need. While we're at sea, you and your team write up a map, her strengths and traits, everything we know. There is a way to beat her. I'm not waiting around for that monster to take our baby from us. There's no better protection for her than inside you, now. Before they find out about her."

"Her?" Quinn managed to find her smile. "I think it's a he. Ornery shit already, like you are."

That wicked smile he knew she loved shaped his lips. "You're the ornery shit. Now, call your team. Let's get this moving. Today." He brushed his mouth across hers before pulling away. Crossing the room, he got dressed while she called her friends. As much as he'd rather they find a secluded cabin, somewhere far from monsters, he knew better. Nothing in his life had been that easy.

His hand on the door, he looked back to find her watching him. She made plans to meet her friends in an hour, and apparently felt the need to torture him, curled up in her chair in nothing more than her panties. Fuck, she was so amazing. He hoped she never lost the urge to sit around naked with him all morning.

"Quinn? You were asking me something earlier?"

"I was?" Her eyebrows drew together in question.

"Yeah. Then I got distracted thinking about you going down on me."

"Oh yeah. Ryan?"

His hand still rested on the door. He chuckled. "Yes, Quinn?"

"Are you going to get around to asking me to marry you?"

Flashing her a wicked smile, he turned the doorknob. "Soon as I get back." He slipped out the door before she could argue. Call him old fashioned, but he wanted to do it right. Maybe he'd swing by the jewelry store as soon as he got back to shore, make it official before they went after Typha.

21

Bennett.

"QUINN'S NEVER LATE. SHE said she'd be here ten minutes ago." Lana sat perched on the stool of their secluded nook, resting her elbows on the back of Bennett's chair. The place was crowded for lunch. Fishing had been great the last few days and pockets were full.

As much as he was moving on, and he really was, Bennett just didn't want the visual and couldn't hold back the nasty swipe. "I'm sure she's still up in her fancy hotel, banging her new plaything," he scoffed, sitting stiffly in the chair, ignoring the voice of worry that was murmuring in his skull.

Lana shot him a nasty glare. "I know you're hurting, to have things turn out so—"

"Look." He felt all the rage, the sadness rising in his chest, boiling into his throat. "I didn't say it earlier. Didn't want to admit it, not after we lost her..." It was time to tell the full truth. Let them know he was the asshole that had risked them all. "Quinn dumped me. Just before Typha."

And... silence. Astrid reached to the coffee table and grabbed a mozzarella stick from the appetizer platter. Chewing slowly, she choked it down to cover the awkwardness of his belated admission.

Vann set down his water, looking across at Bennett with hooded lids. "You've had a rough go."

"I just... she was gone. I was injured. I didn't need any more damn sympathy. Hated that I was wrong. Nearly got us all killed."

Nodding, Vann folded his arms across his chest. "Not your fault. We were all there. We *all* decided to go as far as we did. We all knew the risks. You weren't far from the truth behind the prophecy. Wish you'd said something sooner, you could have used a friend."

"We're with you, Bennett. I, for one, know you'll be ok." Astrid nodded supportively at him, then scowled, looking around. "Seriously, where is Quinn? She'd text us if she was running late."

Bringing a blast of cold from the sinking temperatures of the wintry afternoon with him, Ryan strode back towards their nook. Plopping onto the couch, he grabbed a slider and stuffed it down in a single mouthful. Glancing around, he finally swallowed. He asked casually, "Where's Quinn?"

Burning like the world's worst case of acid reflux, Bennett felt the bile rising in his throat. "We thought she was with you."

Leaping out of the seat like the building was burning around him, Ryan sprinted out the door. Following, the team didn't hesitate. Fucker was fast, but they caught up to him at his hotel room. Done messing with the electronic lock, he stepped back and kicked the door off its hinges.

Ryan stopped dead in the middle of the hotel room. Rapidly applying the brakes as they sprinted in after him, Bennett and the team froze. Lamp crashed on the floor with shards of glass everywhere. Chairs were tipped over, blankets bunched and scattered across the room, and a smattering of tarry drips and puddles stained the floor.

Turning to run, Ryan was like a demon on a rampage.

Stepping into his path, Vann's cheeks were heavy with grief as he reached out her hand and held him in place. "You won't find her. She's in the veil."

"MEET AT THE DOCKS in an hour. Bring whatever weapons you can. We'll be under way by 1600." Ryan was already shoving his and Quinn's belongings into their bags.

Vann was right. There was no way that thing could have dragged Quinn out to sea without being noticed. No way it could have dragged her all the way to Typha in this world. Already, with the amount of its filthy blood on the floor and the damage the room had sustained, she had given it a hell of a fight. Them, in all likelihood, as it would have taken a cluster to take her.

"Our boat is still docked in Dutch Harbor. We can fly out and meet you there," Vann offered, clearly uncomfortable with the entire idea of crossing the entire Gulf of Alaska and half the damn Bering Sea on a Coast Guard vessel... or maybe at the idea of being stuck with Ryan for that long.

Shaking her head, Astrid set her hand on his forearm. "No, we need to stick together. Ryan is one of us now."

Shoving his and Quinn's belongings into their bags, he cringed, bile rising in his throat. "I'm not... You know what, whatever. Just get your shit. If you're not there, I'm not waiting."

On board with the urgency, Bennett was already stepping over the rubble and moving out the door. "Come on, guys. Weather's shit over there anyway, landing in Dutch is a major gamble."

Mercifully, the remainder followed Bennett out the door. Ryan quickly pulled out his phone and dialed Willa. She didn't hesitate. The crew could be back on board within the hour. Each second that ticked by was a lifetime of missing Quinn. The longer she was away, the more torture they could inflict on her.

Somehow, he knew she was alive. The scattered drips of bright red blood, Quinn's, didn't ease his mind, however.

Last, he grabbed their toothbrushes and the floss multi-pack she'd invested in. How many had it taken to bring her down? A massive black hole formed deep in his gut. Nausea pounded over him as he thought about how desperately she would have fought them. Surprised, alone, unarmed.

No, he wasn't dwelling on that. She was fierce. No doubt Quinn was giving her captors a hell of a time. Even if they'd tied her well, she'd still terrorize them with trash talk.

Double checking that he'd grabbed all their stuff, he stormed out and left the keycards on the desk. After he bit the head off the attendant that inquired after his stay, she'd quieted and averted her eyes. "Room got broken into." Quickly, he said, and really meant it, "Sorry." His credit card would take a serious hit. He'd have to find a way to charge the notorious Typha for the expense.

He beat the others to the boat by a long shot. Understandable. They each had an arsenal to pack. A lot of their equipment was on the boat in Dutch, but they still managed to load a few hundred pounds of steel in their gear.

How the hell had these guys come to be a team? Bennett looked as fancy as his name, like he belonged at high tea in London. Vann made the phrase resting-bitch-face look like a tame expression, instead, he carried a resting I-don't-give-a-flying-fuck look. Astrid was one of those librarians that was all bookworm on the outside, but once she flipped that blond hair and ripped off her metaphorical glasses, she'd take you to new heights. Not his fantasy, but he knew a lot of guys that dug that. Lana was pure adorable bubbliness in a small package, the type to dance on the table yet would give her last pair of shoes to whatever pathetic creature needed it.

He had no doubt Quinn was the heart and soul of the motley crew. Embodying traits from them all, she was a friend to everyone she met. School teacher or sailor or scientist or soldier, she'd be a natural at any of it.

Willa politely, but sternly, welcomed the newcomers on board. A formidable captain, she made the chain of command very, very clear. Having his back, she made sure they knew what he said was absolute. Any dissent, and she'd chuck them overboard. Willa being Willa, the language was a bit more colorful. All gulping uncomfortably, they got the message.

Awkward was a gentle word for the scene. Four heavily armed men and women, short, tall, and cavalier-looking demon hunters on one side of the deck, the other side filled with a dozen uniformed, straight-faced Coasties—all but the few that were already gunning the engines on full, charting the fastest course possible. Total strangers, different in their backgrounds, their training, and style.

All eyes looked to him.

"Okay." Ryan stepped in the middle, recognizing he was the reluctant connection here, and his crew was wondering why the fuck he'd brought four more demon hunters on board, and why Quinn wasn't among them. "We all have the same goal. Not the same training or the same style, but we've all taken down our share of baddies. Now, the biggest, baddest of them all is holding Quinn near Zhemchug Canyon."

He swallowed the burning lump in his throat that threatened to hollow him out like a snaggle-toothed jack-o'-lantern.

"Speed and effectiveness are of the utmost importance right now. Quinn is..."

Fuck, this was hard. Sympathetic looks from both sides.

"She's pregnant with our child. Our child may be the key to repairing the rift in the veil that my father foolishly created... or destroy it completely if Typha figures out how to use that power. As you can imagine, that would be pretty fucking awful, end of the world sort of shit."

Bain created the rift, intending to create a single door for a single individual. If even the king of the demon realm couldn't control his own power? With the rage, the fear boiling inside him, Ryan was beginning to suspect he could personally rupture a massive tear in the veil using that same power.

Willa nodded proudly at him from her perch on the stairs. Alone, he stood between his two worlds. As empty as he felt, he knew he had a hell of an army at his back. "We're not going to let that happen. Let's go get her back."

A collection of enthusiastic smiles radiated around the deck. Lana let out a whole-hearted *whoop* and crossed the divide. His crew let out a fearsome battle cry. Vann nodded in assent. Bennett grinned in whole-hearted, merciless agreement at him for the first time, without a trace of distrust behind it. Astrid beamed with a bright smile that lit her up like a beacon.

Ryan took in the overwhelming scene, astonished at the immediate, easy merging of his worlds. Suddenly feeling like the outsider, he quietly escaped to his room.

22

Valkyrie, Gulf of Alaska.

RYAN TOSSED AND TURNED in his bunk, wishing sleep would come. Too many damn long days and nights they'd been at sea. Maybe they should have hopped on the stupid plane.

No. Dumb idea. He needed his crew, his gear, and the semblance of control and familiarity he maintained from taking the Valkyrie. Besides, it sounded like Quinn's boat was still undergoing repairs after her team's emergent departure from Typha's island, and could take longer.

They could always charter. He had no doubt there would be at least one captain crazy enough to take them out to Zhemchug—with enough vodka. Hell, he'd boarded most of the boats in the area for "inspections" while they gathered information about occurrences suspicious for monster activity, and there were one or two cracked enough to take on this mess.

No, there would be resistance, who knew how many sentinels. And he needed to get them all back safely, the cutter was the best way to do that.

The hair on his arms stood on end as the room filled with static electricity. A soft crackling in the center of his room caught his attention. Lifting his head from the pillow, he turned at the subtle sound.

A fist pounded on his door. The static ceased abruptly.

Timely middle of the night interruption. He could use a good fight. His own head was a cluster of unhelpful shit lately.

Quinn would be sound asleep right now. The woman could sleep anywhere, anytime, and peacefully at that. Rolling out of the bunk, his bare feet hit the floor. Throwing on the nearest cargos, he swung open the metal door.

Bennett stood outside, looking remarkably bedraggled, nearly as pale with sleep deprivation as Ryan. "Hey, man. Can I come in?"

Waving his arm as he opened the door wide, he awkwardly welcomed his rival. Bennett was about the last person he expected to be knocking on his door in the middle of the night.

Musing, Bennett inspected the closet-sized room. With a seemingly careless shrug, he turned back to Ryan. Because of the cramped space, the pair were way too close to each other for comfort. Bennett stepped back and sat down on the couch.

"This is the place, huh?" Bennett nodded at the austere accommodations.

Ryan pulled out his desk chair and threw his leg over to sit backwards on the undersized chair. Raising an eyebrow, he questioned the vague comment.

"Had I known it wasn't material comfort Quinn was looking for..." Bennett shook his head and ran his hand over his face, messing up those perfect eyebrows. Guy looked awful. "Sorry. I'm normally not a jerk. Promise."

With a slight nod of his head, Ryan acknowledged the pain his guest was going through. "I figured. Can't picture Quinn putting up with an asshole for long."

Cracking a smile, Bennett looked to be considering relaxing. "No, no she wouldn't. I don't know if she mentioned it, if she even remembered, but she dumped me just before we left for our doomed recon mission." Leaning back on the couch, he stretched his legs and tipped his head back. "I was obsessed with that damn prophecy. She didn't want anything to do with it, and I didn't listen. Now, she's at the center of it."

No idea what to say, Ryan stayed silent and rested his arms on the back of the chair. Midnight confession time.

"She wasn't ready for marriage or kids. Not with me, anyway."

He wasn't sure if Bennett even needed him here for this conversation.

Bennett leaned back and exhaled a heavy breath. "Sorry, man. I don't mean to ruin your night with my own laments, but I needed you to know. I'm the one who fucked up. Quinn was right all along."

Shrugging for lack of a better response, Ryan tried to acknowledge the weirdness of their midnight meeting. "I don't know what to tell you. Can't say I had any intention of settling down for at least another half century either. Then, Quinn splashed into my life and changed everything."

Covering his face with his hands again, Bennett scowled under his fingers as he rubbed his eyebrows. "She... yeah, she's an amazing person. One of my best friends. I realize now that we weren't right for each other. It's pretty obvious she and I were never meant to be, but are you okay with the whole soulmates, foretold to save the world with your love bullshit?"

Ryan gripped his hand in his short hair. "Fuck no. But I suspect that's part of the magic. Neither Quinn, nor I, had any interest in being destined for anything."

"Don't you feel a bit... manipulated?"

"Hell yeah. But I also feel lucky. What if Lana had been the one to splash into my life? She seems cool, and I'm sure we'd hit it off. But, would I have loved her the way I love Quinn?" He smiled, not needing to make eye contact to connect. "You've known her your whole life. That outrageous humor, the fearlessness, that body... damn, that body..." He glanced to Bennett, realizing that might cross the line and coughed to cover his last words. "Sorry. You know what I mean. If she and I weren't destined and all that bullshit... I'd still be frantic to get her back. Lost without her."

Adjusting on the couch, Bennett leaned forward and rested his elbows on his knees. "Yeah, I know what you mean. As much as I loved Quinn. *Love* Quinn—present tense—she still means a lot to me. Now... I know now that she was never herself with me. When I saw you two coming into the tavern that night, how incredibly happy she looked, I knew then that I'd been fooling myself."

"Look, I know I can't change the past—"

Bennett cut him off. "No. And, I wouldn't change it. I really believe this is going to work. We are the team to take down Typha. The six of us."

"No. No, no. There is no six in team. I'm here for Quinn, whatever the fucking prophecy says, whatever my father intended for me. I'm never opposed to taking down a baddie like Typha and know it's not possible to even try without you all. But once this is done, I'm out." Ryan tried to calm his breathing before he hyperventilated and passed out. Rising from the chair, it was time to dismiss his visitor.

Bennett wasn't budging. "Sorry man, prophecy says *team* of six. You don't know Quinn as well as you say, if you think she'd even consider giving up her team."

Pacing didn't work well in the small room, or he'd trip over Bennett's extended legs. Leaning against the bathroom door, his jaw clenched so tight he feared he might break a tooth. "I wouldn't ask her to. Doesn't mean I have to join."

"What's your deal?"

"No deal. I just don't want to be part of any damn team. I'm different from you."

"Not so different. Not the same demon-sire, but the same breed."

"Look, this was a lovely chat. But I could use a few hours rack time before we start training again in the morning. Go get your beauty sleep."

Ryan fought the panic that brewed under his skin until Bennett finally left him in peace. For a while there, he'd been hopeful they might stand a chance of getting along. Dissent wasn't a good thing to carry into battle. Then, he'd blown it with his freak-out.

PULLING HIS BIGGEST, MOST menacing sword from under the couch, Ryan was ready for today's spar with a raging vengeance. Stalking onto the deck without a moment's hesitation, he stood in the center and waited for an acceptance of his challenge.

No sleep. Vice around his heart. He wasn't opposed to self-medicating with a little violence.

One look at the fire in his eyes, and Astrid and Bennett both bowed out from taking him on. Bennett had seen his anger brewing the night before, in his refusal to join their happy little team. Astrid was no fool. Lana seemed to consider for a moment but deferred to Vann.

Eager for a real fight, Vann pulled his monstrous broadsword from his back and flashed a more exuberant smile than Ryan had ever seen him reveal.

Standing back, sword at the ready, Vann was a panther ready to strike.

Full of impatient rage, Ryan came at him with a furious swing of his massive claymore.

Steel clashing against steel, the pair hacked and slashed and ducked and rolled.

A burning slice whipped across his chest. Looking down, Ryan saw blood seep from the wound. Grinning, he held the claymore ready to strike again. Burned like a son-of-a-bitch, but he relished in the sensation, nearly intense enough to distract him from... everything else.

Vann spared him a curious eyebrow raise but didn't slow otherwise.

Taking the offensive again, Ryan swung first, their swords sparking with a deafening resonance.

Spinning, ducking, smiles morphing into sweaty brutality, both were lost in the reckless contest.

Ryan reveled in the guts of it. Vann wasn't giving him an inch, and he was relieved.

With a stiff-legged bash to his opponent's chest, Ryan sent Vann skidding across the deck floor. Vann flipped his body, ready to run back in.

Lana held up her arms and stood between them. The two halted, breathless and bleeding and bruised. "Okay. Vann, you've had your fun. Ryan, I hope you've burned off whatever was eating at you. But, don't injure each other beyond repair. We've got work to do."

Looking around, Ryan realized a crowd had formed to watch. Still fired up, he stalked past the crew. Giving him a wide berth, they stared with worried looks. Ryan ripped off his tattered t-shirt to clean the blade with the ripped cotton and took refuge in his bunk.

POKER NIGHT WAS WAY better than this. Plotting, scheming... never Ryan's favorite part. In the rec room, he leaned back in his chair and listened to everything that went wrong when they'd last faced Typha.

Terrible conditions, yeah, he'd expected that. Rocky outcrops, fierce winds, unpredictable currents. Theoretically, no more whirlpool as he and Quinn had already taken out the kraken responsible. Flights of sharp and awkwardly angled stairs. Darkness. Finally, a vicious monster with squiddy, hydra-style arms and thighs of steel, able to speak without words. As nightmarish as one could imagine.

Deandra was a puzzle. Where was she? Nearby, as she'd been able to talk to Quinn and blast her to him via the world's longest waterspout.

"A dungeon?" Lana seemed to be reading his thoughts. Or, was it that obvious of a question?

Brow furrowed tight, Astrid was clearly figuring it out. "No... no. Nothing of our world would be able to restrain a demon of her power. That blurry wall in the far corner of the room... maybe, maybe veil material?"

"How would that be possible?" Bennett asked.

"Like a little veil bubble." Ryan said. Total Star Trek explanation, but worked for him. First comment he'd made all night. They must think him addled. "Not many can manipulate the veil, but Typha is more powerful than most."

Bennett nodded, nearly going cross-eyed as he envisioned the possibility. "In our world, but not. Obviously not in Bain's world. Not behind the veil, as Typha wouldn't let her get close enough for him to get to her. I'll bet Quinn and Deandra are both being held in veil bubbles in Typha's lair."

Vann shook his head. "Not veil, exactly, or wouldn't Bain have some control over it? Something more of Typha's creation. That awful brimstone odor, her little chemistry set in her lair, the sentinels. She's quite the inventor."

Lana grinned at him. "I miss Quinn. She'd have something snarky to add about now. Ryan, I think you're a perfect addition to the team."

Raising an eyebrow at her, his breath came rushing in and out as he felt the panic closing in. Tooth and nail, he fought to mask it with a bite-me expression. That wound Vann had torn into his chest still ached, a painful reminder that other demon hunters had the power to hurt him. "I think there's been a bit of a misunderstanding. We're together in this mission. We need each other to get Quinn back and finish the mission. But, then, that's it. I'm out."

For all her brains, Astrid seemed a little dense sometimes. "I don't understand."

"I've got a job on this boat. Other fights to fight that don't involve you and your jolly team." His knee started vibrating at a dangerously high frequency, his jaw flexing at rapid speed.

Leaning toward him, Lana tried what was clearly her winsome grin. "What about Quinn?"

"She can do whatever the fuck she wants. We can live our own lives and still be with each other." His stomach roiled, knowing he wasn't getting out of it this time.

Bennett wouldn't let him out of this room without an answer, leaning back in his chair and blocking the door. Not exactly a threat, but the subtle message was clear. "What gives? You don't have a team.

We all like you and trust you, despite my personal misgivings," he added in a poor attempt at humor. "What the hell?"

Ryan couldn't stand being backed into a corner, and he was handling it about as well as a starving grizzly at the end of winter. "I don't want to be on a damn team again, okay?"

"You had a team before?" Astrid asked, her doe eyes all sweet and innocent. *Ha*. She'd spilled a lot of blood, and he didn't believe that naiveté for a moment.

Four sets of probing eyes on him. Fuck. "Yeah, I had a team. *Had*." Shoving back in his chair, he knocked a dent in the wall behind him from the force of the movement.

Lana had just enough shared blood with Quinn to break down the last of his weakened barrier. "I'm so sorry, for what you must have gone through. What happened to them?"

"Ha. *Them*. Bigotry isn't a purely human trait. My peace-loving mother could never have prepared me for the hatred some people carry." He paused, leaning against the wall, helplessly finding himself pulled back to that awful time. "When I was old enough, Mom told me what I was. Not knowing enough, as Bain hadn't been able to tell her much before he had to cross back over, she searched until she found Greg. A decent guy, he served as my mentor. Taught me to fight, everything I'd need to know to serve the role of demon hunter. When I was ready, he introduced me to his team. Initially, they accepted me. Eager, stronger than most, I was a nice trophy for their aging team."

Ryan refused to close his eyes and wish it all away. Might as well let it all out. No other way they'd understand.

Better they heard now why they shouldn't want him either. "Always the first sent into battle. In the beginning, I'd thought it was some sort of hazing for newbies, but later, I realized I was their patsy. Barely survived some harrowing battles a new hunter should never face alone. I was too keen to prove myself, so even when I started to realize something was wrong, I kept fighting."

"Wait, Greg Wallace?" Vann asked.

Ryan nodded.

Vann leaned forward in his chair, a fierce scowl forming across his brow, his lips pulled tight. "Did you guys hear about that team? It was before I joined you. Huge team. Nasty, violent bunch. They'd been on some pretty awful missions, boasting about how they had exterminated all the vampires from Spain. They were extreme."

Nodding, Astrid said, "I remember something about that. A few of their team died suspiciously. Rumors about dissent, but nothing solid. There were a lot of other teams considering investigating, perhaps even taking them out, but I never heard what happened."

Vann looked to Ryan, a knowing dripping from his dark gaze. "I don't remember hearing anything about a new recruit. I imagine they wanted to keep you secret."

Biting the inside of his cheek, Ryan didn't disagree. "Greg didn't realize what was going on at first. He wasn't the brightest bulb. Had pretty much been retired and didn't get out much anymore. When he figured out what was going on, he tried to put an end to it. The leader of their *team* sliced his head off without hesitation. Proving a point, I suppose."

Holding his breath, Ryan fought the searing image that had been branded into his brain. No wonder Quinn passed out at the influx of such intense memories, all at once.

Leaning forward again, Bennett shook his head, his eyebrows raised in horror. "What point could they possibly have been proving, killing one of their own?"

"That any dissent would be punished. That I'd better do their bidding. And, for a short while, I did. Afraid for my life, for my mother—they'd threatened her when I tried to bail. Natural hunters, they kept a close eye on her. Somewhere along the line, they'd grown more outrageous, more cruel, no longer held back by humanity. They'd take pleasure in putting me down, calling me demon-spawn, a pariah. While they hated me, they knew I was different, stronger."

Looking around, Ryan saw the emotion behind each of their eyes. Sympathy. He had constructed some thick barriers and didn't want them to fall. Not now.

Not even Quinn knew what had happened. Why he was so angry. Would she crawl into his lap and kiss the pain away, or would she cuss and threaten in her anger?

"Did they hurt you?" Astrid asked.

"Not right away. I was too handy to have around. They'd say kill, and I'd kill. One monster bloodbath after another." He closed his eyes, reliving the nightmares that still plagued him. "One day, when the blood seemed permanently caked under my nails, I'd had enough. I took Mom, and we fled. Foolishly, I thought I could outsmart them. That they wouldn't be able to find us."

"When they did?" Bennett asked quietly, his heavy expression knowing, as if he already suspected the answer.

Ryan couldn't fight the swath of images that hammered against his aching skull. That awful night when they'd taken her after he'd gone out for supplies.

Following the precise instructions they'd left for him, he'd found Sunshine locked in the darkened basement of a dilapidated house. Her body was weak and bruised, yet her eyes shone bright with an unshakable will. "They took my demon-loving mother. Would have slaughtered her in a heartbeat, but they needed her to get to me."

When he'd found her chained to that wall, the fury that ignited within him had been foreign, almost debilitating in its intensity.

Almost.

They'd laid clever traps for him, bringing him steps away from death's door before they even had to face him.

Lana's eyes opened enough to gage his reaction. "How did you make it out?"

And here's where they'd no longer be able to look at him the same. Why he couldn't look himself in the eye without knowing what he'd done.

"They were there to finish me off. Handy as I'd been, my usefulness had run its course, and their hatred for my parentage ran too deep. Mom and I weren't getting out of there alive. Not when I knew the awful things they'd done, and would do..."

His blood-soaked cheek pasted to the floor, his limbs heavy and lifeless, he'd listened to their voices humming over the damp, stone floor, echoing from wall to wall. Admonishing him for disobeying them. Spitting at him in disgust, son of a demon.

He'd hurt so bad, death would have been a blessing. Every scrap of skin bruised deep to the muscle. Eyelids so swollen he could barely see. Ears ringing as every nerve in his body fired in alarm.

Somewhere, deep inside, he found the strength to keep going. Muscles trembling, coated in lead, at the sound of their derisive laughter, he rose to his feet.

The first that came for him assumed he'd be an easy mark, weak as he was. With a clean, swift blow, he'd snapped her neck. He could barely stand, but they'd trained him to be a proficient killer.

All eyes were wide around the table as he described the awful scene. Too wired to sit back down in his chair, yet Ryan felt the strength sapping from his limbs, the sweat beading on his brow. "I disposed of them as heartlessly and quickly as they had Greg. As they'd trained me to kill monsters. Demon hunters are damn tough. But as they'd shown me with Greg... demon hunters aren't hard to kill if you know what you're doing."

Vann's expression was grave, his deep voice hoarse as he asked, "How many?"

"Fifteen."

Long pause.

"Trust me, it's mutual. I don't want another team, and you don't want me."

Lana looked up at him, not bothering to wipe away the tears that streamed down her cheeks. "Thank you, Ryan, for sharing this with us. I'm so, so sorry that you had to go through that. I understand why you don't trust. I can't say that I would either, and I like most everyone. Please, give us a chance." She rose from her seat and pulled him in for a hug, squeezing him tight. "Does Sunshine like Quinn?"

Astonished by his future cousin, as usual, he found himself gratefully hugging her right back. "Yeah. They hit it off right away."

"Think she'd like me?"

Heart slowing to a steady pace in his chest, he nodded. "Yeah. She'd like you a lot." Taking in a deep breath, he exhaled as the tension under his sternum eased. "She'd like all of you."

Pulling back, Lana grinned up at him. "How about you let her meet us, then you decide if you want to keep us around?"

Fuck. "Okay."

Bennett stood and offered his hand. Accepting with a firm grip, Ryan felt the burden on his soul growing lighter. "Tell you what. We were planning a little get together at my place in BC, when Quinn's and my parents are back in the country. Honestly, I'd hoped it would be to celebrate Quinn and my engagement and Typha's defeat. But, let's just hang out. Our families, you and your mom, Quinn. And Seven."

Finding his first genuine laugh since Quinn had been taken, he let the acceptance wash over him. Voice thick with emotion, gravel came out when he said with a rusty laugh. "Quinn will kick your ass if she hears you calling our baby Seven."

23

A Veil Bubble, Typha's Lair.

QUINN INHALED IN PROTECTIVELY shallow breaths to minimize burn of the noxious mixture that saturated the air. Brimstone. Ugh.

Every limb ached, numb and on fire from the poison of her captors' teeth. A few lacerations were still healing, but the bulk of them had faded while she slept, no more than stings where the poison had seeped under her skin.

Lying on her abdomen, her face plastered against the damp floor, she scoped out her surroundings. Black rock floor and walls. Soft blue light shining in through moonlit swiss-cheese holes in the ceiling. The eerie pall was suffocating.

A trio of the three-headed, twitchy-tailed monsters were snoozing nearby. Wow, they smelled even worse than the brimstone. Like rotten tar, if that was even a thing. Sorry threat that she was, apparently, they didn't seem to be afraid that she may sneak away while they slept.

From afar, a banshee-on-crack shriek pierced into her brain. Quinn flinched at the familiar sound, unable to uselessly cover her ears for the bindings that held her in place.

Hazy. Here, but, not, Typha's multi-armed form seemed to be toiling over a cauldron big enough to take a swim in.

What the fuck? She was even less human-looking now, with bulki-er, more threatening razer-sharp arms. Her dark hair flew wildly over her shoulders from a wind that spun around her. Clearly, it hadn't just been the creatures she had been experimenting with. Had she once been as humanoid as Deandra and Bain?

Rolling to sneak away, in the direction opposite her captors, she struck a nearly imperceptible, curved sort of wall. Sticky without residue, it was like a... a slime bubble surrounding her, yet hard as stone.

Shit, she was on the other side of the veil. No, not quite. She couldn't cross even if she wanted to. Humans, and even hybrids, wouldn't be able to survive on the other side. Just a wall of veil, like the odd-looking wall in Typha's lair that she'd seen before.

Lovely. Trapped in a veil-walled prison with three smelly creatures to keep her company. She supposed she ought to feel flattered that Typha found her threatening enough to need a prison cell and three guards. At least she was alive, unharmed, and her guards seemed dis-interested.

Holding her incarcerated hands over her abdomen, she felt a hint of flutter from Seven. No, dammit, she wasn't naming her baby after a number. Couldn't even be the size of a peanut yet, but something about this place, or the vile company, stirred a powerful reaction from them both.

The sulfuric scent worsened as she breathed more rapidly, fighting the amplifying fear for her child and for Ryan.

Knowing there was no physical escape from her nasty bubble of a prison, she closed her eyes and searched for the lightness that she'd felt when Deandra spoke to her before.

"Please, Deandra, I need you. I'm here." She tried to project her thoughts into her ancestor's mind as Deandra had done to her before.

Felt bizarre trying, knowing she looked ridiculous, but she was out of options.

"You're safe, for now." The serene voice hummed like a lullaby in her skull.

"I don't feel very safe." The trio was starting to stir.

Maternally, Deandra reassured her. *"She needs you alive, for now."*

For now. Again. Her answers weren't very definitive. *"She's waiting for Ryan, isn't she? Knows he'll come for me."*

"Yes." Deandra's voice was sad, but not regretful. *"He carries Bain's same power over the veil. She could drive him to break down the veil entirely."*

"Why did she only take me then? Why not Ryan?"

"She's tried. He's never alone."

Quinn sighed a breath of relief. Of gratitude her friends not only accepted him but safeguarded him as one of their own. She knew he didn't want a team, but they were a tenacious bunch and would break through those rigid barriers he'd constructed around himself.

"Besides, her best shot at tearing down the veil is to shatter his heart."

Great. She was to be a sacrifice. So, all she really had to do to at least prevent the veil from shattering was to stay alive. No problem. *"Tell me how to get out of here. I'll run. We'll stay away so she can't get to him."*

"Nice try. First, you're as stuck in your little bubble as I am in mine. Typha's strength lies here, at the heart of the tear. She's been widening the tear the last few months as she grows more powerful, sapping strength from Bain, her brother, and..." Deandra trailed off.

"What's wrong?" Quinn struggled to make sense of it all. If Typha drew strength from the other side, from Bain, what if she could draw strength from Ryan? Was it a genetic thing or a royal thing? *"It's Ryan, isn't it? She's growing so much stronger because of his proximity?"*

"Yes."

"What about Seven?"

"Some. For now, Seven is well protected inside of you."

Quinn breathed a sigh of relief, instinctively covering her abdomen and the life that was stirring inside her.

"She's been building an army. These are but three of her progenies. If the barrier were to release completely, she could overrun this realm in a day." Great, more bad news. At least her voice softened and sounded apologetic.

"Can't she just call more demons across, as she's been doing?"

"That's not her drawing them across, it's the tear growing wider as she grows stronger. Besides, Typha is no more accepted on the other side than she is here. Like Superman on Krypton, she's nothing special. That being said, there are many that would happily join forces with her to take over your world."

Quinn had to stop herself before she laughed out loud and attracted attention from the troublesome trio. *"Nice pop culture reference. How...?"*

She could hear the smile in Deandra's lyrical voice. *"Things get boring around here, so I channel satellites."*

"Deandra? How do we seal the tear in the veil?"

Long pause. Not good when a multi-millennia-aged demon has to stop and think. Or it's really bad news. *"I don't know."*

Yep. Shit. *"Any ideas? You've had a lot of time to think about it."*

"I've hundreds of theories, but only Dr. Strange would be able to see the correct path for sure."

"Wow, you are a serious superhero fan. Must be in the DNA." Funny, but the silly connection seemed to make Deandra that much more real, that much more hers.

"I'm particularly fond of Thor." Deandra almost sounded a little dreamy.

"Really? I'm more of a Captain America fan."

"Makes sense." Deandra's heartfelt laughter was more reassuring than any promise she could have given.

"Bain tried to create the portal for you. You must have some power, at least over the tear?"

"I've tried to seal it from this end, pushing out from within. But I can't close it."

Quinn remembered the prickling sensation from when the nasty sentinels had ripped her through with them. Like getting sucked into a vacuum, surrounded by static. Only the doorway would respond to her control, not the veil itself.

But if Bain's blood could... She held her hands over her abdomen. "Okay, little one. We've got some serious work to do."

From deep within, closing her eyes, Quinn pulled at the veil with the prickles she'd felt before. A strength, a fluttering stirred deep inside her.

The air crackled around her, static electricity ready to arc. A gleaming silvery doorway glowed in her mind, but she couldn't seem to get close enough to change it, now was she foolish enough to try to pass through it.

She shifted her focus, tracing the edges of the door with her mind. Drawing on the same, prickling sensation, her head pounding with a crushing focus, she focused. Something. Nothing. She kept at it, again and again, until her head throbbed, but eventually, she felt a subtle vibration, and she could almost touch the door.

The tearful hope in Deandra's voice trembled. *"We have time. Keep practicing."*

Quinn pushed as hard as she could, until her muscles ached from exertion and gave out on her.

Valkyrie, Gulf of Alaska.

"ANYTHING?" RYAN DIDN'T JUMP at the sound of Vann approaching silently behind him, but he nearly did. Guy was a deadly quiet menace.

Hours. He'd spent hours upon hours staring at maps, radar, incident reports, and the bottom of his empty coffee cup, for clues as to how to approach the mysterious island without being detected. He was damn sick of the bridge for the first time in his career.

"Nothing. No way she won't see us coming. How did you guys even find her in the first place?" Ryan shook his head and ran his hand over his short hair. "There's been no activity anywhere near Zhemchug in months."

Nodding, Vann pointed to the map that the Valkyrie crew used to mark demon activity. "Exactly. Astrid figured it out. October before last, there was this bizarre storm surrounding the Aleutians."

"I remember that. Lightning without thunder, waves running opposite the wind. We were pulled away for rescue ops. I looked over the data later and couldn't find any sightings, no unusual stories from the ships we rescued. Of course, aside from the bizarreness of the storm."

Both stared at the map, recollecting the awful week while the storm raged. Ryan had suspected something was up but hadn't been able to pinpoint anything.

"No demon activity for days prior and none for days after it ended. We'd called other teams we occasionally coordinate with, and they'd had oddly restful times as well. So, we suspected something was up. There are a handful of stories of similar activity in the last thousand years, all mentioning Typha making a move, in some form or another."

"Why then? Why not wait until after Seven came into existence? Or, why not do something when I was born? Timing was a little odd for her to mobilize." Night after night, Ryan asked himself these questions. Maybe having a team wouldn't be so bad, others to help solve the mysteries he couldn't answer himself.

From the helm, Manuel glanced at him and lowered his eyebrows. "A few weeks before that storm... remember how busy we were? The Valkyrie's first weeks at sea were intense. Maybe something in the veil was, I don't know, broken."

Smiling, Ryan nodded. He had a hell of a team already.

A scowl heavy in his brow, Vann scoured the map again. "Mind?" he nodded to the computer.

Ryan shook his head and shrugged, giving Vann his seat.

Frantically typing and pulling up various programs, Vann looked to be in a trance. "Look at the currents over the past year. The shifting groundfish hot spots."

"Yeah, we've been chalking it up to global warming."

"Maybe. All the increased activity has been radiating from Zhemchug Canyon, a pretty damn big scar on our planet. No doubt, this must be the location of the rift your father made."

Ryan moved closer to the window, staring into the lifeless gray water and grayer sky. "Makes sense. Typha's holding Deandra at the door. She must be trying to break it open. I'll bet the increased activity that started a year ago was when Typha awakened. So, why then? What woke her?"

Turning, he saw Willa at the top of the stairs to the bridge. Face grim, she'd clearly been listening for a while. "You did."

"What?" Ryan felt a sinking sensation deep in his gut as searing acid eroded into his soul.

"This was your first assignment in the area. I was surprised at how crazy things were all around Alaska when we started. At the time, I'd thought it was just that we were paying more attention."

Vann's face dropped as he nodded in agreement. "Your connection to Bain and the other side. Isn't he the demon king? The source of strength and life for demon-kind? Bet she reaps strength from him... and from you."

Fuck. Ryan felt all eyes on him. There was that fear he'd seen too many times. From his first team.

Without a word, hating himself more than a little, he took off. Brushed past Willa at the top of the stairs. He nearly stomped down the stairs and into his room, but heard Sunshine's voice echoing in his head. *You can stomp all you want. But, will that make your anger fade? Will that make the situation any better?*

Closing himself in his quarters, he tried to block out the memories. Erase the faces of his team, the pure hatred and disgust as they locked him in chains in the dungeon they'd built to torture demons. Wipe out the smell of blood, first on his own wrists as he struggled to break free of the chains, and then on his hands as he destroyed every last one of them. The sadness on his mother's face when she accepted the inevitable violence, or risk losing her son.

Breathing slow and steady, pulling in every last molecule of oxygen from the air to fill his swollen lungs, he stood helplessly in the center of his room.

Quinn. She needed him, but he couldn't go near her. His proximity was already putting her in danger.

As memories of the last few months flashed into his mind and dug in deep, he felt his knees weaken and his muscles grow heavy with worry. Fate, destiny, genetics, coincidence... whatever bullshit had brought them together was going to tear them apart.

Bitch of it was, Quinn would be able to make all of this ok. Would make him laugh it off with a clever quip. Kiss his worries away.

Crackling, static electricity in the air around him interrupted his remorseful deliberations. Suddenly his room was overcrowded with massive creatures like the one on deck that day, like those that had taken Quinn.

Nine heads nipped at him. Sharp flippers sliced into him.

Swinging his fists, his feet, he fought back with everything he had. Standing room only, and he was grossly outnumbered.

Risking the inevitable gashes from its sharp teeth, he wrapped his arm around the three heads of the nearest one. He wrenched his arm tight and felt a trio of snaps that ricocheted through him like the crashing of trees falling in the forest, knocking down the limbs of the next tree on the way down.

Still in his clutches, he swung himself over the monster's body to gain some distance from the others.

Dropping into a low squat, he flipped open the couch and pulled out the nearest handle he could reach before they pulled at him again. An axe.

Coming up swinging, he sliced into the nearest piece of flesh. Tough *not* to hit something in such tight quarters. On impact, black goo blasted from the arm of the nearest of them.

Vibrating into his veins, he felt an electricity trying to pull him out of this world as they grabbed at him.

The door swung open. Knowing he wasn't going to win this one, blood seeping from a couple dozen poisoned bite wounds and lacerations, arm hanging limply at his side where one of the flippers had dislocated his shoulder, he tossed the axe across to Vann.

Furious, Vann downed the remaining monsters.

The axe was embedding into the chest of the third monster, its black blood oozing out as Ryan's vision darkened.

Nausea pumped through him.

His limbs heavy, filled with lead.

He forced air in and out of his lungs, struggling to stay conscious.

Too late. Too much blood lost. Venom from the bites burned into his flesh.

His eyes rolled back, and the world faded in starless night.

SLOWLY, BLINKING, THE DIM lights of the infirmary piercing his throbbing skull, Ryan remembered the attack.

Bolting up on the bed, he threw his legs over and fought a surge of dizziness, steadying himself with both hands gripping onto the edge of the mattress.

"Whoa, cowboy. Sit back down. You lost a lot of blood. Plus, I think those teeth were venomous." Lana stood and held her arms ready to catch him in case he collapsed. She looked awful. Hair wild, clothes disheveled, eyes heavy with fatigue.

"How long was I out?" His voice was hoarse, his throat parched. Must have been a while.

"Thirteen hours. The bites, you should have recovered from those within an hour. I'm guessing there was a little more to it. Took a few hours to even get the bleeding to stop."

Once he leaned back and sat on the side of the bed, she plopped back on her chair. Same chair he'd been in a few months back. Quinn holding tight onto the blanket, fiercely calling him on his bullshit while she struggled to remember who she was.

"More than that. I could feel a strange pulling sensation. Think they were trying to take me into the veil like they did with Quinn." He glanced around the room. Must be the middle of the night, maybe later, given the lack of noise outside, aside from the hum of the ship. "Bodyguard?" he asked.

"You got it big guy. None of us is to go anywhere alone anymore. Especially you."

"Figures." He stared up at the ceiling, studying the painted cracks, covering old layers of paint.

Why? He'd already done his job in giving her strength, maybe helping her to widen the tear, albeit unwittingly. Now, Typha had Seven, the blend of Deandra and Bain, and should be able to tear down the barrier, shouldn't she? Or was it something else she needed?

Typha was siphoning power from Bain. From Ryan. Bain was able to control the veil as its protector. Ryan must have some power over it as well. No wonder Bain couldn't go for Deandra directly. Typha held what Ryan loved most, held his heart and soul in her clutches. If he lost control...

Fucking poet inside him was turning very, very dark. No more sonnets.

Rising from the bed, he stalked toward the door on wobbly legs, the lightheadedness threatening to drop him.

He was the final piece of her plan. Typha wasn't looking for a key to cross the veil freely. She'd already been using his strength to slowly widen it. No, she wanted him to shatter it for her.

Nearly to the door, he tried to ignore the dark curtain closing over his vision. Losing the uphill battle, he held onto the door to wait for the dizziness to pass.

Lana chased him down and held him by the arm before he collapsed. "Wait. Harry will be back to check on you shortly."

"It's not Seven or Quinn she's after. She already has Deandra, now Quinn and Seven, and their connection to the doorway. Typha needs me to tear down the barrier for her. She's already got my heart in her grasp. Crush it, and I'll blast a massive rift in the barrier that won't be recovered."

"What are you going to do?"

"I'll figure it out." He shook her off and stumbled forward.

"Ryan, stop. You're not well enough yet."

Stopping in the hallway, he looked down at his black, festering wounds. The bleeding had stopped, but he still looked like he'd been run through a damn meat grinder. "I'll get an hour or two of rack time, then I'm out of here." Ignoring the sensation that he was about to pass out, holding onto the walls, he hobbled back to his room. Spotlessly clean, someone must have spent hours cleaning the last traces of those damn sentinels for him.

24

Valkyrie. Twenty-Four Hours from Zhemchug Canyon.

As the seas boiled, the ship spun a cluster of three-sixties. Ryan bolted up from restless sleep, cracking his head on the ceiling of his bunk with a sharp, throbbing whack. Been a while since he'd done that.

Sleep deprivation was a bitch. He knew he needed the sleep to fully heal, or he'd be useless, but it hadn't come easily. Rolling out of bed, he nearly forgot about his bodyguard.

Vann was sitting on the couch, tying his boots. "Morning."

He spared Ryan a glance before finishing his preparations. Adjusting for the to and fro sway of the ship, he hardly seemed to notice the rocking. "Typha isn't laying out the welcome mat for us this time. We're about a day out, and she's already sending everything she's got."

"Rough entry last time?"

"Actually, not really. We thought it was because she wasn't expecting us. Nope, I suspect she might actually be afraid this time." His voice nonchalant, as usual. Vann didn't appear to ever get worked up about anything.

"Or she wants us to think she is." Ryan rubbed a sleepy hand through his hair and headed into the bathroom. While he meticulously brushed his teeth, he calculated. The team wouldn't be pleased with his plan.

After an efficient shower, he pulled on the cargos he'd brought in with him and headed out to let Vann have a turn in the bathroom. His shirt collection was significantly reduced, as several were still packed with Quinn's things, and the rest had been shredded or tarred.

With a half-assed knock, Bennett swung open the door and entered without a welcome. Not that he would have refused him. He didn't mind him so much anymore. He'd been glad to have someone nearly as desperate to get to Quinn.

Pulling his t-shirt over his head, Ryan grabbed his boots and parked on the couch. Bennett dropped down next to him and nodded at the laceration over Ryan's right eyebrow. "You've had a lousy time of it lately."

Ryan almost felt a bubble of a laugh pushing at his ribs, but that might have been fear. "That's putting it mildly."

"Sorry, man. Really." Bennett leaned back on the couch and scrubbed a hand over his face. Taking a breath, he looked Ryan in the eye, a fire in there Ryan hadn't seen before. "What can I do?"

"That stupid prophecy. It's not just about me, about Quinn, or about Seven. None of us will be there to challenge Typha."

A look of betrayal flashed across Bennett's face. For all that the guy wanted to be the one to be the heart of the prophecy and take out Typha, he wasn't pleased to hear that he had a starring role after all. "Of course you will. Quinn and Seven are right in the middle of it as we speak. Can't imagine you'll turn tail and run away now. I know you think you'll shatter the veil if something happens to them, so we'll do whatever it takes to keep them safe. You're tough, but if it's looking like you're about to flip out and break everything, you'd better believe I'll take you out myself."

The boat rolled with a massive wave that struck the side. "Damn right you will. I'm not running away. Nor will I be with you to take on Typha. Let's just say I'll be taking the back door to get to Quinn while you go straight for Typha."

"How are you going to manage that?"

"Hop up." Ryan nudged Bennett out of the way. Pulling out his favorite great-sword, he adjusted his grip before lowering it to his side. Maybe he'd have to get a cool vest with a sheath like Quinn had. "When the disgusting three-headed things were trying to take me, I felt a weird, almost familiar pull. Last night, I figured out what I have to do. I'll meet you in Typha's lair. Trick is, I can't go near her until you've weakened her substantially. So, get it done."

"Wait." Bennett stopped him as he headed for the door. "Last time we had five and got our asses handed to us. We need you in the fight."

"No, you don't. You've got everything you need. She's just a monster. But, she's a monster that feeds off of *me*. Take me out of the picture, and the four of you can take her like any other demon."

With a curt nod as he came out of the bathroom, Vann agreed. "I'm not sure it will be so easy, but you're right, you can't just walk in the front door."

Dashing out to the deck, Ryan found Willa coming down from the bridge. "We're a long way off still. Why are you all decked out with your finest steel?" Her voice light, Willa seemed to be teasing. Ryan knew better. She was worried.

He quickly explained his plan. "There will be a lot of those nasty three-headed sentinels as you get closer. I suspect she's been spawning them by the dozen. None can get past the Valkyrie."

"We're on it. Harry was up all night studying the things. Three hydra heads. One heart. After the kraken, we're as heavily armed as I could make us." She crossed to the deck and stood back to give him space. "You be careful."

Ryan shrugged and raised an eyebrow. *Careful* was a rather poor word to choose. He had no intention of being careful. Losing wasn't an option.

Standing in the middle of the deck, Ryan closed his eyes and slowed his breathing, letting the zapping pull percolate through him. Pins and needles pricked every follicle on his skin. Focusing, imagining his father, he let the thick, invisible fog coat his body.

Choking, gagging, he inhaled the heavy, viscous air as he was pulled beyond the barrier and into the realm of demons.

Veil Bubble, Typha's Lair.

RAISING HER HEAVY LIDS, Quinn blinked away the dregs of sleep. Testing the walls, bringing up the door in her mind over and over until it became real, combing her power with Seven's, she had been wiped out.

It wasn't enough, but now she was getting there.

"Is it time yet? They should be here by now." Long-ass wait for the troops to arrive.

"Soon."

Settling in for yet another day of nothing, Quinn sat up and pulled her knees in to rest her chin. At least for this long chain of boredom she had memories to reflect on. Some damn good ones.

"Why me?" Quinn finally went right to the source on the question that had been plaguing her since her memories came back. Since Ryan made it very clear he'd have fallen for her without the prophecy.

"Lucky guess." Deandra's soothing soprano lilted in amusement. That woman, demon, whatever, had an absurd sense of humor.

At least Quinn knew where she got it now. *"Guess? Care to elaborate on that one?"*

"I had a one in three chance."

Chuckling softly to avoid attracting attention, Quinn rolled her eyes. Yeah, all this was foretold. Whatever. But... for a destined-to-save-the-world demon hunter, she was beyond happy to hear there was a measure of good old-fashioned luck and lust that hadn't been predestined.

"It's time." Deandra's voice sang into Quinn's imagination.

Slowly sitting up, she feigned resting her hands on her ankles until her guards ignored her again.

Working at the binding, she easily loosened the rope.

Morons can't possibly have intended to hold her seriously with the half-assed wrappings. Typha must have been cranking these creepy things out so fast, she forgot to give them brains or even teach them anything. Temporarily dislocating her thumbs, she managed to wiggle her hands out of the tight wrist cuffs.

Creepo number one turned toward her as she freed her arms and legs. Smiling, Quinn rose slowly and cricked her finger, taunting it to come after her.

Knife-edged arms wind-milling at her, heads bobbing with teeth gnashing, it lunged for her.

Ducking, she blasted her foot at it with a forceful kick.

It recoiled but didn't fall. Asshole was tough.

Intensifying her kicks, she struggled to pummel the thing in the chest. The others started to come at her, helping the first.

Dammit, she really didn't have time to get her ass kicked today.

Knowing better than to let one lose a head, she looped her arm around one of its necks and swung her body around to grab all three. With a flex of her elbow and wrenching it with every ounce of strength, she snapped all three necks at once.

Crumbling, the beast hit the dull floor with a muted thud.

Air crackling around her, the other two came at her more fiercely, and two more appeared behind them. Crap.

Lesson learned.

She dodged and ducked and rolled and tangled them in a mess with each other.

Using a similar strategy, she hooked her arm around a trio of necks again and tangled them, bending in just a way that they didn't snap, merely maim, she took down a second.

No crackling this time. Phew. Just be careful to not kill any, or this could go on until they were nose to nose, standing room only.

Sustaining only a few nasty bruises and a small laceration, she managed to disable the remaining two. Her arm burned where the teeth had cut her skin. Shaking her arm, she managed to return sensation into it. Lucky it wasn't bad. Much deeper and her whole arm would be useless, maybe worse.

With all the power she'd been able to draw from Seven, she couldn't overcome her damn prison walls. *"Deandra? Is there a door around here somewhere?"*

Again, using the power over the veil she'd been practicing, she pushed at the edges of the bubble. Nothing. Sadly, her power didn't seem to extend beyond Deandra's portal.

"Just sit tight. It will open soon enough."

"Come on, there must be some way to get out of here."

A muted thundering of footsteps, then snarky voices, rattled the translucent walls of her veil bubble.

Heart pounding in a frightening combination of terror and relief, Quinn watched as her team entered Typha's lonely throne room. Swords, axes, and maces drawn, the other four swaggered closer.

Shrill laughter bounced off the walls as Typha rose up the opposite stairs to greet them. They didn't even flinch at the ear-splitting sound.

They were prepared this time.

Wait... *"Where's Ryan?"*

"He's in the realm of demons."

"No, no, no. Why would he do something so foolish? Humans can't survive it, not even hybrids." Quinn desperately searched the freaky bubble for a door, a weak spot she may have missed before, anything she could use to get out.

Confidently, Deandra both reassured and worried her more. *"As Bain's son, he can. Bain protects not only his realm, but the veil itself. That's how he was able to create the door in the veil for me. All of his blood share this power."*

The Other Side.

BARELY HOLDING HIMSELF UP on all fours, Ryan fought against the heaviness of the atmosphere. Nausea washed over him. He tasted bile in his mouth as he adjusted to the dense air around him. He struggled to open his eyes.

"It's okay. You found me." Standing above him was a tall, graceful yet rugged man with features remarkably similar to his own.

Kneeling at Ryan's side, Bain looped his heavily muscled arm around Ryan's torso and tenderly pulled him to his feet. Shaking off the delirium that still coated him like a sticky layer of cheap maple syrup, Ryan struggled to concentrate. "Quinn. I need to get to Quinn. And Seven."

"You will. First, I have something for you." His father's gaze was remarkably soft for such a fierce looking demon. Very human in appearance, his charcoal black eyes and sharp features showed his inhumanity. Yet, he smiled. "You look so like your mother. How is Sunshine?"

Brow furrowed, Ryan managed to find his sea legs and stood tall. "She's good. Quinn?" he asked.

As he adjusted to the difference in gravity, in oxygen levels, he felt the urgency of getting to Quinn overwhelming everything else.

"We have time. I'm watching. She's ok."

In Ryan's mind, a heartrending yet reassuring vision of Quinn in a dark bubble covered his vision. *Swinging her body around one of the nasty three-headed monsters, she choked it until it collapsed beneath her, landing next to a pile of their bodies. Brushing her hands of them, she looked around for an escape.*

As much as Ryan felt relief at knowing Quinn was ok, he could also feel something else. Whether it was Bain or being in the realm of his ancestors, he wasn't sure. Feeling the nearby inhabitants of the realm, perhaps, he acutely felt the blood that had spilled because of him, first as a young demon hunter out to prove himself, then to stay alive, and now because he had selfishly fallen in love. The guilt, the ache, throbbed in his skull.

Bain sensed his grief, and Ryan felt his father taking some of the pain and fear to share the weight of it. "I've made a lot of mistakes. You were not one of them."

Gradually, Ryan's vision adapted to his surroundings. Above them stood a great tree with a white trunk and burgundy leaves, amber sunlight dappling through the soft canopy. A warm breeze fingered through the silvery grass of the surrounding field, tickling his nose with the familiar, welcoming scent of summer coming.

Lungs filling with the buoyancy of relief, shoulders feeling increasingly unburdened, he stood tall. At his full height, he stood a good head shorter than his massive father.

Reaching over, Bain rested his hand on Ryan's shoulder, his smile pained, regretful. "I wish I could have come to see you."

"Why didn't you?" Ryan found himself asking, even though he knew the answer. He suddenly felt like the angsty youth that had raged at the injustice when he'd been told of his parentage.

Bain's eyes were as dark as the night sky, yet warm with the affection Ryan had always craved. "Crossing once was dangerous enough. Sunshine's brightness was so much the opposite of Typha, her strength beyond most humans, that I knew the trip was worth the risk. I'd hoped to stay long enough to at least see your birth, but Typha sensed my presence. I'm so sorry I wasn't there to protect you." A thick teardrop trailed down his father's angular cheek.

Nodding, Ryan started to wish he could stay longer. "Me too. I won't pretend I don't understand why you couldn't be there."

"I wish you could stay. So I could show you where you come from. So we could get to know each other. But you are needed on the other side. My granddaughter will need her father."

"Daughter?" Ryan felt a fluttering in his chest, the distant life of his unborn child.

Bain smiled down at him but didn't expound.

"Have they defeated Typha yet? I cannot risk her gaining strength from me. Or, worse, manipulating me into shattering the veil entirely." He searched the horizon for clues, but he may as well be on Antarctica for how far he was from the fight.

"They cannot. It is for you to do. She is my sister. Or, was, anyway. She's changed herself so much in her attempts to gain power. Immortal and stronger than even the fiercest demon hunters. Angrier as well, as she never forgave our father for selecting me as his successor." Bain sighed gravely. "My father was as foolish as I. In his attempts to prevent her from harming me, he bound her power to mine. As my son, you carry this burden as well."

"He was trying to make her want you to stay alive, to depend on you, wasn't he?"

"Yes. I almost wonder if he was protecting her as well. Despite her faults, she was his child as well. She grows stronger because of me, but she also cannot be killed by any but my blood. Banishing her had seemed the safest path for the realm, but I underestimated her."

"But, Seven? Will she not make Typha stronger as well?"

A mysterious smile brightened his sharp features. "Not exactly. Deandra is one of the most potent warriors our realm has ever known. Seven is so well balanced with the power she inherited from Deandra and me both, and her humanity of course, she is already repelling Typha's attempts to siphon her strength." Ryan couldn't help the tug of pride for his peanut-sized daughter already.

His father rested his hand on Ryan's shoulder. The gentle breeze picked up, gusting through the sturdy branches above. At first, the radiating heat from Bain's touch felt heavy, like Ryan had just finished an eight-hour training session. The sensation progressed to a rush through his veins, expanding in his limbs as everything about him became more powerful. Even his mind felt sharper.

What little color lie in Bain's face drained from his cheeks before he disconnected. "I can only hope this extra power I have given you is enough to defeat her."

Appearing from thin air, Bain pulled out a massive broadsword, much like the one Ryan still held. The blade was an unearthly black and its handle a simple, yet elegantly knotted pattern, silver laced with black. Bain extended the weapon to Ryan. "Trade you."

Accepting it, inherently knowing it was critical to winning the fight, Ryan didn't hesitate. Testing its weight, its balance, he discovered it to be remarkably light and perfectly balanced.

"I had it made for you. Imbued with the darkness of our realm, it is the only weapon that can kill Typha. With this, and the strength you have gained from coming home today, you will be able to defeat her."

Holding the powerful weapon, he felt hope. Despite it, he couldn't help but regret this gift from his father meant spilling more blood. He accepted his destiny was to defend humanity, but he eternally regretted the lives he had taken because of it.

Bain stepped into the sunlight, beckoning Ryan to follow. At his father's side, he walked through the soft grass, the orange sun warming his skin. "You know why I chose Sunshine to be your mother. She is passionate and loving and has so much respect for life and freedom. *You* are the best of both of us. A warrior and pacifist both. Yes, too much blood has been spilled because of *me*. You are the balance our worlds need. Be the demon hunter you were born to be, to protect your world and mine." Bain looked down at him with the paternal pride he'd always longed for, a flash of gold in his gaze as the light caught his eye. "You are already famous here, the prince that spares and sends back our lost, innocent souls, while taking down those bent on destruction. Be the man you *are*."

His mind becoming clearer, his body no longer weighed down by the heavy gravity, he could feel Quinn waiting for him.

"How will we heal the tear? Is it Seven?"

"Quinn's on it. You focus on Typha. Eliminating you is her only chance to survive. Your friends should have her weakened, so you can get close enough to drive this into her heart. Tell Deandra, I'll be waiting for her."

Ryan stared up at his demon father. For a brief moment, he allowed himself to imagine how life would have been different if Bain had been able to stay with Sunshine and raise him. Train him to be the warrior he was born to be, but teach him temperance as well. How different his life might have been. Smiling knowingly, Bain stepped back and folded his hands casually behind his back.

Closing his eyes, Ryan imagined the sweet, salty taste of Quinn's skin against his lips, the feel of her hand in his. Again, he felt the prickling dance across his skin. Finally, the pull dragged him across the veil.

25

Typha's Lair.

POUNDING AT THE STICKY walls of her bubble, Quinn tried to get to her team.

Typha swung one of her many arms in a violent loop and knocked into Astrid like a rocket-propelled bowling ball across the room and into the far rock wall.

"I need to get to them. You promised I'd be able to cross when the time was right. The time is now.*"* She pleaded with Deandra, her fists bruised from trying to break through the barrier.

"I said the door would open when the time was right. When Typha is too weak to hold us here. We are equally trapped until it does." At least Deandra had the courtesy to sound apologetic. Not that it was her fault.

"Then send them away like you blasted me through the damn skylight." Quinn dropped to her knees and rested her forehead against the barrier.

"No need. Typha thinks she's winning."

"Isn't she?" She challenged, furious at the blood already spilled. Her team was tough, they weren't nearly out of the fight yet. But, she couldn't help but relive their last visit to Typha's island.

"They can hear me, now that I want them to. They are mine, as you are. You know your friends. Look closer."

Bennett's shield was lowered as one of Typha's blunted fists swung at him. He hesitated, so incredibly unlike him. The force of her blow knocked him back half the length of the great hall.

Lana hadn't even touched her throwing knives yet.

Vann lie on the ground helplessly, but seemed to sense her watching and the corner of his mouth raised in a humorous taunt.

Diving back into the fight, Astrid was moving at half her normal lightning speed.

"They're wearing her out before making their final push. We used the same strategy against the Yeti last year. How is she not as strong as before? I have no doubt they trained hard these past few months, but she's struggling this time." Quinn could hardly believe the difference.

"Multifactorial. Without Ryan's presence making her stronger, she's not so menacing. They have a solid plan. Rather than attacking her full out, as you said, they're tiring her out first. Plus..." Deandra's soft voice wavered, like she was growing dizzy from exertion.

Pumping through Quinn's veins, she felt a buzzing strength channeling into her body and mind. Like when she'd taken on the demon hunter power when she turned eighteen, she felt the power changing her down to the DNA. *"What are you doing?"* she asked her ancestor.

"Sharing my power. I'm not leaving anything to chance. Now each of you carries enough to weaken her."

"Why didn't you do that before?"

"One, it wasn't the right time. Two, I needed that strength to send you to Ryan." Deandra's voice wavered, barely above a whisper.

"Are you okay?"

A weak chuckle echoed in her ears. *"Great. Just a little tired. Not easy passing so much to so many. I'll be fine after a little rest."* Quinn heard a yawn echo in her mind. *"Be ready. It's almost time."*

Limping pathetically unnaturally, her team surrounded Typha again.

Typha panted with exhaustion. Her moves were slower than before, her swings less powerful.

Quinn felt the wall under her hands softening, almost squishy to the touch.

A fierce grin tugged at Vann's lips. Lana's hip was cocked out, and she raised her eyebrows confidently. Astrid held steady. Bennett cinched his shield and raised it high, ready.

Synchronously, they moved at the demon. They could handle the bumps and bruises, even a fractured limb or two. Good strategy. Slashing, kicking, beating her down until she could hardly stand.

As Typha squealed in pain, Quinn paced behind her prison walls. A butterfly sensation tickled in her belly, as the peanut inside her seemed to gain strength, perhaps Deandra's power imbuing the little one as well? Whatever it was, Quinn held steady. Waiting. Ready.

Squish turned into thin air. Salty wind rushed over her skin, filling her lungs with energy. Loud and clear, she heard her team growling and joking as they attacked.

Free of her prison, she glanced around for a weapon. At her feet, her twin swords waited on the ground in front of her, left behind when she'd dropped them last time she was here.

Adrenaline, thrill, anger pumping through her veins, Quinn sprinted at Typha from behind, joining her friends in a pentagon surrounding the beast. With a spinning swipe, she slashed a foot-long gouge across Typha's thick spine.

With a shrill gasp of pain, Typha whipped her head around and lunged for Quinn.

Dodging, Quinn slashed a gouge into the nearest sword-like arm before it slashed her, the blades of her arms coated with a black, sticky tar like her minions.

Remembering the burning poison, Quinn kept her distance.

As a unit, the team brought Typha to her knees.

Still, the monster kept fighting. Her chest impenetrable, any sword that dared to try recoiled back. Weak, barely standing, but she just wouldn't die.

A raging shriek brought rocks down from the ceiling. Quinn felt a pressure in her chest as Typha pulled at her with an angry vengeance, like an iron vice tightening around her lungs.

With a battle cry vibrating from deep within, Quinn tore into Typha with everything she had.

The pressure moved down, surrounding Seven. Lips pulled tight, Quinn felt a savage sneer tighten her expression.

Her team seemed to sense her anguish, her resolve that they were walking away from this one victorious. Fighting with the renewed energy that comes from desperation, they drove at her as a unit.

Knives flying through the air, axes swinging, swords clashing.

They weren't losing today.

Collapsing to the floor, arms drooping as if filled with lead, Typha struggled to catch her breath.

Never-ending fight. Nothing they could do to destroy her completely.

Still, they continued, and Typha seemed to find renewed energy each time she should be dead.

Power buzzing through her, Quinn fought with a fury to surpass any she'd felt before.

From all around, a fresh breath of crisp sea breeze wafted through the air. Snapping, static popped in the air. Rocks fell and crashed around them with violent thunder.

Ryan materialized at her side in a brilliant flash of lightning. Strength and anger and love all emanated off him at once.

Down on one knee, his hands rested on an unearthly black sword.

Raising his head, he opened his eyes, revealing irises black as midnight. His obsidian gaze bore into Typha.

Laughing maniacally in her wicked soprano, Typha pushed up to her feet, her strength increasing in his presence.

Pulsing off him like a warm blanket, his loving glow wrapped around Quinn as he stood at her side.

Limping toward him, Typha smiled, her blood-red lips turned up in a wicked sneer. "Fool. You should have stayed on the other side. One slash and I can crush her. With your wrath, you'll destroy the barrier without thinking twice."

"Oh, you'll feel my wrath." The side of his mouth quirked up in a smug, feral grin. Extending the blacker-than-midnight sword he'd brought with him, Ryan flashed her a lazy, knowing wink.

Typha's eyes grew wide as she realized what he held. Wild, screaming, she slashed at him with dozens of razor-sharp limbs.

Drawing her own swords, seeing her team rolling their shoulders and preparing to engage again, Quinn took her place in the circle of six.

Ryan swung and lashed at Typha.

Fast, feeding on his aggression, Typha dodged his strikes, lashing back at him.

From all sides, the others kept Typha weakened with their fierce strength and humanity. Together, they countered her attacks.

One of her many arms came crashing to the ground as she failed to avoid the slice of Ryan's sword. Charred at the stump, its replacements didn't grow back.

Quinn sliced with her swords, disabling more limbs rather than slicing them off, having learned from the mistakes she'd made before.

Each swing from the team brought her down further. At last, when Typha had only a single functioning arm, her not-quite human legs weak and disjointed, Ryan pivoted.

With a furious growl, he embedded the dark sword deeply into her chest. Oily blood poured from the gaping wound in her ribs.

She dropped to her knees.

Ryan pulled out the sword and swung, beheading her with one final slash of the sword.

Thunder bellowing through the room, Typha's limp form crumpled to the ground, a viscous puddle growing around her. The evil sneer she'd worn softened into an almost innocent-appearing smile.

His chest heaving from exertion, dozens of deep lacerations gouged into his arms and legs from her swings that had aimed at him alone, Ryan started to sway on his feet. Quinn dropped her swords and ran to him, supporting him against her.

Bennett stepped around Typha's missing head and scattering of limbs and ran to Ryan's other side, helping him to stay vertical. "You are fucking crazy, you know that?"

Nodding lethargically, Ryan blinked, struggling to shake off the effects of the venom. Each had a few oozing black wounds, but nothing compared to his.

Quinn felt him starting to crumble at her side. Despite their efforts to hold him up, he dropped to his knees.

Lana came running closer. "It's the venom. He was out for hours last time."

Kneeling in front of him, Quinn pleaded with him to stay with her. Hands cradling his face, she wouldn't let him pass out. "Ryan?"

Pulling his head up at her words, he smiled wearily, a silvery blaze flickering in his eyes. "Yes, Quinn?"

Exhaling the air she'd been holding in, she relaxed into him. Breathing together slow and steady, Quinn felt him growing stronger as she pressed her cheek to his.

The blood from his wounds ran red, then trickled to a stop. There was a strength about him that hadn't been there before.

"Don't scare me like that again. I thought she'd killed you."

Dragging the air in and out of his lungs, Ryan was nearly back. His eyes opened fully now, an infinitely deep onyx laced with silver. Rising to his feet, he kept his arm wrapped around Quinn. A laugh bubbled up from deep in his throat. "You either."

He closed his eyes again, this time a smile tugged at his lips. She felt a power rushing over his skin, like the electrical rush Seven had stirred when she pushed at her veil bubble.

With a smug grin, he opened his eyes.

Soft footsteps echoed from across the throne room. Deandra approached, free from her prison, with tears streaming down her cheeks, and a smile wide across her face. Nearly as tall as Ryan, she rested one icy white hand on Ryan's cheek, the other on Quinn's. "Thank you. Take good care of each other."

Stepping around them, she took in the battered team, her progeny. She hugged each of her many-greats grandchildren and stepped back, turning back to Quinn and Ryan.

"Once I'm across, together you can heal the tear in the veil here, but there are many other, smaller tears across the globe that will still need your protection, many demons still on this side." Looking to them all, she said softly, "Take care, and keep your world safe. I shall miss it dearly, but not my prison. Thank you." She seemed to wait, knowing the door would open soon.

And it did. As Ryan had done, as Seven had done through Quinn, static seemed to coat the room, a sparkling portal widening to the size of a man.

On the other side was a glowing silver field dotted with red and gold blooms. In the center, a tall, handsome man with black eyes stood on the other side, his hand extended.

Deandra granted them all one last wink before stepping across and into the waiting arms of her lover. As she reached him, the doorway to the other side narrowed its aperture and closed.

Turning toward Quinn, Ryan pulled her close. Trailing his hand down her cheek, he bent down and brushed his lips over hers.

Something shifted inside of Quinn and blossomed from within her, extending in all directions. Ryan's skin hummed with electricity. On instinct, following Seven's energy, fueling the static sensation she'd practiced in the long wait in her prison, she pushed out the power within her and spread the sensation far and wide. A prickling, more intensely personal, danced across her skin and blended with Ryan.

Powerful shockwaves resonated from them. That fluttering low in her belly danced like a vibrant butterfly.

Quinn felt the air in the room lighten. A refreshing ocean breeze tickled across her sensitized skin. Looking down at her, Ryan shook his head in wonder. The veil seemed to thicken as the pressure in the air lessened, the air cooler, and the storm outside eased.

Smiling softly, glancing to where his father had been, he smiled and rested forehead against Quinn's. "We make a good team."

Standing on her tiptoes, Quinn cradled his face in her hands. Ryan kissed each of her palms before pulling her against him, resting his lips on hers. Slowly, savoring, he ran his tongue along the crease of her lips.

Melting into him, Quinn kissed him deeply. Hot, liquid steel pumped through her veins as he stirred something profound inside her. The promise of tomorrow.

Interrupting what was turning out to be a momentous kiss, Bennett walked up and tapped each on the shoulder. "Uh, guys? Let's get the hell out of here. No offense, but monster carcasses are a bit unsettling."

Pulling away, Ryan winked at her and grinned. "Fair point. Let's go."

Grabbing their supplies, the team strode across the great hall and into the waiting light of day. Hesitating, Astrid looked back, then to Ryan again. "Were your eyes always so dark?"

Shaking his head, he replied simply, "Nope."

"Race to the bottom of the stairs. Last one to the boat's vampire food." Lana grinned and hopped down the long, steep stairs three at a time.

Throwing his head back with a pout, Bennett groaned and started down behind her. "That doesn't sound so bad. I've been through worse."

Quinn reached out her hand to Ryan. Grinning mischievously, he winked. "Hurry your ass up, I've got plans for you later." Before she could respond, he was sprinting down the stairs with the rest of her team.

Epilogue

Northwest of Vancouver, BC. Four Weeks Later.

"Doesn't sound so bad, huh?" Ryan raised an eyebrow at Bennett before curling up with Quinn on the plush sofa. She melted into his side.

"What?" Bennett asked distractedly as he sank into the nearest armchair, single malt scotch in hand.

"Being vampire food? Sounds like there's a story behind that."

Snorting, Bennett took a long pull on the Scotch and set his feet on the ottoman. "Like hell I'm sharing that with you."

Knocking his feet against Bennett's, Ryan subtly shoved them off the ottoman. "Hey, I've shared more than I wanted to with you assholes."

Reclaiming half of the ottoman, the corner of Bennett's upper lip sneered like a fish on a hook. "For a guy that didn't want a team not too long ago, you sure are keen to share some Kumbaya moments."

Wordlessly, Ryan flipped him off and sported a playful grin.

Quinn perked up at his side, chuckling. "I know this one."

Glaring with a pathetic attempt at Superman laser vision, Bennett failed to silence his ex-girlfriend and oldest friend.

Lana sank into the opposite sofa and wiggled her feet onto the increasingly overcrowded ottoman. "Ha, me too." She earned herself a similar glare.

Ryan raised a meaningful eyebrow.

Clearing her throat, Quinn scrunched her nose in humor. "Adair. I liked her."

Sinking further into his chair, Bennett covered his face in his hands. "Not all vampires are bad."

Vann sat on the couch next to Lana. Ryan didn't think he'd ever seen Vann sit in the middle of a room before. He was normally in the corner or perched so he could watch the room. "This must have been before my time."

Grinning mercilessly, Lana teased, "Our fearsome, strait-laced demon hunter lost his virginity to a vampire. And he rags on me for having a fondness for fishermen. Humans are much tastier."

Astrid shivered dramatically. "Anything's better than a werewolf. Nasty bunch."

From the kitchen, Quinn's mother popped her head out. Sarcastically, she rolled her eyes. "Okay kids. Stop teasing each other and go wash up for supper." After flipping her deeply red hair, she scrunched her nose in humor much like Quinn's teasing grin.

Behind him, a whooshing from the glass slider to the deck preceded the gust of spring breeze that wafted into the room. Sunshine stepped into the house, her cheeks flushed mysteriously. Standing a bit too close to each other for new acquaintances, Vann's father came in behind her.

Scowling, Ryan watched the blushing demon hunter rapidly shove his hands in his pocket. Vann shared an equally suspicious glower and flashed Ryan a conspiratorial eyebrow raise before following the others into the dining room.

Hanging back, Sunshine leaned over the back of the couch and gave Quinn's shoulder a gentle squeeze before heading into the dining room with the others.

Finally alone, for the moment, Ryan pulled Quinn closer against his side and whispered in her ear. Smiling, she nuzzled against him.

"Think you have time to help me pack up the apartment before you have to go back to work?" She asked, her fingers trailing along his upper arm, grazing under the edge of his sleeve.

"You want to move? I love your apartment." A few nights in the homey space and he hadn't wanted to leave. Had loved her in about every square inch of the place.

"We need a place with enough room for Seven."

"We are not naming our daughter after a number," he mocked.

Giggling, Quinn was clearly pleased with herself.

Rising from the couch, Ryan dragged Quinn after him and held her close. Smiling, he pressed his lips to hers. A chuckle shook through her as she was clearly still quite amused with her own antics. Sliding his hands under her shirt, he wrapped his hands around her waist.

Breath catching in her throat, she entwined her arms around his neck. She slanted her lips over his. Pouring all of him into the kiss, accepting her love in return, he found himself in her. In them. In himself. More certain of his future than he'd ever thought possible.

Fate was a tricky monster. One he didn't mind so much anymore.

The End

Carrie Thorne is the author of kick-ass romance novels, specializing in white-hot chemistry, healthy relationships, and a mix of action and dreamily falling in love. Whether it's a sinuous flow down a lazy river or evil bad dudes hot on heels, Carrie's stories will draw you in and ruin your sleep. Happily ever afters are for everyone, and kindness is everything.

She's also an introvert who loves people, travel, fitness, video games, food, and is a true Pacific Northwesterner who lives for rain and outdoors and trees and mountains and ocean, and... she's a total dork. At home, she's lucky to have two creative and confident kids, a witty veteran husband she fell at-first-sight for, and a tiny pup snuggled at her side. In addition to writing romance, Carrie has been a nurse practitioner, a Martian and Earthling geologist, a banker, and she is usually elbow-deep in a DIY project in which she bit off more than she could chew.

Where is she now? Depends on the weather. Cozied up by the fire with a steaming mug of black coffee, or stretched out on the hammock with a frothy IPA in the shade of her forest. Either way, she's working on the next great love story to conquer your TBR list.

www.CarrieThorne.com